The Barricade Diary

B.H. Cameron

ISBN: 978-0-9878474-1-6

CONTENTS

To Hugh Cameron, whose first words encouraged me to try.
To Ron Warne, whose last words admonished me not to stop.

PROLOGUE

It is morning in the square. The small town comes to life in its customary fashion - slow, relaxed and unaffected.

From its Andean perch, in the clear atmosphere, it knows the fleeting nature of history. Once, it had offered its nurturing bosom to nameless tribes, before time became quantified like currency - counted, rationed and controlled. It saw those first immodestly clothed people cling helpless, childlike, to their existence. It watched them grow with confidence, and then fill with arrogance and pride. Mice became men, and men became Masters of Heaven and Earth - Gods of the Sun. It saw their progeny rise, then fall. It saw the strength in their sinewy angles waste away as they became meek and humble farmers, begging and coaxing just enough from their modest plots to keep the hunger pangs at bay. Once, they cowered with timidity. Then they strode tall. Now, what remained of their mortal shells had been cleaved of all fear and ambition. They existed simply to be and little more, barely distinguishable from the bony cattle that clopped along the cobblestone on their way to the butcher.

The man had difficulty becoming accustomed to this pace. Three months of insouciance could not hope to break five decades of rigid and unrelenting determination. He felt the strait jacket tighten on him the more he fought his predicament. Sleep remained a fickle tease. He could only rest after driving his body to the edge of exhaustion, when his body craved the respite more than his mind the retrospection of the days before.

The people frustrated him to no end, but the monotony vexed him more. The weather did not change its routine. Mornings began with a close canopy of clouds, low and laden with moisture. The hot sun stubbornly rose to reign, burning off the greyish white veil

1

into a humid mist that coated everyone with a layer of sweet sweat that thickened into salty grease by siesta. It was occasionally interrupted by the subtle tease of intermittent cool winds trickling down through the passes, like the provocative swaying of the multi-colored skirts the village women wore in the market. They mocked him with the promise of a quenching respite. It got under his skin, even if no one else seemed to bother or care.

The woman in his bed lay still, sprawled onto her stomach without modesty or scruples. Her left leg was bent at the knee and the hip, accentuating her natural gifts. Her hair was black as night, long and rich. It gave a shimmer that reminded him of the flicker of streaming water. The strands stuck to the sweat on her back, the salty rivulets that clung to her caramel skin. She was young and firm, but her body held the truth of a time long since forgotten or even understood.

She turned her head in her sleep, revealing the blackened eye and cut lip from the night before. He looked at her face, and felt nothing - not the angry lust from a few hours ago, nor the remorse for having gotten carried away. He resented her naïve indifference, her animal nature, even though it aroused him so. He assured himself that her situation was preferable to the alternative, and that the predilections of '*el teutón*' were no great secret to anyone, that his generosity was more than adequate compensation for what had happened.

He moved the fine gauze netting of the canopy, and rose with great care from the bed so as not to disturb the girl. He preferred not to engage her in any conversation, even if it was sparse on words. More than a dozen would have been too much of an imposition. The light silk dressing gown wrapped around his naked, scarred torso like a shroud. He was grateful that the simple exercise no longer made his flesh feel searing burns. Tying the loose ends of the waist belt, he made his way to the bathroom.

In time, he left his flat and headed a block west to the town square. Along the short walk, people waved and said '*adios,*' which was their nature. He never acknowledged them, which was also his nature. He continued until he came to the cafe in the square, tucked behind the fountain topped with a statue of Bolivar on horseback.

The man ordered his customary breakfast – a pastry, or what passed as one - which did little else for him but fill the gnawing corners of his stomach. It looked like a lump of dough that had been fried in oil, and then slathered with a trowel full of almond spread and planter's sugar. It did not taste any better than it looked. He missed the pastries he used to get on the Böhringerstrasse, the delicate flakes that melted on his tongue like the first snow. The confection on offer went down like a slice of unbuttered toast, bland and coarse. He took a healthy swig of coffee to wash the masticated ball down his throat.

The man ate in solitude, pausing only to let forth a grunt to summon the owner for more coffee. The man tipped well, but better when left alone, so the proprietor obliged without a word. Once he finished his repast, the man made his way to the Puerto Centrale, and the apothecary tucked in a discrete corner near an alley. He walked in, greeted by nothing more than the insistent clatter of the bell fastened to a spring at the top of the door.

Two women stood at the counter. One sorted through the chemist's ledger book, while the other adjusted a display of stacked jars of Nivea. The man looked at their labours with a mix of amusement and disdain. He wondered who would buy the cream, and what would they use to pay for it.

He said nothing, and continued past them to the office behind the curtain. He made his way to a door, revealing the staircase to the cellar. He swiped his hand against the dark wall, triggering a light and revealing the jagged pieces of volcanic rock that formed the building's foundation.

With great care, he made his way down the narrow staircase. It was mercifully short. The press sat in the middle of the room, like a fat Ottoman Pasha luxuriating among his harem. Its leading edge came within three feet of the bottom of the staircase, and left little more than a five-foot buffer between it and the outer walls. He squeezed past the machine, careful not to catch any ink or grease on his clothes.

A desk sat in the far corner, strewn with remnants of newsprint and jars of red black and blue fluid. Above it was a small window that providing the sole source of natural light for the cavernous room. Along the adjacent wall, behind a chair, a pair of navy coveralls hung on a simple wooden peg, driven into a gap between stones where the mortar had chipped away. He reached for them and prepared to change.

This had not been his choice, but very little had been of his volition for a long time. The only redeeming aspect of life in Chinogallo was that it had some semblance of order and predictability. While he could set his watch to the tedium, it had been good not to have to move from place to place.

His eyes had yet to adjust to the darkness of the cellar. The flicker of reflection from the end of the revolver's barrel went unnoticed, as did the two men who had been waiting patiently for his arrival.

"Señor Steinbrucker!"

The man swung around to confront his uninvited guests. He had no time, no time to reach for the Mauser tucked away in his desk. He raised his hands over his head. *"No disparar...* ", he said in a calm drawl.

"We're not the locals," the stranger interrupted.

"*Amerikanishe?*" he asked.

"Friends of some mutual acquaintances," replied the stranger. "They're quite upset. You didn't keep in touch."

The man laughed. His English betrayed his Swabian nativity. "They don't strike me as the sentimental type," he observed as his hands relaxed, fingers intertwined behind the back of his head.

The stranger's protégé moved forward toward the man. Out of his pocket he pulled a set of handcuffs. The chrome plating gleamed with mocking malice as it caught the light from the window. "Give me your hands."

"So?" the man asked, hands still clasped behind his head. "What do you propose we do now?"

"We're heading to Quito. There's a man who claims to be your son who wants to have a chat. Once we sort all that out, we're going to go on a long trip."

"Sounds splendid," crowed the man. "Travel is good for the soul, they say."

The stranger smiled. "I'm sure they're right."

"What if I don't go?"

"Well, that's entirely up to you, isn't it," the stranger remarked. "I mean, I can pull this trigger right now and I'm through. A little trouble's not so hard to believe."

The man smiled as he shifted himself toward the desk.

The stranger shook his head. His hand waived the gun in short, deliberate movements, like he was swatting at a swarm of gadflies. "Really - a man with your reputation and we weren't going to scope the place out?" he remarked with some amusement. "My associate has your gun. Even if he didn't, the back of your head would be missing before you got that drawer open."

The man shrugged. "Maybe I'm tired of running," he countered. "Maybe I don't care."

The stranger began to laugh. "Oh, that's good! Fake papers and hiding in the fucking jungle for a year! Yep, sounds like you really wanna get caught!"

The man's lips pursed to a smirk. His eyes narrowed, their gaze cutting through the strangers as though they were apparitions of a possessed mind. "Everyone has a limit," came the unaffected reply.

The stranger sighed, then waved his gun. "Yep," he replied, "and you've just reached mine. C'mon, Jack - put the cuffs on him. We gotta go. Need to be in Quito in a couple of hours."

The man extended his arms outward in supplication as the cuffs were applied. The three men then headed up the staircase, through the curtained office, and into the shop. Passing by, the man smiled and gave an exaggerated nod to the women. *"Adiós, mis preciosos!"* he shouted back as they exited out into the street.

The women continued with their work, careful not to make eye contact. They formed no conclusions as to the purpose of the strangers' appearance earlier that morning. Since Doctor Alvarez had first brought the man to the shop three months ago there had been a steady stream of people making their way to the cellar for God knows what. They knew it was politics, but nothing beyond that. They preferred it that way. In Chinogallo, politics got men killed.

They saw the bound wrists of the man and felt an anxious hope, careful to keep it hidden. They had known the man for only a short while, but they learned that he is a resourceful one. Men who got taken never came back, but they knew that if there was ever to be a first, '*el teutón*' would likely be it.

CHAPTER 1

Alexander Merich considered animals superior to people. Without the contrivances of language or tools, they carried on with their business. People, by contrast, needed all manner of sophisticated devices and tutelage to muddle through. It seemed peculiar to him that the most evolved needed so much help to accomplish what simpler creatures did without scruples or ceremony.

The sparrow that landed on his window ledge the week before had already constructed her modest nest. She knew instinctively that spring was set to arrive. Nothing in his own trained mind, or the deeper primitive recesses that still recognized the inflections of nature's song, gave him enough to either agree or disagree. The bird simply knew these things, and he gratefully deferred to her judgment.

He had left his window shut, lest he disturb the creature's attempt to make a home for herself and her own. He could not begrudge her that, even if it meant having to breathe in the same warm, stale air in his flat for a few more weeks. It was not that much of a sacrifice, though. The oily and acrid smoke that belched from nearby factories was no great improvement from the fine soot of coal dust that wafted out from his small ceramic lined hearth. Besides, it was much colder.

The frequent tapping of the sparrow's wings against the window pane had also ceased to be annoying to him. It gently stirred him in the morning, and would rouse his attentions when he became too engrossed in his reading or study. It had become a pleasant interlude to a routine that otherwise felt dull and pedantic. He took it as an opportunity to forget where he was. The bird, unlike man, had no ulterior motivations and no preoccupations to torment it. Hunger, fear, fatigue, and love – not even love - but some sense of a greater responsibility embedded deep in the bone. Merich's envy of the small creature had softened his heart, albeit for the briefest of moments.

Five days of cold, wet drizzle did not seem to have fazed the sparrow, but it served to compound Merich's generally foul mood. Getting a taxi to the centre of the city was difficult enough, with the lack of roadworthy vehicles and the continuance of petrol rationing. Finding one to take him through the early spring gloom would be something short of an improbability. He knew that he would need to walk the distance or, in his particular case, hobble painfully through it.

Rubbing the sleep from his eyes, he peeled back the heavy wool blanket and coarse sheet that had been his sole protection against the morning chill. Merich groaned at the prospect of another day that served as nothing more than a continuation of the one before. He preferred to extend his rest, such as it was, in the relative comfort of his bed. The other, more insistent, part of his brain had nevertheless compelled him to rise and ready himself for another day. Slowly, he made his way to the toilet. The harsh light of the overhead bulb created the most unflattering of portraits in the mirror - the tousled hair, the whiskered stubble. His eyes went in and out of focus at the sight, distracted by the fine white specks of dried splatter that had come from the sink below. For a moment, he considered the chasm between expectation and reality - a routine as regular to him as his morning shave. The indulgence did not last long. After getting dressed, and partaking of a light breakfast, he made his way out of the flat.

The noise in the hallway was ever present. The cacophony varied in pitch and tenor, but the composition had not yet reached anything resembling a climatic crescendo. The ungoverned screams of children continued to collide with the frantic, stressed yelling of their parents, reverberating out into the staircase like disembodied specters seeking to torment the living. Pungent smells of spiced meats and boiled vegetables were harder to get used to. He had developed some tolerance for it, knowing that he would be assaulted with far more offensive odours from the street along his journey. Merich was grateful that much of the noise and smell could not penetrate his front door. Only a muffled din managed to seep through the lathe and plaster. Against those errant sounds, the sparrow's rustling had been more than a match.

Balancing the curved hook of his cane on his right wrist, he grasped the thick oak railing and carefully descended the long staircase leading to the street below. He had no umbrella – or at least one that was in working order. He relied on the protection that was offered by the old fedora hat and mackintosh that had looked so distinguished on his father many years before. Merich had reasoned that they fit well enough, and were no less comfortable than any hand-me-down tailored to satisfy the taste and build of another.

In truth, the coat looked awkward on him. It barely concealed his pant legs from the all too frequent splashing that came from passing cars. Merich leaned slightly forward in order to lower the hem of the coat. The hat did a far more effective job, covering his sandy brown hair and casting a shadow that hid his sunken blue eyes, making his cheekbones and chin appear more angular and dramatic. With the cane, the transformation was complete, and men old enough to be his father gave their deferential pardons and salutary touches of the brims of their hats as they passed him by. Merich's boyish visage belied the truth that he had never actually been a boy. His good fortune had been to have come into the world at a time and place that offered no such interludes, fleeting as they might have been. Gentle tutelage and innocent play were the stuff of books and the remembrances of old men who sadly acknowledged the deficiency of their dowry.

He was tall and lean, much like his father before him, and was therefore prone to slouching to compensate. He had inherited his features mostly from his mother's side, including the hair that would transform from vibrant ginger to a patina of auburn.

His face was one of rare import in that it held the outward expression of emotion with relative ease. Joy and pain were displayed through his blue eyes with great alacrity, and he could pull a person into his world with no more than a telling glance. He knew this to be true, and attempted to refrain from such conveyances. The condition of his soul was a matter for him alone, and a matter to which he preferred the utmost of discretion.

A heavy sigh manifested itself into a tiny mist of fog, quickly dissipated by the steady rain. Every tentative stride taken forward produced a momentary shot of pain radiating up through his right knee. It was much worse in the mornings, when the air was particularly thick with damp. Like a heroin addict who had inoculated themselves for the umpteenth time, the searing fire was now more of a sore annoyance and a discomfort. What once stopped him dead in his tracks now merely slowed his pace. Regardless, pain was pain, and it still had the ability to catch his breath when he let his guard down.

In his nearly thirty years on this earth, Merich had lived under a dysfunctional republic, two foreign dictators, a Commissar, and...and then what? Freedom? Finally? They all promised freedom. Freedom from mob rule, freedom from the unclean and the impure, and then freedom from the exploitative bourgeoisie. Freedom from this and freedom from that. Yes, you knew you had to be prepared for something – anything – when they promised you freedom. That is usually when things always went wrong. The streets were remarkably busy, he thought to himself. It almost passed for what most people might have taken for normal. For so long, the city's traffic had alternated between extremes – between phrenetic anarchy and dead quiet. The former usually came when the people voiced their displeasure with the powers-that-be, while the latter followed in the wake of the consequent rebuttal.

The sidewalk had always been another matter entirely. It held a throng of people who could be counted upon for their punctuality. Another month was ready to pass, and with it a number of ration coupons. Families that had shown restraint in their consumption now found themselves left with a number of unused coupons that would soon be as worthless as a *Republikakroner*.

Every shop had a queue that ran up to twenty deep outside the door, the visible part of a serpentine of undeterminable length. What was quantifiable was its voracity, its head for self-preservation. It coiled itself tightly, stubbornly on the sidewalk. Strangers invaded personal space without scruple, while mothers drew their fidgeting brood ever closer, like the tensive muscles of a predator that smelled its own mortality. It showed Merich its cold resolve to defend its quarry by forcing him to make his path in the storm flow on the edge of the street. Satisfied that the challenge had been met, the crowd once again relaxed its collective sinews.

It took about forty minutes for Merich to make his way to Nyitry Palace, and another five to navigate his way past the constant flow of pre-War Fiats and Skodas that circled the Mall in front. There were the odd Daimlers, but very few people had the courage to drive one in public, for fear of vandalism, or worse. It would take much longer than six years to get over that kind of bitterness.

Nyitry Palace had begun as the ancestral home of the Royal family, then the Presidency, before serving as the administrative headquarters for the Gestapo and Waffen SS. After the war, once the Red Army had ended its interregnum, it served as the executive offices for the First Secretary and his Cabinet. Now, it was just a large building full of damaged artifacts, smashed furniture, and paper strewn in every direction. More significantly, it had become the bane of Merich's existence.

The armed guards at the front gate, recognizing him instantly, had opened a small passage in the massive wrought-iron fence to let him through. If he had really been a stickler for detail and protocol, he would have given them a proper dressing down for not having checked his papers first. Rules were rules, after all. On the other hand, it was miserable enough weather to walk in, let alone having to stand in it for a second longer than necessary. These guards, these boys, had been there for hours and would be there for hours more. Merich said his thanks, careful not to sound irritable about it all, then proceeded toward the front entrance.

The palace was an awful mess but, for the time being, it was his mess. There were countless others who, for a myriad of reasons, wanted to have free rein of the place, but they would all have to wait. He represented the Justice Ministry, which made him *primus inter pares*. There would be plenty of time and opportunity for clerks to count the silverware.

The front entrance to the Palace led to a cavernous reception hall. Ornate Corinthian columns of marble rose from the floor that stubbornly held a large fresco up to the firmament. Sad cherubs continued to float among the dappled clouds, defiantly grappling ribbons of faded indigo and gold despite their scars of exposed plaster that bled dust.

As he climbed the enormous staircase in the centre of the hall, he could feel the soggy slush of the plush crimson carpet beneath, made almost black from the saturation. Holes in the roof, and in the once ornate stained glass windows, gave surrender to the elements. Treading it was difficult, but preferable still to the slick marble and wood parquet floors elsewhere that were near impossible for a man in his state to navigate.

Merich was a poor supervisor, and he knew it. He felt best when left to his own devices - alone, with a clear task to achieve.

No interruptions or distractions. He had been fortunate early on to have identified some talent among his coterie. By his estimation, there were three or four rather intelligent self-starters who could be relied upon to keep a careful watch on the others. It afforded him the freedom to busy himself with projects of his own choosing. Determining his own routine seemed to be the only tonic for the monotony.

At the end of the second floor hall, in the far corner of the south wing, stood the private apartments of the First Secretary, or what remained thereof. Merich had made this the focus of his attention for almost a week. It had been a slow effort due to his limitations, but he had been reluctant to enlist any help. It would all be finished on his schedule, and besides, there was far too much to be done elsewhere. Pulling men away from their tasks would only have served to slow down the entire project.

The living quarters consisted of a large anteroom connecting three smaller rooms - a bedroom, a study, and a lavatory. It lacked the intricate gilding found in most of the formal reception halls on the first floor. Everything was painted in a particularly drab shade of beige. Occasionally, there were bright patches, demarcating the portraits and other wall hangings that had once protected the paint from the western sun. Along one wall were a series of holes, ranging from a couple of inches to three or four feet in diameter. Snapped ends of lathe lay exposed like the cracked ribs of an injured man. Some displayed stains of soot that streaked upward like the flames that had spawned them. He had reasoned these had come from looters. A shell big enough to do that sort of damage to an interior wall would not have bothered to leave anything else along its trajectory.

Large multi-segmented windows formed the outer side of the room. Many of the individual panes were cracked, if not outright shattered. Slivered remnants lay on the dirty carpet, shimmering the reflection of the errant rays of light they could find. The tattered remains of crimson drapes fluttered like a cat o' nine tails in the constant breeze, giving the room its only flourish of colour. What remained of the room's furnishings had been scattered haphazardly in every direction. Sofas and ottomans were sliced open like roast pigs before having been overturned and cast aside. A large curio cabinet stood defiantly amid the chaos. It had been mostly emptied of its contents, with the remaining trinkets framed within a wreath of jagged shards of glass.

Merich gave a sigh of resignation. The destruction meant nothing in itself, but it represented a greater challenge in finding and retrieving papers for the Ministry. Broken spindles and torn chintz were inevitably someone else's problem. For the time being, though, they would be his.

Near an emptied bookshelf, beside an overturned side table, a pile of papers had taken his notice. Most bore the seal of the former regime. Merich was surprised to not have seen it earlier, although the dreadful condition of the room and its contents made it difficult for even the most determined mind to maintain a precise focus. Leaning heavily on his walking stick, he carefully stooped down to pick up the documents.

He had bent past the point of return when his balance suddenly gave way. Merich lurched forward and down, his right shoulder smashing into the exposed upper edge of the table top. Twisting to the side, he landed hard on the floor. His temple glanced a pile of books, leaving the right side of his head with a cold, stinging sensation above his right ear.

Merich lay still for a moment, stunned and sore from his sudden fall, he turned his head to see the cause of his misfortune. The cane still marked the spot where he had been, standing erect and plunged half a foot or so through the floorboards, as if a farmer had positioned a stake to delineate the row where he had planted his cabbages. He groaned as he crawled ahead, his hand slowly pushing him up to a sitting position where he could survey the scene more clearly.

The parquet slats had been previously cut clean from the rest of the floor, leaving a square of about one foot that acted as a removable panel. Merich's cane had landed on one of its corners, and the downward pressure had lifted the rest of the piece up on a pivot, bringing him down. Still unable to rise completely to his feet, he brought his upper body forward and slid himself over to the opening to get his cane.

The hole appeared to serve as an access panel, positioned over the spot where a large chandelier in the room below was anchored. He could see the large iron plate with a half-dozen well worn bolts rising about three inches past the fastening nuts. Fascinated by the discovery, Merich lay flat on his stomach and peered down into the shallow hole.

Immediately to the right of the assembly, he saw a reddish-brown object, slightly obscured by a thin film of dust. Reaching down into the opening, he grabbed the item and pulled it up onto the floor.

Bound in a fine patent leather, it appeared to be a ledger or journal of some sort. He swiped his hand gently over its surface, feeling the fine texture of the treated hide. A strap made of the same material formed a closure – sewed into the leading edge of the back cover, and adorned with a brass fastener that clipped into the front. There was no lock, just a snap button. Merich pushed on it with his thumb.

The closure released and he opened the cover to reveal an inscription: *"To my beloved Johannes, from Eva – 27 November 1937."* Merich stared at the page for a moment, his eyes transfixed on the name "Johannes". Johannes – Johann – Johann Licht. He felt a nervous sensation course up his spine to his brain. *Was it him? Of course. "From Eva" – Eva Licht – and in this place?*

He thumbed past the first page, revealing dozens more handwritten pages. A journal. A diary. Licht's diary.

He looked to the first entry, and began to read.

"29 November 1937
We gathered at the Café Sforza for our usual supper. Stern was his sullen self, but Eva took all of that away. She has always been good at that. It is almost impossible to feel melancholy with…"

"Herr Merich? Are you in here?"

Merich immediately slammed the book shut. "Uh…yes…I'm here. What do you want?" he stammered. He quickly slid the tome into one of the inner pockets of his coat as one of the guards came into view.

"Herr Merich! Are you all right?!" he shouted, as he made his way into the room, darting and weaving his way through the piles of debris. He stopped in front of Merich who, by this time, was on his knees and attempting to pull himself up to his feet with the aid of a nearby chair. "I'm fine. I'm fine," he grumbled, motioning him off with his one free hand. "What do you want?"

"Uh…Minister Hartz wants you to come to his office immediately," the guard explained, almost apologetically.

"I can't," huffed Merich, finally managing to pull himself

erect. "Hand me my cane...There's too much to do here. Tell him I'll be there tomorrow."

"Sorry, sir," came the fretful reply. "He said you would say something like that, and for me to tell you to come anyway."

Merich shot a look of frustrated consternation to the guard who, by this time, had been eyeing up the doorway and hoping for a merciful dismissal. The anxious look on the young sentry's face made him wholly aware of his demeanor. "Fine," he said with a resignation. "I'm not going to get anything done here anyway."

Stepping forward, he could feel a new and unfamiliar pain in his side, one that made him wince slightly.

"Are you alright, Herr Merich – should you see a doctor?" said the guard. Obediently, he held out his forearm for support.

"No, no doctors – I've had enough of them," sighed Merich, mindful of the need to sound more conciliatory to the young man. He grabbed hold of the guard's arm and strained to push as he was being pulled up. "Besides," he added, "you said that the Minister wanted me there immediately, right?"

The guard, satisfied that his superior was in good stead, began to adjust his tunic by smoothing his hands down the front. "Uh…yes, sir…immediately," he answered. "That's what I was told."

Merich nodded and proceeded to hobble past the guard toward the door. "Come along then," he called out. "I expect you're going to give me a ride, *ja*?

"Yes - of course, Herr Merich."

CHAPTER 2

The Justice Ministry had been reconstituted in a non-descript building just on the fringe of the city's centre. It was not a particularly inspired choice for either the sake of aesthetics or convenience, but it was nonetheless highly practical. The previous location had sustained far more structural damage than the Palace during the counter-revolution. Indeed, that building was nothing more than a gutted brick shell, streaked with black soot that trailed up from empty frames where windows had once stood.

Merich's understanding of the pedagogy of such things led him to appreciate that it was likely to be one of the first targets for those displeased with the status quo. Not only had it been so thoroughly hated and despised for its actions, but its massive depository of surveillance files constituted a tempting enticement for those wishing to make a clean start of the rest of their lives, politically or otherwise. It also offered an irresistible prize for those who sought to gain something – anything – at the expense of others. What had not been destroyed or stolen in the initial phases of the counter-revolution was secreted away to an undisclosed location, or so he understood. While he had no reason to dispute this narrative, Merich knew that the underground vaults of this particular building, a former mercantile bank and depository, were more than sufficient for that purpose.

Unlike the detail at the Palace, the guards that lorded domain over the front entrance were the hardened veterans of many battles. Hand-picked for the task, they were physically imposing in size and comportment. They would brook no compromise. Working in shifts of four, two would take position on either side of the twin oak doors while the others stood at the bottom of the four stone steps connecting the passing sidewalk. They held a gaze that

15

immediately told you more than you cared to know. Merich had seen that look often enough. With the right amount of deference, he showed his identification and, after a few moments of intense scrutiny, was allowed to pass through.

The lobby of the building was clean, if only that. No public place – particularly those associated with the preoccupation of accumulating and securing wealth – fared well over the past few years. Any adornments of decorative elements had long since been removed, leaving a Spartan space. The smell of disinfectant was strong in the air. He could see that an older gentleman had been mopping the expanse of the lobby floor, and the soapy concoction that he generously ladled on the marble surface reeked of chemicals.

Careful not to slip on the still glistening area, he slowly hobbled to the elevator. He asked the attendant to take him to the fifth floor. He closed his eyes, as the lift – an old wire cage of dubious vintage – gave a jerk and headed upward. Merich had never been good with heights, and the meshwork that surrounded the elevator cage gave an all too expansive view of the cavernous foyer that reached up to the top of the third storey.

The Minister's Office sat at the end of a wide and gloomy hallway. While not the most spacious or well-appointed suite in the building, it had been favoured mostly for its location. The back wall abutted the neighbouring building, which saw a steady and regular stream of armed troops. Its only outside exposure overlooked an alleyway, also heavily guarded. The size of the window, and the possible – or impossible – trajectories of a sniper's bullet to reach a target inside had made it a logical choice.

There was no ante room or secretary. Merich opened the door to reveal his employer sitting behind his desk. His hulking frame leaned into his papers, his shoulders drawn forward as if to shield it all from the wind and rain outside. Merich thought he looked like like a vulture ready to devouring some fresh carrion.

Georg Hartz was an old man in more than one way. Merich knew very few of that generation who were not. He was in his early sixties, but his visage was more that of a latter day Methuselah. His hair - or what remained of it - was a shock of white. It stood on his head like tufts of cotton pulled out a child's stuffed animal. His face was not wrinkled, but his eye sockets were deep-set, underlined with skin so thin that it retained the pallor of a bruise.

Pale blue eyes, while pleasing on a much younger man, made his gaunt features that much more exaggerated. Without a natural predisposition to smiling, he would have cut a most grim figure.

Hartz had been born in the time of monarchy, when even the most egregious of situations seemed, with hindsight, to be ephemeral. His father had been a clerk, while his mother taught school in a small town located in the western provinces. It was a comfortable home, and life, with Tuesday night salons and Sunday afternoon picnics.

He had once explained it all to Merich by referencing Bertrand Russell, that they were all like a Christmas goose, fed and fattened every day of their lives. They assumed that tomorrow would be like today, and the day before. Blissful monotony. They didn't count on a day where it all changed.

Still young, Hartz found himself commanding an artillery group during the Great War on behalf of the Emperor. A shrapnel wound to his right arm at Gorizia, the loss of three toes on his right foot at Vittorio Veneto, and a strong and enduring degree of cynicism were his reward.

After the armistice, he resumed his studies in Vienna, then returned home to the fledgling republic to begin his career at the University. Over the years, he had taught the law to countless young scholars, including Merich's own father, Franz.

Merich begrudgingly admired the fact that whatever the political climate, Hartz was consistent and resolute in his predilections, even if he was somewhat pragmatic in their execution. During the last war, he managed to keep one step ahead of the Nazis, continuing to do the same when the Reds took over. Throughout the counter-revolution, Hartz had become a guiding - often moderating - influence. More often than not, he had been able to prevail upon the reason that lie hidden deep in the more zealous of the partisan commanders. It had not been easy. Late in the final push eastward, he had to intervene personally lest the village of Tiestrea be erased from the map.

When the smoke had finally settled, he found himself named as the Minister of Justice in the Provisional Government. Many had expressed their congratulations and support, but he knew better. The Minister of Justice, whoever they might be, would have to deal with two of the most contentious issues of establishing a new government – drafting a new Constitution and deciding what to do with the former rulers, most of whom survived to await some form of trial.

Merich had first met the man when he had returned from Switzerland. His father had introduced the two, and they had been in close contact ever since. Hartz was among the first to visit the Merich home when Franz died, and quickly recruited him to the Ministry after the overthrow was complete. Merich had assumed that a personal offer extended from such a family friend would be to serve as some sort of protégé. Early on, he learned that the Minister did not work that way.

Hartz had never been specific with his offer, but Merich had hoped that it would be in relation to the Constitutional Convention. Instead, he was moved in and out of assignments with all of the alacrity of a stagehand who placed objects before the curtain rose and the aria began. He knew deep down that his real purpose was to be Hartz's eyes and ears. Unfortunately, so did everyone else.

"You wanted to see me?" he asked.

Hartz looked up from his papers, his eyes peering just over the wire frames of his spectacles. He gestured to the chair in front of his desk. "Come. Sit."

Merich hobbled over and, with some maneuvering as he balanced on the cane, he obliged.

"Your leg giving you any more trouble?" asked Hartz with the dispassion of an adroit school headmaster.

"No more than usual."

"I was told that you had a fall at the Palace," he continued. "Didn't you think to go to the doctor?"

Merich shrugged with an equally casual air. "You said that you wanted me here immediately," he reminded him. "I didn't think that meant me taking any detours along the way."

Hartz smiled knowingly. "If only you were so literal in your interpretation of every request I send you…Anyway, how are things progressing on the site."

"I would think you'd be better off building a new Parliament than trying to resurrect that death-trap," observed Merich. "It'll take years to sort that place out properly. We've had teams in there for almost eighteen months, and it's still a mess."

"That's a decision for the politicians and the structural engineers – not for you or I."

"But you're a politician."

"A politician," corrected Hartz. "Not the only one. The President of the governing council wants it to be Nyitry, and so do most of the rest. They may have to wait a long time for it, but wait they will."

"If you don't mind me saying so, it's all superstition. Nyitry's not the centre of the universe," grumbled Merich, shifting ever so slightly to one side as to accommodate his leg.

"It's the centre of power," replied Hartz. "Always has been. If you want to govern, you have to govern from Nyitry."

"Is that your slogan?"

Hartz picked up his fountain pen with his right hand. Balancing it between his thumb and forefinger, he began to flick it back and forth. It tapped against the leather desk pad like a snare drum. "No," he replied. "It's a direct quote from the President. This issue is closed. Your 'suggestions' are duly noted."

Merich frowned as he let out a brief sigh. "Fine, but that still leaves the reason for me being here. You're not expecting some great progress report, because I haven't got one."

"Yes, of course, and no, I'm not looking for a report...I'm reassigning you...subject to your consent, of course."
Merich looked at the Minister casually. The past allowed him some latitude in his dealings with Hartz, but there were limits. "I'm almost inclined to say 'yes' no matter what it is, but something tells me I shouldn't. You've never given me a choice before."

"Most likely a good idea," confessed Hartz. He rubbed his chin. "Always trust your instincts."

Merich grimaced as he tapped gently on his right thigh. "My instincts always seem to lie," he said. "So, what's your proposal?"
The Minister leaned back in his chair. He stuffed his hands down into the pockets in his jacket. Merich noticed he did this whenever he was moved to make some grand statement. He imagined that this was how he used to conduct his lectures at the University. "The Tribunals will be beginning sooner than expected," he explained. "There are a lot of people who want to move them along – get it over with – but there are 'considerations.'"

"Such as?" asked Merich.

"I'm sure you appreciate that it's in our best interest politically to move fast, but if we're too hasty, it'll backfire - badly. We'll be accused of sanctioning nothing more than a lynching."

"The people who throw Molotov Cocktails and shoot at motorcades are going to think that anyway," observed Merich, with a smirk.

"I couldn't give a damn about them," declared Hartz. "Just a bunch of malcontents that Stern used to recruit to bust heads. They do it because they don't know how to do anything else. Believe me, they'll be caught... It's the other people I worry about."

"Being?"

"The Russians, for one. They are waiting to see whether we become vigilantes. They're willing to go along with some things - surprisingly so - but you can only push them so far. And then, of course, there's the Americans – they're concerned about the same thing, but only because of appearances. They want to know that we are serious about rights and the rule of law."

"I always thought we were," replied Merich. "I mean, wasn't that was the point of it all?"

"It doesn't really matter, does it?" answered Hartz. "It's how the whole process looks to them. The Soviets will tolerate some direct justice where it eliminates people who are an embarrassment to international socialism, and the Americans will go along provided it's in a venue that shows justice was done. If we fail, then the Russians will re-occupy us, and the Americans won't lift a finger to help."

"That's all well and good," he shrugged, "but I can't see what this has to do with me. I'm just a simple clerk."

Hartz gazed at Merich intently, giving him a weak smile. "I want you to serve as defense counsel for one of the men on trial," he said.

Merich smirked. He shook his head, and started to laugh. "I never understood your sense of humour, and it's a bad day...".

"It's not a joke. I didn't drag you all the way here for a punchline. We're both too busy for that."

The smirk gave way to a frown. He shifted his weight in the chair. "Why me?" he asked. "I don't have any courtroom experience. You should be talking to someone else."

Hartz shook his head. "No, I'm going to talk to you," he replied. "You're the perfect man for this job."

"Perfect? Based on what? Because you think I'll lose – is that it?"

"I have my reasons."

"Being?"

"For one - you are the son of a well-respected legal scholar. That legacy goes a long way."

"He's dead," remarked Merich. "Just in case you hadn't noticed."

"Yes," answered Hartz. "And don't think that the way he died doesn't count for something. Hell, there's a move to rename the law library at the University in his honour...Then, of course, there's the matter of your leg. It's not like you haven't given greatly for the cause yourself."

"Others gave more – still no reason to give me a case."

Hartz leaned back, clasping his hands together as if to make a supplication to the Gods. "The truth is," he began, "that we - I - have very few good options. Most of the top legal minds this country produced are either dead, or living abroad. Those still here are unable to take up the task."

"Unable...or unwilling?" countered Merich. Hartz never showed his hand unless he meant to. That is what his father had once told him.

"In my opinion, both. Quite frankly, I don't care. The point is I'm giving you the opportunity of your career. You say you want to argue cases? Here's your chance."

With that, Hartz took a file folder that sat on the cabinet to his right and laid it on the desk. Merich looked at the plain light tan colour of the folder. There was no notation or label to indicate its contents. He reached forward and pulled it toward him. Opening the folder, he examined the brief summation and the photograph that had been paper clipped to it. His eyes widened as he studied the picture in the file. Giving a slight sigh, he closed the cover once again, and pushed the folder back toward Hartz.

"If this isn't a joke, then you're far more desperate than I thought!" he remarked.

"Everyone is entitled to a defense, counsellor," reminded Hartz.

"Not by me, they're not!"

"Why not you?"

"For God's sake, do I have to come out and say it?! I've never actually defended a client in my career. Mock trials in university are not a substitute for the real thing. The fact that you would even suggest me is perverse - especially for this one? You've lost your mind!"

"Do you want to try a case or not?"

"Yes - of course - but not as the lead and not for this one! For Chrissakes, can't I assist on a couple before you throw me in the pit?"

Hartz shook his head. Despite his doddling appearance, there was a clear strength of will that stood behind his words, one that Merich knew was not to be lightly dismissed. The old fox had not survived this long without learning a few tricks.

"Alex," he explained. "I have spent the last four days considering how this should be handled. I've considered every angle – every option. In a perfect world, we wouldn't be having this conversation. The ideal lawyer for this case is either dead, in exile, or in hiding. That doesn't help me right now... This isn't a joke, but it's a choice – for you."

"I still think you're daft," sighed Merich. "It's a poor choice, and I'd be a fool to do it."

"Yes…maybe," said Hartz, nodding his head. " I suppose you would…Personally, if I were you, I wouldn't go anywhere near it."

For the next couple of moments, both men were uncharacteristically silent. Hartz stared at Merich who, in turn, could not pry his eyes away from the closed folder.

"If I agree," Merich began slowly, "and for the record, I haven't – but if I did, I would expect some sort of recognition for this service."

"Well…of course, you would have the gratitude of a great number of people – including myself…"

"The bench," interrupted Merich.

"Excuse me?"

"You are going to appoint me to the bench – make me a magistrate."

"Absurd," countered Hartz, shaking his head. "You can't be serious."

"No more absurd than this conversation."

"You said it yourself – you've never defended or tried a case in your life...Besides, how old are you?"

"Almost thirty," answered Merich. "That's not the point. You said you couldn't find a more qualified lawyer to defend this case. If you can't find a better defense counsel, then where are you going to find a better judge?"

Hartz leaned forward, frowning. He placed his hands back on the desk. "You realize that I'll face a lot of opposition to this."

"From who? The people who want to erect a statue of my father, or those too scared to do the dirty work themselves. I suspect that they're one in the same."

The comment elicited a slight grin from Hartz, and a softening of his expression. "I could think of a number of other possibilities," he replied. "Some far better suited to your experience, your...situation."

"My situation?"

"Well, you do speak French and English, yes? You also lived in Switzerland for a time. I would think that a diplomatic posting would be more to your...liking. We're short on those too."

"I've seen all there is to see there," said Merich. "Nice place, but I'm not interested."

"It doesn't have to be there - maybe something in Vienna, London..."

"Stamping passports by day, and sucking up to dilettantes by night," Merich muttered. "Thanks, but no thanks - the law is my profession. I'd much prefer the bench."

"Yes, but a young man in your situation has to take other things into account."

"You mean other people, don't you?"

"Well...yes...don't you think you should discuss the options with her before you decide?" asked Hartz.

"We're not married," he countered. "Besides, I would never dare to give her career advice, and I would expect the same courtesy."

"But it's not just her, is it?"

Merich had dealt with the insinuation almost from the moment of the overthrow. "I don't take career advice from him either," he said, the resolve firm in his voice. "I'm my own man - I thought you would have known that by now, Georg."

Hartz pursed his lips, as though he had caught taste of some bitter drink. He grimaced ever so slightly, before he let out a shallow sigh. "Fine," he said slowly, leaning back into his chair. "I will make you a magistrate...It won't be easy, but I will do it."

Merich surveyed the Minister, his eyes narrowing slightly. "Then, I suppose I will take the case," he said as he pulled himself to his feet. He leaned forward to shake Hartz's hand. "I'll come by tomorrow to pick up the letter."

"What letter?"

"The one from you that confirms our 'understanding'."

"That seems a bit unnecessary, don't you think."

Merich smiled. "I think," he pondered, "that without contracts and agreements, there would be little need for the likes of either one of us. God help the legal profession if a handshake was ever to become an ironclad guarantee - for anything."

Hartz grunted his assent. He sat back down and, putting his reading glasses on, he waved his protégé out of the room. "You'll have it in the morning – along with the briefs for your client… Congratulations, counselor."

CHAPTER 3

Merich arrived late. Emi had been waiting for him for over an hour by this point. As much as he regretted the delay, he was relieved to arrive in as much time as it would take to have their meal. He had no doubt that she had already ordered for them both.

The Klosters Atrium was her favourite establishment in the city, and she always insisted that they dine there when they did not eat at her parents' home. The idea of supping at his apartment would not be entertained, unless she supervised the meal. He readily conceded that his culinary skills were such that insisting on cooking for them would be akin to a blasphemy. Given Emi's tastes – both in décor and in dining – the Atrium stood alone as an acceptable destination.

As the name suggested, the Atrium had begun as a minor rectory for a small order of Benedictine monks, with the blessing of the Pontiff and the will of the Grand Duke. It had remained a modest mission for generations. Over time, under more inspired - and artful - leadership, it had become prosperous, with a modest distillery, a winery, and a study for the production of theological texts. It also housed a small academy, subsidized by nobles in exchange for the edification of their children. It grew in scale and opulence until it was chosen as the palace for a late Renaissance cleric. It was a time when many city-states were run as bishoprics, and one could have easily confused a high-ranking clergyman with an aristocrat, both in taste and manner.

As the old order gave way to the power of the Hapsburgs, the Atrium passed to a family of minor nobility who, in the waning decades of the 18th century, would rise to become the *de facto* rulers of a semi-autonomous state within the Empire. Within two generations, the family moved to the newly commissioned Nytriy Palace, while the Atrium passed into the hands of a family named Delabarge, whose culinary patriarch had been lured away from an aristocratic family in the Dordogne of France to serve the Royal household.

The Atrium lacked many of the normal accoutrements befitting such an august crowd of patrons. On the other hand, more than a decade of rationing had left every other establishment in the same modest situation. The food was no longer the attraction. The architecture and design of the establishment, however, remained more than a suitable backdrop to satisfy the whims and fancy of a Versailles courtesan, even after years of decline and deprivation.

The granite floors had been polished to look like wet glass, making the brass inlay along the seams of each piece look dull and tarnished by comparison. Gold sconces marked every other panel of dark oak that fenced the room, broken only by the high glass doors that led to the terrace. Carved podiums, painted to look like ancient Greek columns, were strategically placed among the assorted tables. Each was topped with a potted fern that flowed over like a bucket with the last handle push from a hand pump.

The grandson of the founder, a seemingly affable man named Delabarge-Majdic, managed to keep the enterprise running over the years. Merich's father had always said that despite the words and intent of those who sought power, they all had some predilection for comfort and, on occasion, a degree of indulgence. Nazi officers and proletarian Commissars enjoyed their fine wine and gourmet food as much as the doyens of the *ancien regime*. There was always a place for someone who made the right people feel as though they were the centre of the world as they knew it.

Merich felt conflicted about the proprietor. He knew that the polite and courteous manner shown to him would have also been extended to people who had no compunction about sending men, women and children to a certain demise. He imagined the same salubrious affectations being offered to a Gestapo chief, or an EBI Colonel. Even the most gracious *bon mots* from the man made him feel uncomfortable.

Notwithstanding its pedigree, Merich still did not welcome the experience. The restaurant's ambiance, meant to put its patrons in a state of comfort and ease, had the opposite effect on him. It felt altogether contrived, and one did not have to venture far past its brass and stained glass adorned oak doors to have that illusion broken.

A block away, he had passed a rag-tag collection of men and women, many with very young children. They slept in an adjacent alley, having constructed makeshift shelters with whatever materials they could scavenge – broken timbers and mattress slats, wired and nailed together and covered with dirty canvas tarpaulins. A week before, he had heard that a mother and her six-year-old child had burned to death when they attempted to use a small kerosene heater. The covering of the enclosure had been permeated with petrol over years of use, and set ablaze once the latent fumes hit the open flame.

They were sad gatherings where a ration card, some chocolate, or a couple of spare crowns could get you a body or soul for hire. There had always been an element of this for as long as anyone could remember – just not as much of it. People from the countryside came in anticipation of a better set of circumstances, only to learn it was much worse when a retreat home was rendered impossible. The alleys and ghettos of the capital were sticky strands of a web that snugly ensnared their prey for whatever predators happened to be about.

It had been much worse under the Nazis, but it had barely improved under the Socialist Republic. The Provisional Government, eager to show both its compassion and its competency, had tried some temporary fixes – hostels and settlement camps – but to no avail. For over ten years, government offers of food and shelter usually meant an early and ignominious demise. Everyone knew someone who had boarded a train never to return. Half a life was better than none at all, and all of the good will in the world would not dissuade them otherwise.

This may have been just as well. The camps were notorious for other things - gangs that ran the shanty settlements with impunity. Rampant crime, rape, abuse, and the more than occasional murders were commonplace.

Police were nowhere to be seen much of the time. What few constables there were in the national force had their hands full keeping government buildings from being firebombed. The rate of pay did not help matters either, and a good portion of the force found it more advantageous to moonlight as paid security for wealthy clients than to show up for their shifts.

As he handed his coat and hat to the attendant, he began to formulate the excuse for his tardiness. This was not the first time and every possible alibi he could think of had already been used. Previous offerings to this point had been met with a curt indifference. There was only one that he had never used. He readied himself as he neared the table.

"I'm sorry, Emi. I completely lost track of time," he said immediately, leaning down to kiss her on the cheek. He took his place opposite, drinking in the faint scent of lavender that seemed to follow her everywhere. It was so omnipresent, so enduring that he wondered whether it simply exuded naturally from her pores. It was too intoxicating to have been disconcerting.

Emiliane Stolzer was pretty without the aid of adornment. She had the good fortune to inherit the best aspects of her parents' physicality, with all the compromises working to her favour. Her skin was light, but not pale, and smooth. It carried just enough natural blush as not to look gaunt. Her face was framed by dark auburn hair, worn at shoulder length, with a naturally waved bob. She disliked her hair longer than this, and detested its natural predisposition to curl even more.

"You didn't lose track of anything," she replied matter-of-factly. "He took it from you."

"Please," defended Merich. "The old man needed to talk to me about something." He took the embroidered linen napkin and began to spread it on his lap. The silk thread gave it a reflective quality, like the sheen on a string of pearls.

"About what – did he need his floors mopped?"

"Emi, we've been through this," he frowned. "We need evidence for the trials – anything that we can lay our hands on. If the wrong papers get burned…"

"I know, I know. You told me all that. But you're a lawyer, and a very good one at that," she countered. "Why can't Hartz find some clerk to do this?"

"Because he knows how important it is."

"You mean because he knows that you will say yes to anything," she corrected.

"I'm not even going to dignify that with an answer," he began to mutter.

"Alex, I'm not trying to be difficult," Emi continued, as she attempted to soften her tone. "Truly, I'm not. But your talents are being wasted by a man who'd sell you out for the right price. He has no appreciation of what loyalty is."

Merich shook his head. "We've had four kinds of government in this country in the past forty years," he pointed out. "I doubt that anyone here knows what loyalty really is!"

"Some people do."

"Yes," replied Merich, "but they're all gone now. We're just the survivors clever enough to save our own skins."

"That's not fair, and you know it," she countered.

This is what politics had become. Things had become so chaotic and complicated, that even the most generalized and benign of statements could become a point of contention – and, more often than not, a violent one.

Bruno Stolzer was the son of a wealthy industrialist who had made a pragmatic assessment of his prospects, and acted accordingly. If people were honest with themselves, they would have done the same thing if those options had been available. Merich did not expect Emi's father to have taken a vow of poverty and deprivation. When the Nazis left and the Soviets arrived, his own father had elected to stay. Stolzer had, instead, opted to stay in Bern a little longer – to keep his powder dry – in his own words.

It was all very well and good, but Merich had always felt that Stolzer's triumphant return depended largely on the sacrifice of others – like his father. Like him.

No - not like him. Not really, anyway. Franz Merich had taken up Stolzer on his offer to go to Switzerland only where it had concerned his son, and Emi's father had more than fulfilled his best friend's wishes. Alex could have stayed in Bern – should have stayed - but he did not. The struggle - his family - was back home. So, too, were two bullets – the one that penetrated his father's skull, and the one that shattered his tibia. The truth was that he could not moralize without hurting Emi and exposing some measure of hypocrisy on his part.

"I'm sorry," he said apologetically. He reaching forward to gently grasp her forearm. "It's been a difficult day, and I'm not in the best of moods."

Emi raised an eyebrow as she took a small delicate sip from her wineglass with her free hand. "Hartz puts me in a foul mood, too," she remarked dryly.

Merich shook his head. "You barely know the man, and he's been nothing but a gentleman to you."

"And I don't intend to get to know him," she countered. "I know how he treated father when he was in the university, and I see how he works you. That's enough for me."

"Do me a favour, Emi – hate him for your own reasons. Neither your father nor I are in need of defending."

Emi shrugged. "I defend the men I love, and I'll make no apologies for it," she stated. "Besides, you men sometimes need to be saved from yourselves. If we waited for you to ask, it would be too late."

Merich grinned ever so slightly. To most people, Emiliane Stolzer seemed flighty and superficial – a privileged girl who would not, could not, embrace anything weighty. He had known her for what seemed like an eternity - long enough to understand that she followed her own set of priorities. It was there that she made her stand. Everything else was negotiable. At its best, one might see it as a ruthlessly efficient way of viewing the world. At its worst, it led to seemingly schizophrenic segues, from compulsion to indifference, then back again. Merich thought her to be very much her father's daughter in that respect.

"I appreciate your concern," he offered. "Truly, I do – but this really isn't the time or the place to make a stand."
Emi's eyes narrowed, her lips tightening on the corners. "That's a curious choice of words for you to use."

Merich remained resolute. "I don't know what you mean," he said before taking a sip from his water glass.

"What did he say?"

"Who?"

"Your boss. Seriously…"

"Just that I was finished at Nytriy."

"And?"

"And what?" he shrugged. "Like you said, I'm a lawyer – he wants to put my talents to work."

"Doing what? Trying a case, or carrying someone else's valise?"

"Neither, if you must know," he declared.

The frown that had begun to form on Emi's face had now reached its apogee. "Alex, you're always cryptic for some reason.

Just come out and say what it is."

Merich peered over to the man sitting at the nearest table who spent much of his attention on the young couple. A large, lumbering figure clad in an ill-fitting suit, he looked out of place. "I thought that we could discuss this…in private," he whispered as he leaned in toward Emi.

"Jaromir can keep a confidence," she scolded. "You know that."

Merich rolled his eyes. "You know I don't feel comfortable with…him. Why is he here anyway?"

"He's protection," defended Emi.

In light of the present circumstances, it would have been an act of suicide for her to have ventured out without a minder. Killings were common enough, but relatively rare. Kidnappings and ransom demands were not. Money could be had by those who dared, and the Klosters laid out potential targets like it did crudites - on a silver platter. Merich had no dispute with the logic of having protection – only the choice of protector. "He's a Neanderthal. A simian," he grumbled.

Emi showed no interest in compromise. "I've known him longer than I've known you," she countered. "He'd take a bullet for me."

"Only because he's paid... I just don't trust him. Never have."

"People put their lives on the line every day."

"For a cause," he argued, "not for money. Die for your family, for love, or for a better world, but not for a bag of gold crowns. He's a mercenary."

"Maybe that's how he defines a better world – did you ever think of that?"

"Then he's an even bigger idiot that I imagined."

Emi sighed deeply. "Excellent segue, counselor," she declared, "but I still want to know what Hartz said – what he offered you."

Merich took hold of his wineglass and took a healthy gulp. Emi's eyes were trained directly on him. He could feel them burning a hole through him. "If you must know," he swallowed, "he offered me a case."

Emi's expression relaxed. "That's wonderful! Finally! You can get the chance you've always wanted. What court?"

"No court – the Tribunals."

The enthusiasm dissipated as quickly as it had come, as if she had found a roach on her plate. "The Tribunals... Alex, please don't be offended, but I would think that as talented as you are, that is more than what either one of us would have expected."

"I know, I know," he nodded. "I was just as surprised, but he's giving it to me anyway. Lawyers are so rare around here, it's a wonder they're not selling us in the alleyways too."

Emi began to rub her hands together - something that Merich knew was a reaction to stress. "So...do you know who you will be prosecuting?" she asked, with a slight lilt to her voice.

"Defending," corrected Merich, in a voice muted, but clear.

Emi sat silently for a moment. A look of incredulity began to spread across her face. She cleared her throat, then repeated what Merich had just said.

"Yes, I am a defense counsel," he reiterated.

"For who?" she asked with the gravity that he had come to expect, or at least anticipate.

Merich paused ever so slightly, then in a barely audible tone, he answered "Johann Licht."

Emi sat silent for what felt like an eternity to him. Her face went pale, her eyes large and dilated. Finally, she cleared her throat once again with growing resolve. She shook her head slowly and with emphasis. "No...no, you are not!" she intoned.

"I've already agreed. Hartz will be signing the case over to me in the morning."

Emi stared at him with a mix of bewilderment and anxiousness. "How could you be so foolish? So...stupid?!"

"I have my reasons, Emi," defended Merich. "Besides, I don't remember ever having to consult you on these things – especially where they involve my career."

"You don't have a career anymore! He took it – and you let him!"

Merich felt the tension build in him as his jaw began to clench. "Please lower your voice - you're being emotional," he cautioned as he leaned forward, his eyes nervously darting about the dining room.

"And you're being completely delusional!" she continued. "What in God's name would compel you to agree to something like this?!"

"I'm to be appointed as a magistrate once the case is done."

"Right," she said mockingly, "and you believe him?"

"Of course not – not entirely. I'm having it put in writing."

Emi shook her head dismissively. "Worthless paper," she grumbled.

"Not worthless," argued Merich. "He's bound by what he signs!"

"Only if you're around to collect it."

"I have no idea what you're talking about."

"Of course you do. The day people know what you'll be doing is the day someone will come after you."

"That's not going to happen," defended Merich.

"No – it'll happen. It happens every day – just like Djurevic." Franko Djurevic was the Provisional Government's Minister of Public Security, the man responsible for ensuring the safety of his colleagues. Three weeks before, as he headed to a meeting with the Chief of the capital's police force, his car had been ambushed. The Citroen had been saturated with automatic gunfire, then pelted with a couple of Molotov Cocktails. Elements of the former regime were quick to take full credit for the attack. Anywhere else, he would have been a tragedy, or at the least a sorrowful statistic. Here, he had the great fortune to become a cliché.

The difficult truth was that the challenge of dealing with housing and food was eclipsed by the problem of maintaining order. The Provisional Government may have had 'official' jurisdiction, but it lacked the resources to effect its will over the whole country. Its hold was strongest around the capital, as well as the two provincial centres in the west. Everywhere else bordered on anarchy.

The mountainous eastern region still had pockets of loyalty for the socialists, and groups of vigilantes would often thwart attempts to establish authority. The police and militias in those areas were notorious for selectively applying the law, demanding a percentage on the trade out of the area, and sheltering the socialist cells who would agree to mount their hit and run operations somewhere else.

Supporters of the Provisional Government, not wishing to wait for official protection, took to organizing their own response. Pro-government militias, trained and resourced by certain benefactors, exacted their own form of justice, differing little from that exercised by their foes. It was commonly recognized that a person in need was better off contacting these paramilitaries than their local constabulary. The killers of Franko Djurevic were eventually placed in the custody of the authorities – or what remained of their bodies after one particular pro-government squad had gotten to them first.

"The people who killed him won't touch me, and the others won't touch me either," he said.

"You can't say that! You don't know!"

"Between my client and your father, who's going to lay a finger on me?" he asked with a lilt of sarcasm.

While Emi had grown to expect these rejoinders, she had not acquired any great appreciation for them. "We've been through this - my father has nothing to do with those animals!"

Merich said nothing as he gave a knowing glance back toward Jaromir, whose own gaze had not wavered from their table the whole time.

"I'm telling you he doesn't have anything to do with the militias!" she again defended.

"Well, he has his fingers on everything else," Merich said wryly. "Is it so hard to believe that he didn't gift some rifles and hand grenades to some of his friends?"

Emi's frown that told Merich that the debate had come to an end. "Whatever you think of my father, he is a good man! He did his best to protect you, and I would expect some courtesy for it – for me! That's the least you owe him!"

Merich shrugged, grunting his assent while he cut into his food.

"And another thing," she continued icily. "This doesn't change the fact that what you agreed to is beyond comprehension! I know you, Alex. When you think you have something to prove – you throw caution to the wind. This time there might not be anyone around to pick you up off the ground...or what's left of you!"

Merich held his tongue, refusing to challenge her on those points. He wanted to ask where she was when the bullets shattered his leg. He wanted to say a great deal, but no good would have come of it. If he wanted the discussion to end, it was best to face the full brunt of what she intended to deliver.

Merich was no stranger to this situation. He remembered the moment he told her he was leaving Switzerland to return home. The more he argued his case, the more entrenched the argument became. The whole affair only turned a corner after he sat and listened through her objections and complaints, on why it was an idiotic decision. In the end, nothing more was said. She had burned through her fuel and he was packed and on his way back.

The talking ended, their attention turning back to their meals. A waiter appeared to remove their plates and offer recommendations for dessert. Once he had stepped away from the table, the truce expired.

"So," began Emi. "When will you tell him?"

"Tell who what?"

"Tell Hartz that you changed your mind?" she volunteered, her voice seemingly depleted of angry energy.

Merich calmly placed his napkin on the table, grabbed his cane and began to lift himself out of the chair. "This is pointless, Emi," he intoned. "I made my choice, and I'm going to see it through. Like it, don't like it – it's not going to matter. If we're just going to argue about this all night, then I might as well go home."

"Don't be silly," she chided him.

Merich held firm. "In one sentence, you question my judgment and my ability. What's more, you just expect me to do what you say. If that's the way the evening's going to go, then let's just finish it now."

Reflexively, Emi placed her hand over the back of the hand pressed into the table for support. "Sit down – please. You wouldn't leave without me?" she asked.

"You're joking!" he remarked. "You hardly sound like someone who wants my company. Besides, you just said you might not be there. Can't be any clearer than that."

Emi's expression softened, the corner of her mouth upturned ever so slightly. "Sit down," she scolded gently. "You're pig-headed – and reckless – but I still love you. Come. Sit. Let's finish our dinner. No more talk about the law, or that horrible troll you work for. Let's start over...please."

Merich hesitated, fighting the urge to refute Emi's last fusillade. Finally, he lowered himself back into the chair. After a suitable period of time passed to push the previous talk aside, their evening began anew. No talk of politics or trials - just Emi's day in the Gallery.

After they finished, Emi nodded to her minder, which was the traditional cue to bring the family car - one of the family cars - to the curb in front. Then followed the other peculiar rituals of the evening. Merich would attempt to pay for the dinner, despite it costing nearly two weeks of his Ministry salary. Emi would intercede after a suitable amount of time to establish Merich's bona fides, paying the bill under the pretext that - in all fairness - the meal and the venue had been of her choosing. She would quickly suggest that Merich leave a generous gratuity - if he so wished - and he would readily, and gratefully, oblige.

Such were the well choreographed movements that made up their lives. Indeed, Emi had never known a time when Merich was not a part of her life. He, too, also had scant and vague recollections of their first encounter, although he had managed to narrow it down to when he was five years old, and his parents had taken him to the Stolzer's house in order to meet the newest member of their family.

The casual contacts, the childhood games at picnics and other outings, marked their relationship until the day that he found himself boarding a train bound for Prague, Vienna and points beyond. The long years of exile brought Merich from childhood to manhood, and his relationship with Emi had changed more than once. The youthful playmate, who became like a sister to him, once again transformed into a vivacious young woman, and the object of affectation and desire.

Emi, for her part, had always been infatuated with Merich. She had shown her feelings in the typical fashion that remains such a mystery to a man. She teased and annoyed him up to her adolescence, then changed her strategy to one of equal measures of flirtation and premeditated indifference. It was in his final year of law school, when she had begun her studies at Zurich, that the forced absence had brought Merich around, and their romance had begun in earnest.

There would be many times when it came close to ending, but Emi had always found some way to resolve the situation. She had invested too much of her head and heart in this enterprise to let it slip away. As Jaromir pulled the car up to the curb, she smiled demurely at Merich while he opened the door for her.

The last eight months had been a particularly rough time, but when put against all those other years, it was the kind of challenge that Fraulein Stolzer would never shy from.

She leaned back in the seat, turning her head away from

Merich to look out the window to the busy street beyond. She knew that all would be forgiven long before they arrived at their destination.

CHAPTER 4

"January 15, 1938 -

I am still not convinced that this diary is a good thing. Eva believes that momentous change is coming, and people need to get our story right. I believe that committing anything to paper makes it more likely that we will all land in prison - or worse.

I don't believe in destiny, and it's not clear to me that anything will come of what we may do. She sees promise, but all I see is danger.

Nevertheless, I am using this book out of respect for her, and the need to purge my thoughts and keep myself sane.

We have all been together for five years now - Eva and myself, Stern, Vlasik and Klimsky. Most of the time we talk - probably too much. I am thankful for Hugo, though. Of the group, he seems to be the only one who appreciates that words without deeds are meaningless.

He can be a coarse man, and he lacks the tact to deal with the others. He started out different than the rest of us, and I try to remind others - and myself - of what that means. Most times I have to intermediate, such as last week when he and Klimsky got into a fight. I am sure that Stern would have done his worst had I not stepped in.

Eva is another matter. She says little about Hugo - good or bad - but I've noticed that she goes out of her way to avoid being left alone with him. If the three of us are talking, and I turn to leave, she follows me away. I think that his roughness makes her uncomfortable, but there is little I can do about that.

She has said nothing, but the others want Stern to go. I understand their feelings, but I cannot forget that Hugo was the one to bring us in contact with Moscow. Without that, I know that the Red Star militia would have surpassed us in men and material. That alone has proved his worth..."

Merich bent back the corner of the page to mark his place. He closed the book and gently slid it to the side of the table. Placing his left elbow on the table top, he rested his chin firmly in the palm of his hand. His index finger pointed up along his face, its tip touching against his temple. The other fingers curled back into themselves, holding his cleft as if it were a handle. His eyes fixed themselves upon a narrow crack in the plaster in front of him, just below a wall calendar that still pestered him with the month before. The crack had become visible from the black soot that had steadily layered itself from weeks of errant hearth smoke.

He tried to summon a thought, but nothing came to mind. The crack in the wall seemed to draw every image and impression out of his head like some ethereal vacuum. He felt frustration well up inside from not being able to draw so much as a basic opinion on the matter.

"What are you doing up?" asked Emi, entering the kitchen. She moved in quietly, as though hovering in midair over the floor, stopping just behind Merich's chair. Her hands were busy tying up the sash of his old housecoat around her waist. "It's cold out here," she declared as she let forth a slight shiver. "Come back to bed."

"...In a minute," he replied casually as he placed his hand over the book.

"What's that," she asked, nodding to the diary.

"Nothing," he said, as his hand gently patted its cover. "Just a journal I keep for Hartz. You know, the things we found in Nytriy."

"Anything I would be interested in?" she asked, placing her hands gently upon his shoulders.

"Like what?"

"You know...like portraits...statues...things we could use for the Gallery."

"Not from what I've seen," he joked, "unless you need to stoke the furnace."

"I was afraid you'd say that," she sighed, as she began to

knead at his shoulders with her slender fingers. "You wouldn't believe how difficult it is to find late period...Alex, are you all right? Your neck is as tight as a knot."

"It's fine...I'm fine," he said reassuringly. His hand came off the book and reached back, softly covering hers. He squeezed it gently. "You worry too much - you know that."

"I know nothing of the sort," she declared. "Seriously, Alex, the only good thing about you taking that damned case is that you don't have to do this anymore. It's tedious, and it's demeaning. You need to hand that report to Hartz tomorrow and tell him that's it." Merich craned his head around to her direction. "That's it – as in Nytriy, or the other thing too?" he asked.

"You asked me not to talk about it, and I'm keeping my word. And I did mean the Palace. It makes you miserable – everyone can see it. Please finish with it. Tell him."

Merich sighed with some relief. "And I will - tomorrow - I promise. I just need to make sure that everything's in order before I give it over."

Emi leaned down and gave him a gentle kiss on his cheek. She turned her head slightly in the direction of the book "Are you sure there's nothing I'd be interested in?" she whispered in his ear. Merich placed his hand back on the cover. "Not really...unless you want Licht's toothbrush...only slightly used from what I can see!"

She slapped him gently, playfully on his shoulder. "You can hang onto it. Maybe you should take it with you to Shostoi. I'm sure he misses it...Now, you can come to bed."

"Okay, okay...I will, just let me put this away."
Emi smiled. Feigning the look of a scolding school matron, she turned and walked back to the bedroom. Her hands moved to her front, loosening the sash with the most fluid of motions. Merich turned to look back, and caught sight of the drop of the robe at the threshold, revealing the slender, smooth curvature of her naked back and buttocks. From his angle, the light affected a silhouette of her side profile. It reminded him of the lines of the edge of a cello, like the ones he saw at the Philharmonika as a boy. He thought of the deep tonal echoes, warm and soothing in their confident power.

"I'm getting very sleepy," she purred, her voice gradually trailing off as she disappeared into the black.

Once he heard Emi move the bedcovers and sheets, he took

the diary in one hand, and his cane in the other. He groaned slightly as he lifted himself out of the chair, and moved slowly to the parlor. Reaching to his side, he found the switch to the overhead light.

The room may have been intended for entertainment or leisure, but Merich had repurposed it as a makeshift library and study. That intent would have been lost on an outside observer who would have seen nothing more than a narrow gauntlet of crowded bookshelves. To his left and right, the shelves were fully packed with all manner of volumes. A few scant inches separated the shelves from the ceiling above and the floor below. Only the outer wall of the room was devoid of this collection, and as a result, provided a venue for nearly everything else, including two large windows that revealed the vast north vista of the city - Nytriy, the Cathedral, and the tower that marked the University quarter. Merich moved over to the shelf on his left. He scanned through the row that sat at eye level.

"Alex," called the voice from the other room. "Are you coming in?"

"Yes," said Merich in a tone faltering with distraction. "Just give me a moment." His eyes rapidly glanced the spines of the books - big and small, thick and thin, ornate and plain. A foot to his left, he finally spotted what he had been looking for. Reaching up, he pulled out one of the books out. Beyond the back of the shelf was a hole that stretched about fifteen inches in diameter, positioned just above a rough cross piece of wall studding. Slipping the book on its side atop the adjacent volumes, he took the diary and pushed it in through the opening. Then, he took the other book from its temporary perch and shoved it back in place. Satisfied with his effort, he turned to leave the room. He rubbed his hand over the light switch in a downward sweep, like he was grooming the mane of a horse. Today was done - mercifully. *Tomorrow would be different.*

Merich limped down the hallway to his room, to his bed, and to the comfort of his lover.

CHAPTER 5

Shostoi Prison was the darkest place in the entire country. It was said often enough and it may very well have been the only thing that people were willing to agree upon. It had been declared a thoroughly miserable place, and widely acknowledged as such for so long that it passed for what could be considered as an article of faith.

The massive Gothic structure had originally been built as a fortress to thwart the forces of the Ottoman ruler, Mehmet IV. To that end, it had done its job admirably. Numerous times, legions of Janissaries had tried with valiant might to penetrate the walls of Shostoi, with no avail. The only ones of their ranks managing to gain entry did so at the tip of a spear, and their time within the fortress was sadly typical of Christian men who fought in the cause of the Mohammedans.

Its utility in those struggles had proved apocryphal. Rulers were quick to realize that if nothing could break in, then nothing could make its way out either. Over passing generations, its sturdy and seemingly impenetrable walls had found greater use as a prison – both for enemies of the rulers of the day, as well as for them when the fates had decided to shine their favour on another.

From fiefdom to empire, from republic to annexed territory, from a people's commune to whatever this new 'age of democracy' was to become, those with power had all come to appreciate what Shostoi could offer. Merich mused that the first thing that the freed lodgers of the prison were wont to do was to place their captors in the very same dungeons and cells. That every ruler, or cabal of rulers, for the past three decades had spent some measure of time in the fortress was an incontrovertible truth. Nytriy was where they aspired to go, but Shostoi was where their journey would end.

The fortress was two hours drive northeast from the edge of the city. The road was maintained well enough for about thirty kilometers, but then devolved into a gravelled route with potholes and a washboard texture that made the trip as uncomfortable as it was long.

The final stretches of the road snaked their way along a seemingly impossible path. It hugged the sides of minor mountains, hovering defiantly over the gorges and rivers below. It was not uncommon for the way to be blocked by boulders, and great care was taken to avoid debris that might give way without notice.

Over the past few weeks, those occasional piles of stone and gravel were joined by the burned out shells of passenger cars and delivery trucks. Insurgents and partisans from the old regime were largely the cause of these occurrences. Merich had heard that most were the work of criminal gangs or groups of peasants who were keen to grab something of worth for themselves. The Public Security office was aware of the issue and its import, but had squarely laid the attacks and violence at the feet of the 'Bolsheviks'. They intimated that each new event was orchestrated to either test the defenses of Shostoi, or to free one of its new guests.

Merich made the trip in a late model Mercedes provided by the Ministry, including a driver and two escorts. Each of the men wore holsters under their overcoats, securing the British-made Webleys issued them. Propped on the front passenger side seat, pointing muzzle down into the floorboards, were two Thompson machine guns. Beside them was a Model 1897 Winchester pump action hammer gun – still plentiful more than three decades after they had been brought by American soldiers to the trenches of the Somme. Merich knew this particular weapon far better than he cared to admit. The fact that it was in the possession of one of his minders gave him no particular ease.

He leaned forward until he was about four inches from the back of the driver's head. "How long before we get there?" he asked.

"A few minutes – why?" came the gruff reply.

"I need to relieve myself, and the bumps on this road aren't helping."

The driver pointed to the charred remains of a Skoda to their right as they passed by. "Maybe they had to stop for a piss too, *ja?*" he chortled.

This exchange elicited the first words that the one minder, to Merich's right, had uttered the whole time they had been driving. "What a way to go," he goaded. "They find you with a bullet to the brain and still holding your *ćurák*!"

The men continued to laugh with no attempt to mask their derision. Merich slouched back into the seat, attempting to take his mind off his aching bladder by considering his meeting with his client. He tried hard to form some sense, some expectation. Next to the Lord Almighty, everyone knew of Johann Licht. Even with that – even with the man's own words to draw upon – Merich saw nothing. *Tabula rasa.*

Within ten minutes they finally reached the first guard house that sat on the outermost perimeter of Shostoi. As Merich would learn, much to his increasing discomfort, there would be two more checkpoints, each staffed by sentries whose main qualification was an obsessively compulsive personality.

Even if Shostoi had not been meant for such a grim use, it certainly gave the impression that it was. Other castles in the country, whose light grey facades and elegant parapets dotted fertile valleys, were the stuff of elegance and romance. Shostoi bore no such beauty. Its slender columns of dark reddish brown volcanic rock reached up from the side of a mountain like long scraggly claws, as if the Devil himself were attempting to pull himself up from his hellish pit. The dark rusting patina of the rock made the walls look as though the pain and sorrow of many had bled into it, soaked into its pores. It was utilitarian, by purpose and by design. It never apologized for what it was, and was not likely to begin now.

Once their car had pulled in through the portcullis, it wheeled up to a small outbuilding at the far end of a cobblestoned courtyard. Standing at its door were three men - two uniformed guards and another dressed in a pale blue suit. The car stopped and Merich's entourage assisted him to make his way to the reception party. The combination of the cane in one hand and his valise in the other made Merich's steps look even more measured and ponderous, like a tightrope walker clutching his pole to retain equilibrium amid the uneven rocks underfoot.

The man in the suit was slightly older than Merich, although the effect of his obvious predispositions had left their obvious trace. His jacket was ill-fitting against his girth, which would not have been as noticeable had he not done up the buttons. As it was, slight horizontal creases formed where they had fastened.

His face was plain and unadulterated, a noticeable gradient beyond lean, and framed by a mantle of dark brown hair that held ever the slightest premature dusting of white.

He stepped ahead of his escorts and, with a slight efficient bow, he reached forward with an open hand. "Herr Merich? My name is Szatmáry. I am the Deputy Governor of Shostoi. I trust that your trip was uneventful."

"Yes," replied Merich. "Mercifully so. I understand that there have been a number of incidents along the road."

"Not as many as before," the official answered confidently.

"Still, the bandits manage to mount an attack every so often."

"Isn't there something you can do about it? I mean, this is an important facility."

"We've made requests," sighed Szatmáry, gesturing to one of the guard turrets near the portcullis. "So far, nothing. The government can't spare the soldiers, or even a detachment of police. My men are too busy looking after this place, let alone the land around...but we improvise."

"Improvise?"

"*Ja*, when we can, we spare up some resources and we put the bandits on notice."

A frown crossed Merich's face. "You mean you investigate these gangs, correct?" he offered.

Szatmáry grimaced as though his tongue had encountered something tart. "Yes...you could say that," came the halting reply. "Within our limited means."

"Could you elaborate?"

"You're from the Justice Ministry, Herr Merich. I report to the Ministry of Public Security. Unless I have been directed otherwise, I would think it imprudent to discuss any details regarding our operations."

Merich's eyes narrowed. "Of course," he answered purposefully. "I certainly would not wish to discuss matters that would reflect badly on this facility...or its staff."

Szatmáry smiled back and nodded. "Please," he said as he gestured toward a large deceivingly ornate entranceway. "We have your client waiting for you in one of our anterooms. It will be my pleasure to take you there. In the meantime, your friends are welcome to wait in the mess hall."

Merich quickly explained the immediacy of his comforts, and his host led him to a nearby lavatory just inside the arched passageway that led into the fortress.

Once he rejoined Szatmáry, he was led down a wide passageway, walled with enormous slabs of whitewashed rock that were roughly chiseled only for the sake of providing a consistent surface. The joints between the segments were hastily mortared, and seemed so more for the sake of preventing moisture from making its way into the passage, which travelled on a slight incline as it moved further inward.

The corridor was eerily quiet, save for the steady gurgling and hissing that echoed from the strands of steam piping that were fastened along the wall, just beyond arm's reach. Every few feet, he could see 'patches' applied to the lines - nothing more than rags and bits of cloth that had been tied around the pipe, then covered over with a metal coupler. Stains of reddish brown moisture marked their locations along the way.

Merich could detect the pungent smell of urine and excrement that emanated from deep in the fortress. He fought the increasing urge to vomit, and turned his head slightly back in order to capture what little fresh air creeped into the entrance from behind.
The interview room was located to the left, thirty feet beyond the mouth of the passageway. A young guard marked its location in the dimly lit corridor. Szatmáry addressed the sentry in Czech, and by what Merich could understand, his guide had asked whether the inmate "had caused any trouble."

The guard gave a perfunctory, yet assuring report that his charge had behaved himself "for a change." Then he turned and unlocked the thick oak door, swinging it open for the men to pass.

The room was brightly lit, from the overhead florescent lights, as well as the reflective qualities of the walls. They had been painted in a shade of green so pale that it could have been mistaken for a discoloured beige. All that sat in the room were a large wooden table, two metal framed chairs, and a man.

Merich stared at the prisoner for longer than what would have been considered as polite in another circumstance. His brain tried to reconcile what he was now viewing with the countless images he had seen over the years - in newspapers, in cinemas, and in books.

The man before him was noticeably taller and slenderer than

he had imagined, his face withdrawn and pale. His hair was mostly grey, but still showed the touches of black that Merich recognized. It was closely cropped, like the stubbly regrowth that came a couple of weeks after being shaved off completely. Evidence of the attempt on his life was also easily viewed, the scarring of skin on the right side of his neck, extending from just below the jawline and running down. It resurfaced from under the cuff of the grey cotton shirt to the back of his right hand, just below the knuckles.

The light blue irises of his eyes were surrounded by tinges of reddish yellow, with one socket slightly lower than the other, just enough to throw off the symmetry of his visage.

He sat quietly, his hands clasped together, except for a brief moment when he adjusted his eyeglasses, round lenses mounted in a thin gold wire frame.

"Herr Licht?" said Merich as he came forward to the table and held out his hand.

Licht sat motionless, his hands remaining on the table, palms down. "Yes - and who are you?"

"My name is Alexander Merich. I have been appointed as your defense counsel for the trial." With that, Merich sat down on the chair opposite, and opened his valise to extract his memo pad and a pen.

The prisoner raised his hands from the table, pressing them together and holding them to his mouth, as if in supplication to the Almighty. "So... Which are you?" he asked.

"I'm sorry. I don't follow."

"Desperate or stupid?"

Merich grimaced. "Actually, neither," he intoned coolly.

"Well then, your bosses must hate you, " observed Licht, his voice full of mechanical confidence. "I've wondered what kind of...man they would send."

"I can assure you that none of those things apply to me," came the reply. He removed the cap from his fountain pen, and drew it carefully over the pad of paper in a figure eight pattern until the dark blue ink began to leave a trail.

"I see," answered Licht thoughtfully. He removed his glasses and, taking the open edge of his shirt, just below the collar, began to rub the lenses. He peered up at Merich for a brief moment, then placed one of the lenses at his mouth and took a heavy breath on it. He continued to polish them for a moment, then carefully placed them back on. "Well, being oblivious is just another form of stupidity as far as I'm concerned...You may leave."

Merich stared at him, trying hard to fight the puzzled expression that he felt coming across his own face. "Herr Licht, I don't think that you understand, " he said calmly, methodically. "The trial has been set, and I am your lawyer. Now, I don't expect much from our meeting today. I mostly wanted to introduce myself. Make no mistake though - I am your counsel."

Licht stared at him, nonplussed. "You are my counsel...You know, when I was First Secretary, each man in this country had a right to his own representation in court."

Merich drew in a deep breath, trying to keep to his plan. He had anticipated much of this, but that was just that - anticipation. "I'm sure you are referring to those lucky bastards who managed to make it that far," he remarked sarcastically.

Licht glared at Merich for a moment, his eyes flickering with intense activity. Then, almost as suddenly, his gaze lifted. A smile began to cross his face. "What's your name again?"

"Merich, Alexander Merich," came the quizzical reply.

Without ceremony, the prisoner got up from his chair, then nodded to the guard at the door. "Fine, then, Alexander Merich. You'll have my answer tomorrow." He walked past Merich and headed to his minder.

"What answer?" asked Merich, as he shifted in his chair and turned back to face Licht.

"Whether or not you'll be my lawyer, Herr Merich," he replied. Licht held out his arms in an obedient supplication while the guard placed a pair of handcuffs on the slender scarred wrists of his charge.

"I don't think you understand how this works, Herr..."

"Tomorrow," interrupted Licht, as he nodded to the guard to indicate their departure.

Merich stared at the men as they left the room. Then, he turned his attention to his blank writing pad, still blank, save for the figure eight in the top left hand corner that he had made.

His eyes quickly darted about the room as he considered his situation. For a brief moment, he wondered whether Hartz would still be in his office by the time he returned to the city. Dispelling that option, his brain began to lean in on its training, its honed instinct. His left hand raised to his face, kneading over his mouth and chin with a deep and vigorous rub.

A few minutes more passed before Szatmáry entered the room. "I see your meeting went well,' he chortled.

Merich looked at the man, at his bemusement. He swallowed to keep down the feeling that always put a flush to his face. "I'll be back next week," he announced, as he began to place his belongings back in his briefcase.

"Of course," answered Szatmáry pleasantly. "The Ministry gives us the schedule every..."

"Forgive me," interrupted Merich. " I'm not making myself clear. I'm giving you advance notice."

"That's really not necessary, Herr Merich," came the ebullient reply.

"Actually, I think that it is...You see, when I return my next meeting with my client will be in his cell."

"But this is the interview room," explained Szatmáry. "This is what we use for all of our inmates when they meet with their counsel."

"Yes - so it is. Nevertheless, unless you choose to house Herr Licht in this room, I would prefer to meet with him in his cell - where he sleeps, where he eats, where he's expected to make toilet."

The thin veneer of Szatmáry's smile was began to wear. "Herr Merich, there's no reason for that kind of arrangement. I hope you're not implying that our care of this inmate has been lacking," he said.

"No. What I'm saying is that it's my right as his counsel to see every aspect of his care in this facility. You know your procedures - I know the law."

"Well, I can assure you that his needs are tended to properly. We take our responsibilities very seriously!"

"Yes...I saw that. I noticed, for example, that his head injury has started to heal quite nicely. The bruising and swelling are gone. It's a shame that your doctor couldn't repair the skull fracture better."

"I have no idea what you are talking about!" defended the official.

"Come, come, Szatmáry! You know, the skull fracture! The one that's causing his right eye to droop so much. He didn't have one when he came here - I've seen the photographs they took before he was shipped here!"

"That is a very serious allegation, Herr Merich!" he growled.

"Indeed it is, indeed it is!" Merich shot back, as he pulled himself to his feet. "I expect that there would be a lot of explanation needed as well."

Szatmáry paused, then gave a smile and a shallow laugh. "Well," he said, "it seems to me that so long as they'll hang him, they could care less what his face looks like."

Merich's mouth contorted slightly. "But, my dear Szatmáry, do you know who does care?" Turning slightly, he pointed in the direction of due east. "Beyond those mountains, there are five mechanized divisions of the Red Army. They are just sitting there, waiting. Do you know what for?"

"I haven't a clue," commented Szatmáry nonplussed.

"Of course you don't! They are waiting for a call - the one that tells them to drive their tanks west...drive them down the road to your front gates, or head back home to Ukraine!

"Do you know who else cares?! Those bandits out there in the hills - the ones who manage to kill a couple of guards and blow up a convoy every week - yes, I know all about them!

Merich paused for a moment, a grimace forming on his face. "I'm sure you appreciate the fact that everything you do here has to be justified and defended elsewhere."

"Goddamn you politicians!" spat Szatmáry, the facade fully lost. "You're the ruin of us!"

"I'm not a politician," countered Merich. "Just a lawyer. I work for them just like you do. But you have to know they would hang you faster than my client if it meant keeping the Soviets beyond the border!"

The official stepped closer to Merich, well within arm's reach. "I don't mind telling you, but I don't like you much!" he growled.

Merich smiled bitterly at the man. "Well, from where I stand, that would appear to be a Public Security problem. Since I'm Justice, it would have very little to do with me." He poked his finger into the man's chest. "You remember this, *ja*?! Now get my car!"

CHAPTER 6

Once they arrived back in the city, Merich instructed his escorts to drop him off at his flat. It was nearly dusk, and there was nothing in his office worth retrieving. This was more rationale than they needed, and they readily obliged. Pulling up to the curb outside his building, they waited until he had fully passed through the front door before they made their departure.

Merich was tired, and in a measure of pain. His upper leg continued with its almost relentless dull throb, but was joined by sporadic shooting spasms of sharp pain in his lower abdomen. A modest degree of caution in his diet and physical activity had managed to keep those symptoms at bay most of the time. The stress of the day, the rigors of the journey, and the fact he had not taken a meal that morning had all conspired to punish him for his neglectful self-abuse.

Once he had entered the flat, he set to making a fire in the hearth. The room was damp and cold. Merich felt as though a lifetime of summers would never draw out the chill that had set deep into his bones.

The coal scuttle was nearly empty, and he contemplated the chore of getting it filled. The caretaker's wife was always happy to oblige, but the price would be a couple of hours of social niceties and a bottle of plum brandy. An extra wool blanket seemed to him to be the easier option.

Taking great care, he sat himself down on the ottoman adjacent to the fireplace. He stretched out his lame leg as if pushing down on an automobile's brake pedal. Discomfort welled up from his groin and extended its coarse touch down to his thigh at the midpoint. He spat a curse with every jab of misery his body inflicted upon itself. Would every trip to Shostoi would end up this way?

After an hour of diligently tending the flames, the heat began to penetrate beneath his flesh. He gave a slight shiver of contentment, like a cat purring in supplication for a saucer of cream. It had yet to seep into his bones, displacing the damp that accumulated like poison in his blood for weeks.

Merich was tired, and he struggled to fight it. His eyes wandered, almost dreamlike, around the room until they settled on the entrance to the study. Grabbing his cane once again, he pulled himself up, and made his way into the darkened room.

He went to the bookshelf. His eye scanned the spines of his collection. Ibsen. He pulled it out and glanced at the hole he had left in the line. He took a couple of more volumes out, widening the chasm, then reached beyond. His fingers glanced against the fine leather of the hidden tome, which he grasped and pulled into the light.

Licht was a code - complex and challenging. He needed to break the code. Merich stared at the cover of the diary. Was this the cipher? He took the book and set it on his desk, then sat down and turned on the lamp placed on the corner.

Judges would not call it a 'cipher'. They would call it 'evidence', and decree that it be shared and shared alike. They would also inquire as to the exact circumstances by which such a book would have made its way from Nytriy to a cubbyhole behind his bookshelf. They would no doubt mention the fact that one moved throughout Nytriy on behalf of, and in service to, the government.

Merich felt uncomfortable in his thoughts. Guards who had engaged in their own personal activities while at Nytriy were dealt with quickly and without compromise. Had he not personally sanctioned firings and fines against some of the young men who had been detailed there?

That was different, of course. They were profiteers and trophy hunters. They fed from their single-minded purpose to pursue their filthy lucre in spite of their duty. This book before him was not a trophy, or a month's wages, or a stack of petrol ration cards. It was a key, and it opened a door. Justice demanded that the door be opened.

Carefully, he opened the book and leafed through the pages

until he had found the one he had left dog-eared.

"March 21, 1938 -

Yesterday, Eva and I were wed.

Given the situation we found ourselves in, we could not have a proper ceremony - as Eva had wished.

Borsch agreed to meet us at the old hunting lodge that Eva's family used to visit as a girl. Her parents have refused to bless our marriage, and have chosen to stay away. Being at the lodge was the closest thing that she could have to their consent. I had never been there before, but it was just as beautiful as she had described it. On the front step, with some of our friends, we exchanged our vows.

It was a pleasant enough time, and we managed to find food and drink at a local haus in the village.

I did not want a ceremony, owing to my feelings about the church. On the other hand, my feelings for Eva are stronger than that - stronger than my politics. This is what she wanted, and my only precondition was that Christoph do the honours. He has been so kind to all of us for many years, and I could not endure what I consider an empty ceremony unless I had his integrity to rely on.

Stern was the only one absent from the occasion, which I must freely admit was a relief. His decision to stay away allowed me to avoid telling him that he was not welcome. On this point, Eva was unbending. I cannot count the number of arguments that began with Hugo - what he said or did. I understand how people feel about him personally, but the Party is not a club or society dinner party - it's a movement that depends on work and sacrifice. We would have been finished long ago had it not been for his efforts, and I find myself having to remind others of this.

I always ask them - including Eva - to separate their personal life from the struggle. As important as our work is, we have the right as human beings to feel joy and love. That is our own private matter, and should remain so. But it is just that - private.

I have also tried talking to Hugo about the situation. He is prone to anger in many cases, which I believe comes from his notion that his contributions are not respected. Where Eva is concerned, he is never abrupt or rash. Indeed, he has asked me to intercede on his behalf, and talk to her. If it were only so simple. I may be able to turn the sentiments of a crowded room, but restoring the good graces of a woman is something beyond my talents."

Merich took a leather bookmark and laid it on the page before closing the book. Was it really a cipher, or just ramblings of a man recounting who he loved or hated? He rubbed his chin, then leaned back in the chair. His eyes flickered back and forth as he scanned the semi-lit room. The interplay of the dark in the room with the light from the lamp and the street below created amorphous shadows that moved with an envied fluidity. Disembodied. Unencumbered.

The dull ache in his leg was beginning to return, and he felt his body become more sluggish and heavy. It was still angry for his neglect and would no longer be denied. He pulled himself up from the chair and returned the diary back to the safety of the hole. It was time for sleep.

CHAPTER 7

Merich arrived before six the next morning. The sleep that
normally accompanied fatigue had not come. Frustration fed the
insomnia and the vicious circle had been joined. After lying in bed
for an extended time, it made more sense to just get on with things.

He allowed himself the indulgence of a taxi ride. Since the last
surgery, Merich had been diligent with the advice of his doctors -
lots of exercise, walk wherever and whenever you can. The moist
damp had turned to frost overnight. Until the morning sun got
around to burning it off, this seemed to be the healthier option.

Once past the guards at the front door of the building, he was
alone, save for the elderly janitor who was sweeping out a corner of
the lobby. He hobbled over to the man, whose attentions were
seized by his work. He startled at Merich's immediate presence.

"Good morning, Emil," Merich said to the man.

"Good morning, Herr..."

"Merich."

The old man smiled politely and shook his head. "Ah, yes...I'm
sorry - not so good with names."

"How are your grandchildren?"

The old man grasped the handle of the dust mop with both
hands. The skin on the fingers was tight, and hugged the bones
beneath. They looked like slivers of wax with bluish wicks threaded
beneath. "They're well - as well as many," he replied slowly.

Merich reached into the breast pocket of his jacket and
extracted his billfold. He took a ten crown note out and held it out
to the man. "For them," he said.

"I can't, Herr Merich," he said apologetically.

"It's a birthday gift," insisted Merich. "For the little one..."

"Angela?"

"Yes...Angela...I'm sorry I'm late with this. I've been away on business and you finish up so early."

Bewilderment showed on the man's face. "Her birthday?"

"Yes. We spoke a couple of weeks ago. I understand why you're so proud of her."

"Yes...her birthday?" the old man said slowly.

"I'm sure of it," replied Merich. He took one of the man's hands and pushed the banknote firmly into his palm. "Please...give her my best wishes."

The old man smiled kindly. With a slight nod, he thanked him on behalf of his granddaughter. Then, without ceremony, he returned to his duties. Merich knew the man would forget the conversation by the time he was out of sight. To have expected him to remember a professor bringing sweets to a colleague's son years earlier would have been too much. Hartz was right, he thought. All the good ones were dead, or might as well have been. Merich continued to the elevator and pressed the button to his floor. He watched Emil through the cage as he began to rise higher. He wondered whether the broom handle worked as well as his cane.

Being the first one on the floor, he spent a couple of moments searching for the switch that controlled the hall lights. He left the gate of the elevator open for a moment so that it would illuminate the wall opposite where the switch was set.

He continued to his office, unlocking the door and turning on the light. All was as he had left it, with the exception of a cardboard filing box that sat on the desk. The box was plain, with no discernable markings other than a filing code written in large black figures on the end that faced him - 'JGL - 057.'

Merich hobbled over and pulled off the lid. The box was packed tightly with files, each an inch or two thick. Atop them was a single sheet of paper, emblazoned with the letterhead of the Ministry. It read:

> *'Licht, Johann Gerhard*
> *With compliments,*
> *P.B.'*

The contents of the box reeked of smoke and the onset of

damp mold. He took the letter and placed it on the corner of his desk. He ran his thumb carefully over the raised tabs of the folders, studying the typewritten labels of each. They covered everything, and nothing.

Knowing that he could spend too much time equivocating over where to start, Merich stopped his hand at a point midway in the box and proceeded to pull out the folder at his reach. It was documentation covering the 1947 Plenary of the Central Committee. He grimaced. His hand proved no more helpful than his client.

He sat down and began to read through the file - a laundry list of factory production quotas, judicial appointments, and self-effacing platitudes. Merich spent the next three hours combing through its contents, as well as some of the other files, determined to find a single sentence or word that kept this search from being a waste of time - who said what, and when.

A gentle wrap on the smoked glass pane of the door snapped Merich out of his thoughts. "Yes," he answered, not even bothering to look up from the files.

"I hope I'm not disturbing you," said Hartz, as he stepped fully into the office.

"No," he sighed, as he leaned back from the desk and rubbed his eyes. "I could use the break."

"Ah...well...how is this working for you? There's not a lot of good space available."

"No, no - it's fine," Merich politely assured him, trying not to draw attention to the tin bucket in the corner that was half full of condensate from the leaking steam pipe above. "I've been working out of a briefcase for so long, it's nice to have somewhere to work out of. To be honest, it's more than I had hoped for...although what I could really use right now is a clerk."

Hartz smiled. "If I could find a law clerk, I could probably have found an experienced lawyer to take this case," he laughed.

"You'll have to be careful, just in case all of this flattery goes to my head," replied Merich, with some amusement.

"Well, they say that in the land of the blind, the one-eyed man is king."

"Or Minister?"

"Yes...or Minister...Anyway, I came down to talk to you about the date of the trial."

"Perfect," replied Merich, leaning forward as he clasped his hands together, still managing to hold the pencil he had been jotting his notes with. "Actually, I wanted to speak with you about that."

"That's fine. I'm going to call it for the end of May."

A crease formed on Merich's brow. "That only gives me six weeks," he said coolly.

"Yes," answered Hartz. "I'm well aware of that."

"I can't be ready that soon. I'm sure you heard about my meeting with Licht."

"Yes," shrugged the Minister, as he came forward and took the seat opposite his protégé. "I can't say I' m surprised. Nevertheless, you'll have to be ready to go by then."

"Well, maybe if I had the clerk you're not giving me. Not when I have to do it all myself."

"Yes, yes - I know. It's not ideal, but the prosecution hasn't had much time either. I see you got his package."

"Yes - been pouring through it all morning. Who is it?"

"Petr Bŏsek."

"You're kidding," said Merich. He shook his head, as he tossed his pencil on the desk. His eyes took sight of the memo still laying on the desk. "P.B.," he sighed.

"No, Bŏsek will be the lead prosecutor."

Merich laughed derisively. "Seriously? I almost believe you're trying to give me a shot at this after all."

"Bŏsek's a good trial lawyer," defended Hartz. "You can't deny that."

"Sure, provided he's not pissed or trying to keep a jealous husband from shooting him."

"He makes a big impression in the courtroom," cautioned Hartz. "You'd do well to remember that."

"Only because he's a clown. He treats it all like some pantomime performance. Spends more time fighting objections than cross-examining witnesses. I can't possibly imagine why you would have named him. I thought you were all about credibility."

Hartz chuckled a little. "Alex, I deal with the way things are - not as I wish them. Years ago, we produced some of the greatest legal minds the Empire ever saw. Two wars and three revolutions - now what do we have? The best lawyer this country produced in the last fifty years is dragging a broom across the lobby as we speak, and that's pushing his abilities...Maybe years from now we might have reason to be proud again. In the meantime, we do our best with what we've got."

"You don't have much respect for the lot of us, do you?' observed Merich.

"On the contrary. I think you and a couple of others might just be the ones to bring it all back - sooner or later."

"Including Bŏsek."

"Good Lord, no," said Hartz, with more than a little bemusement. "You're right about him. I just don't want you to get overconfident, make mistakes...He wasn't even my first choice."

"Who did you have in mind?"

"Someone better...but I'd already assigned him to the defense."

Merich grimaced. "You old bastard - why didn't you give it to me?"

"I did what I thought was right. I still do."

"Well, Bŏsek's going to cock it up, and you know it."

"Everyone has their part to play," lectured Hartz. "Even him."

"Well, that's good for him. In the meantime, I'm killing myself trying to defend..."

"The man who had your father killed? Smart lad, and you haven't figured it out."

"No...no, I don't get it. I'm not a politician. I don't get half of your games. I seriously doubt you understand them either," Merich said categorically.

Hartz cleared his throat loudly. "Look," he explained, "when I asked you to take the case, I told you how important it was, yes? There are a lot of people who want us to fail, and Bŏsek is the kind of hack that would do it...Alex, you give them something they don't expect."

"A scapegoat?" he replied sarcastically.

"No. A trial - a real trial. I picked you because I knew you wouldn't let Licht hang without a fight...You have no idea how important that is."

"One man's life, Georg," sighed Merich. "In the end, that's all it is."

"Now, you're either being modest or flippant, because you know that's not true. Our government - every person in it and backing it - is on trial. I told you that we're being watched, but I don't think you know how close.

"This country is going to be invaded - either with Russian soldiers or American money. How we conduct ourselves - what we show the world - is going to make the difference. You make an effort to save him - a sincere effort - and you'll be doing your part."

Merich shook his head. "You wanted me because I'm naive and sincere," he argued. "Not because I'm any good."

"You'll be good enough because you're sincere," came the reply.

"Not a quality normally associated with our profession."

"Perhaps - then again, the best of us try to win at all costs."

"Really - sincerity as a courtroom tactic," mused Merich. "Has it come to that?"

"For now it has," smiled Hartz. "Anyway, that's not all I wanted to talk to you about. We will be announcing the presiding justices next week."

"Who have you picked?"

"We," emphasized Hartz, "are naming Eduard Nagy as the Chief Magistrate. Radek and Litmann will be the associates." Merich frown deepened. "Then you have to delay the trial," he declared. "Nagy won't give me a continuance, and you know it."

"He's a fair man."

"He's also tough to deal with. I know his reputation."

"But he's not unreasonable," countered Hartz. "Besides, this is the biggest trial that any of you - including Nagy - have ever been in. I'm not sure that the past is a fair measure."

Merich shook his head. "It tells me that unless you hold off the date for another two weeks, I won't be ready - and don't think that's going to go over well with your jury."

"There's no jury in this case," corrected Hartz.

"You know what I mean," said Merich.

Hartz looked at Merich for a brief moment, then past him to the window over his shoulder. "I'll see what I can do," he sighed. "But no promises. If you can't get Licht to cooperate, it won't matter anyway."

"Thanks, Georg," said Merich. "I wouldn't be pressing so hard if it wasn't necessary."

Hartz smiled politely, then got up to leave. "I want you to understand something," he said. "Regardless of what I just said –

regardless of all the other things – this is a case that has to be tried right, and it has to be defended right as well. You want to be a judge. Well, I'm not going to hand it to you on a silver platter. You're going to work for it. If you expect me to do all the heavy lifting for you, then you'll end up empty handed."

"I know…Thank you, Georg."

Hartz waved his hand as he headed out the door. His voice trailed as he left the room. "Don't thank me - just get him to talk."

CHAPTER 8

The cafe was tucked in an alleyway leading off of the Böhringerstrasse, deep in the eastern section of the city. The police stayed away from this neighborhood for obvious and compelling reasons. Others were enticed there by the same motivations.

Every block had at least one bar - legal or otherwise - where the strains of gypsy music fought with the equally raucous sounds of drunk men fighting over their women, their money, or their offended reputations. No woman would walk through this area without some sort of chaperone. Assaults begat acts of revenge, and a life lost often meant honour restored. A constable would arrive just in time to find out if anyone had witnessed the events leading up to the latest example of justice by other means. It was a good beat to have if you tolerated violence better than paperwork. If you had an entrepreneurial bent, all the better. Merich had no business being in this bar, let alone that part of the capital. Yet there he was.

He had been careful enough to choose a place he had been to before. No mobsters held court, and the alcohol came from a sealed bottle, rather than some corrosive liquid rendered from a backroom that could kill you or make you go blind. There were still the other people in the establishment. Merich knew that if he kept to his business, they would keep to theirs

A large man, dark haired and barrel-chested, held court over the bar. The healthy glow of his skin showed some gypsy or Mediterranean lineage. His arms were thick and muscular, and Merich knew that they had been employed for purposes other than serving patrons or polishing glasses. "Hello, my friend," came the affable greeting, as he took his place at the edge of the counter. Everyone - young or old, rich or poor - was 'friend' so long as they could pay for their drink and hold it.

"Vodka," said Merich, firm, but polite.

"Yes, my friend," the owner replied, reaching for a half-emptied bottle of Kapitanska. "Just Poland," he explained. "The last of the Stoli is gone."

"That's fine," assured Merich. "Polish goes down just as well as the Bolshevik."

"You sound like one of the new bosses - dress like one too," the barman said, pouring Merich his drink. "For that, I give you clean glass!"

"Unfortunately, I don't have the money they have," he joked as he handed the barman a ten crown note. "Keep it all - just give me drinks until it's gone."

"You want to drink very much, yes?"

"If I don't give it to you, someone's going to roll me for it out there. At least with you I get something in return."

The barman smiled and leaned in. "Show some American dollars and they won't even let you out of this room."

Merich nodded as he tilted back. He downed the contents of the shot glass with a hearty gulp, giving a slight shiver as the fiery liquid ran down the back of his throat. "I wouldn't know what they looked like much less where to get them," he said.

Lies, of course. They were all that the Stolzers had used while he was with them in Bern. On occasion, he would accompany Bruno on one of his regular visits to the offices of Julius Baer, where just enough of them were converted into francs in order to meet the expenses of the household. Most people thought that the Stolzers had more gold than Croesus to begin with. Just on the appreciation of the dollar after the war, Merich knew that Bruno had increased his already sizeable wealth significantly.

"Sometimes I see them," offered the barman. "They buy things crowns won't get."

"Like Stoli?" volunteered Merich.

"Like things that people should not wish to buy."

Merich drew his index finger around the rim of the shot glass. "I hear that some buy penicillin with them."

The barman shrugged and nodded. "They can – if they want. You see that man over there?"

Merich turned his head slightly to the left, in the direction the barman gestured. At a table against the wall sat a tall man, his face sunken and withdrawn. He hovered over a tumbler of clear liquid. The man's eyes held the look of one who had just died before the doctor had the chance to palm the lids shut.

"He had many American dollars," continued the barman. "He also had a sick boy."

"And?"

"He wanted much. He gets ten crates of Irish whiskey, and boy is dead."

"You know your patrons well."

"Not so much," said the barman. "I know him because his whiskey is now mine. The guilt I let him keep. That means he buys back whiskey from me - at a fair price, of course."

Merich sighed, as he turned his head back to his host. "You don't...feel..."

"Feel bad? No - I didn't kill his son. He was greedy. I have two boys myself. I don't let them die - ever. I lose this place first... No, they are in Turkey. They get good school, maybe be lawyer, yes?"

"I could think of better things to do," muttered Merich, as he took another sip from his glass.

"Yes!" laughed the barman. "I think this too, but never as bad as this. Someday, someone will kill me. I don't think - this I know. I only make sure I shoot them before I die." With that, he tapped the shelf below the bar top. Merich could hear the sound of a metal object rattling against some glasses. "They get really bad stomach ache for their trouble," he smiled.

"I don't think I could live that way."

"Why? You will die someday - all of us will. God willing, we don't burn for what we do. That is my only fear."

"On that, my friend, we can agree," replied Merich, as he handed his empty glass over.

The barman smiled and refilled the shot glass. "You know, if I were you, my friend, I would drink this and then leave," he intoned in a voice barely above a whisper.

"Why?" asked Merich. "My money's still good."

"I think...," he replied, his eyes flickering past Merich's head, "I think you have an admirer, and not the kind you want to take home."

Merich's expression turned sober, as he drew the glass of vodka toward him. "I won't turn around," he answered softly, "so you need to tell me exactly where they are."

The barman quickly turned his gaze back to Merich. "Large man - looks like a Slav. Doesn't belong in those clothes. Somebody who used to work for EBI or the Vopos, I think."

Merich picked up the shot glass and swallowed its contents whole. "Where is he sitting?" he asked, with a slight cough.

"Table closest to door. You won't get past him."

"Is there a back door?"

The barman smiled like a mischievous boy. He placed the cap back on the bottle, and turned to set it back on the shelf. "We're in an alley, my friend. That is the back door."

Merich frowned slightly. "Then a front door - you've got one of those?" he asked, clearing his throat.

"Yes. In through my flat."

"Not sure how this will work, " he sighed.

The barman smiled. "Take my lead," he said. With that, he called over to a young waitress serving a table near the bar. "Sima, I need you to cover this for me!"

He removed his apron and set it in a pile on the bar. "Come!" he bellowed to Merich in a deep garrulous voice. "You don't get to leave before you say hello to the children! It's been far too long!"

Coming around the side, he gestured for Merich to follow him across the room, toward a door to the rear of the establishment. Careful not to turn his head in his admirer's direction, Merich walked in lock step with the proprietor. "How do I know I can trust you?" he murmured.

"Because killing is bad for my business. If you have any friends, I don't want to meet them," came the equally muted reply.

"Come!" he continued in a voluble boom, patting Merich firmly on the shoulder. "Nicoleta has been cooking all day! You stay for supper, yes?"

"Yes, of course," replied Merich in an equally effusive tone. "It's been too long, my friend – far too long."

The men made their way across the room, stepping carefully past the couple of tables between them and the door. The barman stepped forward and, opening the door, gestured for Merich to go in. He promptly followed, then closed the door and slid the deadbolt.

The passage brought the two men into the kitchen of the residence. An older woman stood at the table, kneading some dough. She looked up at them briefly, then returned to her work, saying nothing.

The proprietor pointed down along a narrow hallway. "The door at the end takes you to the street. Go now!"

"Thank you," said Merich, holding out his hand in appreciation. "You don't know me..."

"I don't have to," interrupted the barman, as he continued to gesture in the direction of the Böhringerstrasse. "I know his kind, and that's enough - now go!"

CHAPTER 9

Merich's return to Shostoi felt less stressful from the start. He had
the same minders, but they were quieter than before. He reasoned
that they had expended all of the humour and irony their minds
could contain. Having drawn that well dry, there was nothing left
to do than drive and watch for trouble. Regardless, he knew
enough not to provide them the opportunity to use him for their
bemusement.

His arrival was different as well. Szatmàry was nowhere to be
seen, and his regrets had been duly conveyed by another prison
official. The new man's friendly demeanor was off-putting, forcing
Merich to change tack in his own responses. Of course, Herr Licht
was waiting for him, and yes, he would be in his cell. He also had
the booklet and pencils that had been requested the day before.
Merich could not decide what bothered him more – this man's
diffidence or Szatmàry's contempt.

Merich was placed in the charge of a guard who led him to
Licht's cell. He could not help but notice that his escort was much
older than his colleagues, almost fifty by his estimation. It was
practice, he would later learn, that only the older guards dealt
directly with the prisoners. The official rationale was seniority - a
reward for having not been picked off one of the outer guard
towers by a sniper. Merich thought it had more to do with a higher
toleration for the fetid smells in the lower cells, as well as the
lowered likelihood of letting the authority go to their heads.

The guard led Merich down a narrow corridor, and through a
large iron plated door that groaned with a pained indignation when
it opened. It seemed as though even the building itself had resented
his presence.

What lay ahead was a rounded chamber whose floor and

ceiling were comprised of fine metal gratings. They managed the trick of blocking the light while still allowing every putrid stench and groan of grinding steel pass forth. Merich recognized the structure to be one of Shostoi's imposing turrets, repurposed as a stairwell to the various floors.

Two levels down the turret, and one more within the substructure, brought the pair to another even more slender corridor. Bare lightbulbs hung from thick black wires, surrounded by an eerie halo that looked like a mixture of dust and moisture. The dampness chilled Merich's bones on contact. He knew that he would pay a price for it later.

The whitewashed stone gave the corridor an ethereal glow, like the faded florescent dial on a watch that had lost much of its fierce radiance. Light was brightest along the slate floor, where beams of brilliance shone out from below the cell doors, like emaciated fingers clawing to make their escape.

The guard stopped at the third door on the right. Taking his modest ring of keys, he slipped one into the lock mechanism. With a harsh sudden twist of the wrist, the bolt emitted a loud clang. He pushed the door open, and with an indecipherable smile, he gestured for Merich to enter.

Licht was sitting at a small wooden table. He was busy scribbling notes in the booklet with the intensity of a young student attempting to complete one last question before the proctor's signal. "Herr Licht?" said Merich, announcing his arrival.

Licht stopped writing and raised his head. "Ah, Herr Merich. I'm glad to see you. Oh, by the way, thank you for asking them to let me have this book and pencil. I used to keep a diary and, I fear, I have become accustomed to the habit."

Mention of the word 'diary' threw Merich for a moment. "I understand," he said in a slow, ponderous voice. "I hope you don't mind the interruption."

"No. Not in the least," replied Licht, politely closing his book. "I only write about my day. Since I came here, the entries have gotten much shorter."

"So, if you don't mind me asking, what exactly do you usually write about?"

"My travels," said Licht.

"Travels?" asked Merich. "Just how far do you get in the course of a day?"

"I travel in here," he replied, tapping his right index finger against his temple. "As far and as fast as I wish to go."

"Daydream?"

"Daydream is such a common term," corrected Licht. "It's what schoolboys do to pass the time through their arithmetic lessons. I prefer to consider myself a metaphysical traveler."

"I'm sorry," said Merich, sensing that this direction was leading back to where their last meeting went. "I didn't mean to make light of…"

"It's quite all right, really," Licht assured him. "I wouldn't expect you to understand. I'm a free soul entombed in stone walls and metal bars. I don't travel to escape, mind you. I travel so as not to forget."

Merich took a seat on the wooden stool across the table from his client. "To be honest, I can't for the life of me see what would be worth remembering," he observed.

"That's fair, I suppose. Your memories obviously differ from my own. It's all subjective, after all."

"Subjective usually doesn't get you locked up," replied Merich.

"Or kill you?" offered Licht.

"Some things you can't wish away. Whether you think that's good or bad isn't a matter of perspective. It's how you deal with it. It's a matter of conscience."

"But that same conscience has no qualms with seeing me dangle on the end of a rope?" asked Licht. "Even when your priests teach you to 'love your enemies'?"

"I wouldn't know. My job's to keep that from happening. Besides, I'm not a particularly religious man. My father was though – he used to say that logic was often the devil's language."

"Clever man," remarked Licht. "Anyone I would have known of?"

"Your people had him shot, so, yes, I would think you were familiar with him."

Licht looked straight into Merich's eyes. He leaned in to the table, hunching his shoulders forward. "Ahh, so that is your grievance with me," he replied. "And all this time, I thought it was on account of you being a cripple…"

"I don't know how you justify yourself," muttered Merich. "To be honest, I don't really care. My job is to defend you in court, not plead for your soul."

"Well, if you are going to defend me, you better learn," answered Licht. "How do I justify myself? Very easily, as a matter of fact. You might be a clever lawyer, but your memory is flawed. You forgot about life before the revolution – even before the Nazis. Tell me, when some poor peasant farmer had to suffer seeing his wife raped before the government troops put them out of their misery, did you cry for them? Could you feel as much outrage for them as you do yourself?

"You don't realize this, but while you and your kind were in the capital swilling champagne and speaking flawed French to one another, there were a great many of us being clubbed or shot. When the war started, your people left for Switzerland or England or America, while we fought Nazis in the back alleys.

"This prison – Shostoi - You use it for people like me, but so did the King, and so did the Germans. Truth be known, I sent far fewer people here than any of you.

"You know nothing of me, or what I represent, so drop the moral outrage. Only saints and hypocrites use it, and I'm quite certain by how you got your injury that you're not the former." Merich kept his demeanor. "I know what I know, inmate Licht," he answered, as he opened his case, extracting his notepad and fountain pen. "The law doesn't inhabit your world of grey. My world has limits; absolutes you just don't dare to cross. Play with your past - that's entirely your business. I have a job, and I intend to see it through."

"Given the current state of affairs, I find that hard to argue with," remarked Licht with some amusement. "Your colleagues call the tune, and you play the music."

"I'm sure I have no idea what you're saying."

"The history books are always written by those who win," he continued. "Spoils of war and all that."

"You don't seem to have much faith in people's ability to reason for themselves," observed Merich. "Pretty strange coming from someone who's so dedicated to their plight."

"No, actually I do," countered Licht. "I have great faith in a human being's ability to think and discern things for what they really are. The problem comes when you put more than two of them together in the same room."

"You aren't the first person I've heard say that."

"The truth is quite evident for anyone open to it."

Merich picked up his pen and began making notations on the legal pad. "Before we begin," he said, "there's one question I have to ask. This is the second time I've come here, and the second time you've tried to goad me into an argument. I'm trying to defend you – why are you trying to make me angry?"

"You've just answered your own question."

"I'm not in the mood for riddles…"

"No, no riddles. If I've learned one thing, it's that you can't defend a cause that you don't believe in.

"You dislike me, but I'm not bothered by that. I'd be worried if you didn't. What I need to know is whether you can still do your job. You seem ambivalent as to whether I should live or die. That gives me some hope, but not much."

"Hope?" asked Merich.

"Well, you couldn't defend me if you wanted me dead, could you. Since you seem on the fence about me hanging, there's a ghost of a chance you'll do what it takes. You may not like me - I can deal with that - but what's worse is if you don't understand me.

"Until you get past it all, you can't do your job. So I argue with you…I want you to confront your anger. If you acknowledge it…If you can see even the slightest justification for my life, then I think you might just fight for me."

Merich shook his head and began to laugh. "My dear Brother Chairman – you've put far more thought into this than I ever will," he chortled. "It's a trial. There's a tribunal, and lawyers, and witnesses and evidence. At the end, there'll be a decision. If I do my job well, you'll live. If I don't, then none of this is going to matter.

"You're so concerned about what I think or feel. Well, cards on the table – I didn't like your government and I paid a price for not liking it. You can't change those things, or fix them, and I don't expect you to.

"If you want my sympathy, then you're wasting your time and mine. You'll never get it. What you will get is my professionalism. You'll get my best because it's what I need to do. You don't want my understanding – you want my self-interest. Now, can we please begin?"

Licht paused, then shrugged. "Of course. I'm ready," he replied.

"Good. Now, the tribunal is modeled on the example from

what the Allied powers had used at Nuremburg. The main charges, of course, will be crimes against humanity. They haven't formally released them, but I' m privy to a number of details. From what I understand, there are over one hundred counts, so the trial will take some time. Even if we don't know the specifics, I think it would be helpful to construct a theme to the defense."

"You mean 'my' defense," corrected Licht.

"That's what I meant...Anyway, as I see it, our theme would be comprised of three possible components, if you will."

"Which are?"

"Well, first, we would need to associate the more egregious abuses with someone else – someone who the Court would view as a credible suspect – someone like Stern, or another individual in your government."

"I'm not willing to do that," stated Licht. "I won't betray my friends, even in death."

"Are you saying it was all you - that Stern didn't do anything you didn't order him to do?"

Licht paused for a moment, his eyes quickly flickering to the cell door before returning to Merich. "I was President and Party Chairman. I believe that speaks for itself," he said assertively.

"Actually...it doesn't," countered Merich. "You're not saying anything."

"I'm saying no. Clear enough for you?"

"All right, but I have to tell you that's our best option. Without that, our case is very weak. Besides, what harm is there in implicating Stern? Most people believe he was the worst of your commissars."

"I'm still not interested."

"Look, everyone knows that he was your muscle," argued Merich. "They might not like you, but they hate him with a passion. I really think it would be in your best interest to agree to this."

"Tell me the other two," said Licht, still unmoved by Merich's explanation.

"Fine...," sighed Merich. "The second is to argue that many of the so-called atrocities were handled within the parameters of the existing law. That is, that due process was in place, and that the alleged lawbreakers were fully aware of the consequences of these actions."

"This is true."

"Yes, but the Magistrates may question those laws in light of the United Nations Charter on Human Rights. Also, there are the penalties. Things changed after the war. There are limits to the kind of punishment you can impose."

"Regardless, the law is the law," declared Licht.

"Using that logic, you were a criminal before you took power, and you are guilty now. The prosecution is going to point that inconsistency."

"You don't understand. The killing, the suffering - there was a moral imperative to act."

"Sure, and the same argument is being used by the government now to justify your overthrow...I know this is the line you want to take, but it's the hardest one for us to defend. I have to recommend against it."

"Then, tell me the third."

"Essentially, we attempt to convince the tribunal into the merits of commuting your sentence."

"You propose bribing them, then?"
Merich stared at Licht, shaking his head. "Bribing? I don't even know what to say to that."

"Of course...my apology," smiled Licht. "I shouldn't assume that sort of thing goes on with your people."

"What I mean," Merich continued, "is that we argue that killing you will create a martyr, and that your supporters may react – killings, reprisals, bombings – you know, general disruptions of daily life.

"That may work on one level, but I can foresee problems. It's indirect - I - we - have to trust that they read between the lines. I can't really do much in open court, except make some speech about 'national unity.' They'll rule me out of order before I get the first sentence out. If there were a jury, I could play it to a mistrial, but we don't have that. The main problem is that we don't address the charges directly, so a mistrial's unlikely. You'll get a new lawyer, though.

"They may decide to go ahead and rule - execute you just to show a strong hand. Even if they don't, the option of exile in a neutral country gets taken off the table. After all, they wouldn't want you and your followers organizing outside their sphere of influence. The best that you could hope for is life imprisonment"

Licht sighed. "It doesn't seem as though you've given me any decent alternatives," he said.

"I've given you the best of a bad lot," defended Merich. "It's not like you stole a cow, or left an unpaid debt. Your situation is on the sunny side of hopeless. Mind you, had you spent less time playing games and more time discussing strategy, we'd be further ahead."

"God save us from trivial people," muttered Licht.

"I thought you didn't believe in God?"

"I said that I haven't seen any evidence," he continued. "For someone so omnipotent, you would think that they would have a better class of people representing them."

"I thought we were talking about the courts - not the Almighty."

"Neither are particularly well served by their employees, if you ask me. Poor oversight."

"Observation, or experience?"

"Pardon?"

Merich slid the notepad to one side. He clasped his hands together as if in supplication. "Before I was assigned to collecting documents from government buildings, I spent the better part of six months in the field on behalf of the Ministry. You know, I think I've been to every village and town in the central province." Licht's mouth contorted into a smirk. "I'm so pleased for you. Spent your days drinking beer and eating sausages, did we?"

"There wasn't a week that went by where we didn't find a ditch out in some farmer's pasture," continued Merich. "We'd try to enlist some of the locals to help dig. Most wouldn't dare. You'd walk through a village - the old women would cross themselves, run off to God knows where.

"Eventually, we'd talk a few of the men into helping us. We had to pay them a lot, and we always had to have a priest there - to give them forgiveness before the shovels even hit the dirt. Most times, we had to have them keep praying and burning incense, or the men would run off.

"Usually, you'd only go down a foot or two before you would find them. Mostly men, but women and children too - layer upon layer. The smell was gone, but they were pretty badly decomposed.

"In the beginning, we did our best to separate them, identify them, but that got to be too much. The bodies - they would come apart when you tried to lift them out, like a piece of boiled meat.

74

We lost most of our help when that happened.

"We wanted to give them all a good Christian burial, but in the end, we'd just end up filling the ditch with kerosene and cremating the remains.

"The first site I went to was the hardest - threw up all that beer and sausage you talked about...Before I was done, I had been to five more - all pretty much the same.

"The old timers - if you asked them what killed those people, they don't say bullets or knives. Do you know what they say? Brother Chairman's tears. They say that when your wife died, you cried so hard that the tears poisoned the souls of men, drove them mad, made them kill and kill again. Funny thing to say...Well, they're uneducated, superstitious. Can't expect much from that lot, *ja*?"

Licht stared vacantly at Merich, the paleness in his face making the partially visible scar on his neck appear almost a shade of indigo.

A moment of silence passed before Merich began to place his writing pad back in the case. He grabbed his cane, and pulled himself out of the chair.

"Where are you going? asked Licht, his voice distracted.

"Back to the city."

"We haven't finished talking."

"About what?" shrugged Merich. "The case? Your political views? We didn't talk about the trial the last time I came here - it didn't seem to bother you then."

"You're not taking the case?" asked Licht.

"Last time I came here you walked out on me," said Merich. "I know a play for power when I see one...You need to understand that I'm your counsel. I'm not your mouthpiece, and I'm sure as hell not your apologist."

"But you're still going."

"Two days, Brother Chairman - two days for you to decide how this goes. I'll be back for your answer."

Merich called out for the guard to unlock the cell door. He turned back briefly to Licht. "Time is always wasted on the foolish. You and I both know better than to waste ours. Maybe our next meeting will make a difference?"

He turned and walked out of the cell.

CHAPTER 10

Merich woke from a rest in name only. He felt far more fatigued than when he had retired the evening before. A flushed feeling came over him, through his cheeks and forehead. He dreaded the thought of catching something. Ever since his injury, he found it hard to fight off even the most benign cough. The first sign of lethargy had Merich brewing numerous pots of an herbal tea loaded with bits of dried Echinacea. It was what his mother had done on such occasions. He was not entirely convinced of its efficacy, but felt some compulsion to do it all the same.

Once the tea had had time to steep, he poured some of the contents into a large earthenware mug, stirring in a couple of rounded tablespoons of honey. The crystallized mounds of whitish gold bobbed atop the dark liquid as they slowly melted away. Merich sat at his table, staring at the pieces of solid dissipate, mesmerized by the transformation.

The loud knock on the door startled him back.

"Herr Merich?" came the accompanying voice. "There is a call for you."

"Uh…Thank you, Frau Fischer," he hesitated. "I'll be there in a moment…I'm not decent yet."

Fastening the tasseled ends of his dressing gown, he made his way into the hall. A few feet down sat a small oval table, where the communal telephone was located. Its receiver was laid carefully to the side. He picked it up. "Hello?" he answered.

"Herr Merich? This is Marta Kysely. The Minister asked me to call you. You had a meeting with him this morning."

"Yes…sorry…I've been in bed all morning…Not feeling well."

"He was expecting you," she repeated efficiently.

"Please…give my apologies…I'll make myself available anytime when I come in."

"He is a busy man, Herr Merich…"

"I realize that, Marta, but I'm sick, and standing in a drafty hallway talking to you isn't helping! Unless you want me to come in and cough and vomit all over the Minister's office, I suggest you stick to whatever job he pays you to do! Pass on my apologies!"

Merich slammed the receiver down hard on the cradle, muttering 'bitch' as he hobbled back to his flat. He had met the woman on only a couple of occasions. She appeared to be unremarkable, yet efficient. Nevertheless, she possessed the kind of personality that put him on edge from the start. Having seen a cursory glimpse of the department, and the occasional miscue of superiors, they conclude that they are the indispensable intellect running the show. He had never really noticed the phenomenon until Bruno pointed it out to him. Now, he could see just how prevalent it was.

Grabbing his mug of tea, he grumbled some more as he made his way down the hall to his bedroom. He felt tired and restless all at once. No sooner did he position himself in bed, he would get up and move, or adjust something he found to be bothersome - his pillows, or the closed curtains that still allowed a sliver of light to shine through.

For what seemed an eternity, he lay still and awake. He turned on his table lamp, and began to stare at the ceiling. He noticed the cobwebs that had gathered on the light fixture and the far upper corners of the room. The soot from the coal had stuck to the silk, turning the strands of the webs black. They looked like the errant pieces of thread that occasionally creeped up from the back of Emi's dresses when he had to help her with a stubborn fastener or zipper. Merich thought about how the shadows they created against the ceiling were more visible, more pronounced, than the webs themselves. Just like people, he thought.

He rubbed his hand gently over his thigh. A pant leg usually hid the scars, which were significant. The damage of the initial wound had only been compounded by a number of corrective surgeries, the nature and immediacy of which many were debatable.

What remained after the scalpels was a large reddish colored scar that radiated from the front of his leg around to the once fatty inner thigh. The outer covering of skin was drawn taut over the leg like the casing on a sausage. Every sinewy contour the remaining muscles and ligatures formed presented bumps and lines along the patch. When alone and naked, Merich did his best to avert his eyes from it.

It had affected his relations with Emi. Even if it no longer felt a burn to the touch, he would never let her near it. When making love, he insisted on darkness. Not even the glimmer of an overcast crescent moon could be permitted to pass beyond the window drapes. Beyond this, he had also taken to wearing loose fitting pajama bottoms that allowed him to engage without disrobing below the waist.

Finally, the boredom overtook him. He resolved to get up and began to make his way, ever so gingerly, to his study. He hobbled over to the bookshelf and, after counting off the requisite book spines, pulled back the four he had removed a number of times already. Steadying his shoulder into the shelf, he reached in behind and extracted the diary. Placing the other books back in their spot, he hobbled back to his room with the object of his attention.

After a short detour to the washroom, he climbed back into bed. He stared thoughtfully at the book that lay on top of the quilt by his side, then picked it up and began to read.

To this point, Merich had found Licht's handwriting to be challenging to read. His lettering was tight and economical, and it was often difficult to discern an accent from an errant ink mark on the page. He reasoned that the only solution, like in so many other pursuits, was time and practice.

For the next hour, he carefully read through each page. In time, the tight script began to open up, and he felt a flow develop. He found the cadence to the words. They began to evoke pictures in his mind - hope and sorrow, exhilaration and despair. He saw the youthful passion, for love and for a cause, and knew it unto himself. He wondered whether he could have written the same words himself a few short years ago.

He saw pain and sacrifice, despair and despondency. It was a detailed recount of the days of occupation. He had been spared any direct knowledge of it, and those who held those memories – like his parents - were reluctant to share any but the most sanitized and redacted fragments of the time.

There was Licht, his wife, Stern, and a close circle of

confidantes who shrank, one by one, with every journey entry. For a stretch of time - nearly three years by the date count - the diary read more like a collection of obituaries. One man dies by firing squad, while another gets sent to one camp or another - Dachau, Bergen-Belsen, Sobibor. A woman is detained by the local Gestapo head with no proof of the outcome, only a reasonable expectation of an end most ignoble. The content of each entry differed only in the identity of the victim and the nature of the vulgarities.

In the beginning, the descriptions were perfunctory, almost an aside. Somewhere in the midpoint, the more egregious details of torture and murder were revealed in increasingly blunt language. The handwriting form in these entries became tighter, more rushed. Merich could see the indentation of the pen nib on the paper. Writing with anger? Anger at your enemies? Anger with your lot? Yes, he knew that feeling. It was not writing. It was shouting without the volume.

Every one of the entries through the middle began with a simple sentence - 'In hiding.' The only variation was 'Still in hiding,' but this only seemed to last for a period of three or four months. Then, it was back to the original. It was as though the circumstances could not justify the luxury of a single superfluous word.

Merich recognized the sadness. He slammed the book shut and tossed it on the bed. What was so different? These poor, poor people - they would endure. They would go on and take power. Before long, they would do the very same things that caused Licht so much hurt. He shed tears for his compatriots. Did he shed any tears for those people in the unmarked graves here and there? Did he shed a tear for Franz Merich?

He sighed and shook his head. Empathy, pathology - just the matter of flipping a switch. Merich had read psychology before taking on the law, and was not unfamiliar with the subject. People could turn, and often did. He knew that it did not happen in a vacuum. Freud or Jung - whatever your inclination - there was always a foundation, a pretext. They only disagreed on the cause, not on its existence. If Licht had turned into a psychotic bastard, maybe it was because it had been in the man all along? The sense of disconnect was foremost in his thoughts as he drifted to sleep. It was the briefest of interludes before he was startled out of his rest.

"Alex? Alex, are you in here?" The voice lilted as it echoed from the direction of the front door.

Still groggy, he looked about the room. "Uh...just a minute," he shouted back.

He heard footsteps moving down the hallway to his room. "Seriously, you pick the strangest time to be modest," called out the voice, gaining volume and tone with each approaching pace. Merich took sight of the diary that lay beside him. "Wait!" he called back. "I'm sick - at least let me sort myself out!"

"That's why I'm here," answered Emi. "I called your office, and they said you were home with something or another. Thought I'd play nurse."

"I'm out of tea!" he called out quickly. "I could really use some more."

The footsteps stopped a couple of feet short of his door.

"Okay," she replied, "do you want anything else?"

"No...thanks...just the tea."

The steps began again, retracing in the opposite direction. Once he heard the noise enter the kitchen, he grabbed the book and looked about for a place to put it. Not under a pillow. Not the drawer in the night stand.

Merich dropped the book as carefully as he could on the floor.

"What was that?" called out Emi.

"Nothing," he said quickly. "The headboard - it's loose."

"Well, you better get it fixed soon," she laughed, "or I won't be able to show my face around your neighbors!"

"I doubt that's a big concern for them," he groaned as he leaned over the side to grab his cane. He placed the rubber end on the book, pushing it under his bed. Satisfied it was hidden from view, he took the cane and laid it on the bed across his legs. Emi soon entered the room, carrying a steaming mug, taking great care not to spill any. "I have no idea how you or your mother make this stuff," she remarked. "All I did was boil some water and add it to the pot."

"Thanks," he said, reaching out to take the mug from her. He took a long sip.

"Seriously," she added, "how much of that should you be drinking? The pot was nearly empty as it was."

"It's not going to kill me," he sighed, after swallowing the mouthful. "I've gone through more than that in a day."

Emi frowned. "Maybe so, but you should be a lot more careful," she said. "I'll tell you one thing that'll get you, though."

"What?"

"That," she added, pointing to his cane. "What if you roll over on it?" She picked it up and leaned it against the wall still within reach.

An impish grin came across Merich's face. "Well, you're a hell of a lot bigger than that, and I haven't got hurt rolling over you!" he laughed.

"You're a pig - you know that?" she said with feigned offense.

"I take it you're feeling better?"

"Not for that, I don't...Still a bit queasy. I'll stick to the tea and toast for now."

"You need some broth," asserted Emi. "You also need to get out of this drafty place. Come home with me. Mother will make up a guest room for you."

Merich sighed as he shook his head. "No - I can't. She means well, but I don't want her hovering over me. Besides, a good night's rest, and I'll be fine."

"You won't get it here," she replied. "Seriously, Alex, just come back with me - for a day or two."

"Please don't ask me again, Emi. I'd rather stay here...Please."

"Fine, at least let me go to the chemist and pick you up something. That tea isn't going to do anything except rot a hole in your stomach."

"Later," he said. "There's no rush." He held out his arm to her. "Come here."

"I'm not here for that, you dirty boy," she said with a playful scold.

Merich shook his head while his arm remained outstretched. "That's not what I want – not right now," he said, as he gently patted the pillow. "Just lay here with me for a little while."

Emi looked at Merich, and after a moment of reflection, she climbed onto the bed and moved herself in to his side. He cradled his arm around her as she placed her head on his chest. "I'm warning you," she said. "If your hands move anywhere, I'm getting up."

"My word as a gentleman," he replied. "This is all I'm looking for."

She raised herself slightly so as to turn to him. "You really are sick, aren't you?" she said.

"I'm not dying, if that's what you mean."

"Seriously," she continued, "what's wrong?"

"Nothing," said Merich, gently pulling her back to him. "I guess…I miss this."

"Miss what?"

"This," he said. "Whatever it is."

Emi burrowed herself back into the spot. "When was the last time we did this?" she asked.

"I don't know," he answered. "Feels good, though. Whatever it is, I think I miss it."

"Is that you or the tea talking?" she laughed.

"Just me," he said in a soft tone. "Just me."

They lay still in their embrace – seconds, to minutes, to hours. Still until the steeped liquid in the mug went cold and the room turned dark.

CHAPTER 11

Merich had tried to avoid this particular meeting for as long as he could. He sensed it was going to be awkward and uncomfortable, much like his first experience with Licht. Regardless, it was much more than a social nicety, and he had taken some time that morning to consider his approach.

The offices for the public prosecutors were, conveniently enough, in the same building, two floors above. Merich had not been there before, but presumed that the layout and the accommodations were similarly modest. He made his way down the hall, stopping at the identified door. He sat his case down, and then raised his hand to knock. The light wrapping still seemed sufficient to knock the frosted pane from its glazing.

"Come," replied the casual voice from the other side.
He turned the knob, pushing the door open before picking up his valise. "I hope I'm not disturbing you. I think I might be a bit early."

"Not at all - Herr Merich?"

"Yes. Please - call me Alex."

"Then you can call me Petr."

He was constructed on the perfect frame for his demeanor – compact and muscular, with large forearms and a conflated chest. He resembled those breeds of dog that men put on one another for sport. They waddled awkwardly, like mechanical automatons, until they entered the arena. It was only then, in the pell mell moments of sweat and furious blood that their movements assumed their natural and fluid poetry. He stood and reached out to shake Merich's hand. "I'm surprised that we haven't crossed paths before now."

"Actually," volunteered Merich, "we have."

"Really? I'm sorry...I don't recall..."

"Almost two years ago," he continued. "You were at a lecture my father gave on pre-republican jurisprudence."

Bŏsek nodded. "I remember that it was a very select group," he replied as he took his seat, gesturing for Merich to do likewise.

"And a very obscure location," added Merich, as he set his case on the floor and sat down.

"Yes...mind you, the Vopos would manage to fit someone in if you had held it in a telephone box...They got him shortly after that, didn't they?"

"About a couple of weeks after," sighed Merich. "Not that it would have stopped him."

"No," replied Bŏsek thoughtfully. "No, it wouldn't have. I am sorry for your loss."

Merich nodded politely. "Thank you," he replied. "Of course, I came to talk about the trial."

"Yes - I hear that we're going to be facing off against one another."

"Thank you. I prefer to look at it as conducting a case."
"Sure," replied Bŏsek, "but there's only one outcome, and we're both looking for a win."

"You mean for justice?" asked Merich.

"I think my meaning's obvious."

"Regardless, I wanted to meet to discuss the evidence being presented."

The prosecutor gave a puzzled look. "I believe you would have gotten the list already. I had the paperwork sent to your office."

"Yes - and thank you," answered Merich, "but I have a few questions about it."

"Well, I'll try to help if I can."

"I think some things are missing."

Bŏsek looked at him with unmistakable incredulity. "Missing," he said.

"A few things, by my count."

"By your count...Tell me, what is it that you think is missing?"
Merich shrugged. "Well, I'm not sure..."

Bŏsek leaned back in his chair and held up a hand. "Okay, just so I'm clear on this," he interrupted. "I sent three boxes of documents to your office - about 500 items - less than three days ago. You've got nobody to help you go through them, but you're confident that some things are missing...but you don't know what."

"What can I say? There are some gaps in what you've sent."

The prosecutor's face hardened with the clenching of his jaw "Honestly," he muttered. "I don't have time for games..."

"I'm not playing games," defended Merich. "I'm dead serious."

"And so am I!" spat back Bösek. "I don't like what you're hinting at!"

"Your counts - over 180 - all between January 1947 and March 1948 - why are they only over that year?" asked Merich. "Is there any significance?"

"Not to me," came the reply. "It's what we have. The investigators have pulled everything they could find. You should know that. It was your crew that dug it up in the first place!"

"Of course, but none of them date prior to February of 1947. My client was First Secretary from June of 1946."

"Your point being?"

"My point, Petr, is that you don't have anything between Licht taking charge and the attempt on his life."

Bösek smirked as he shook his head. He clasped his hands together as if to meditate. "Alex," he began slowly, "you're new to this, so I'll give you some friendly advice. Don't tell me your strategy - you've got a hard enough job as it is."

"I'm not giving anything away," countered Merich. "I just want to know what I'm not getting."

"Well, I hope you didn't come here to suggest I'm holding things back from you. That's professional misconduct. Not the best way to begin a trial."

"I'm not suggesting anything of the sort," asserted Merich. "All I'm pointing out is that you're arguing that for a year he was as bad as the Nazis, but for the six months before that? Nothing. Put yourself in my shoes."

"He lost his wife. He snapped. What can I say?"

"Seems unlikely to me. Sure, he's angry...but unhinged? Besides, he's only one man. That's a lot to put on him."

Bösek laughed derisively. "You're his lawyer - not his friend! Maybe he has you fooled, *ja*?"

Merich knew Bösek's reputation as a street fighter – both in and out of the courtroom. He had grown up poor in the eastern reaches, well past Shostoi and deep into a frontier that remained one step shy of anarchy. Vocations related to the law were common, but usually not from Bösek's chosen perspective.

The ground was rocky and sparse, so farming meant herding - and conflict. Two of Bösek's uncles met a premature end in this hard-scrabble struggle. One died from what had amounted to an argument over five sheep, while the other was shot over the right to grazing on a plot of land that would not have been able to fill the belly of a goat. Bösek's mother had attended far too many funerals, and her insistence on a different path for young Petr could not be assuaged or diverted.

Hundreds of years of mountain blood do not purge easily, and to pursue a career in law, certain compromises were necessary. Through it all, he had exercised more caution and discretion than his forbearers. That changed when the counter-revolt came. Bösek proved to be disturbingly effective at the tasks at hand, and in a part of the country where their forces were at a decided disadvantage.

He remembered what Franz used to say about the truly uncouth. Life and circumstance may force you to live in the filth, but you did not have to give in to it. That was your choice. Bosek not only gave into it, but he luxuriated in it. It made him reek like the prostitutes off the Bohringerstrasse who cut their cheap toilet water with alcohol. Merich could not help but feel that the stink would get on him, that it would never fully wash out.

He neither liked nor disliked Petr Bösek as a man. He knew what he knew, but that was precious little. His training taught him to be wary of the persona, and it was on that where he had made his opinion. Where others saw bravery, he saw weakness - insecurity, and self-doubt. Franz taught him that aggression was fear in action. By that measure, the great Petr Bösek was possibly one of the most frightened men he had ever met. He hoped that he was right about that.

"You want to win?" he replied. "Well, I'm going to make you work for it."

The smile dissipated from Bösek's face. He leaned forward, his gaze making Merich feel as though he were naked and exposed. "You listen to me - as far as I can tell, you got this case either because you're Franz Merich's son, or because you got crippled in the cause. Either way I don't care. It's all going to end the same."

Merich took a moment to get his bearings from the sudden

swipe. "If that's part of your opening statement," he observed wryly, "then I think you might have a problem."

"No problem, boy!" came the defiant reply. "I'll win, and that sonofabitch will hang! What's left of him can burn in hell with Stern and his whore wife! Get in my way and you'll join them!" Merich grinned. Without a word, he reached into his case and extracted a sealed bottle, which he placed on the desk in front of Bŏsek.

"What the fuck is that?"

"Lagavulin. From Scotland," Merich said in a measured tone. "Sixteen years old. I think we got off on the wrong foot. Please...Consider it a peace offering."

Bŏsek's face turned pale at the sight of the bottle. "Where'd you get it?"

"Oh, that. Well, you mentioned all of the usual things - my father, my leg. You didn't mention how I was Bruno Stolzer's lackey...Sorry...I shouldn't have said that. Please...no hard feelings. Let's have a drink."

As Merich reached to break the seal, Bŏsek stopped him. "I don't drink."

"I'm sorry. I was informed to the contrary," replied Merich, picking up the bottle. He held it for a couple of seconds before placing it back on the desk. "On second thought," he continued, "maybe I'll just leave it with you. You know, for guests...with my compliments, of course."

"Of course," muttered Bŏsek, as he glanced away from the bottle.

Merich grabbed his case and lifted himself to his feet. "You know, you're probably right - about the gap in time. It's just that it's my first case. I want to do it right...You understand..."

Bŏsek said nothing. The anger melted away from his face, the muscles in his body relaxing. The predator at rest.

"So," continued Merich, "I'll leave you then...Good luck, counselor."

Merich moved out into the hall, leaving the office door open. As he made his way slowly to the elevators, he could hear the clinking of glass echo in the corridor.

CHAPTER 12

Merich arrived home just after seven o'clock. It was still early enough in the year that darkness had already made its suffocating presence known. He removed his coat and went to the kitchen, set to fixing a simple meal of broth and bread. He felt ravenous, but his stomach was still queasy. He knew anything more substantial would have set him over the edge.

Sitting down at the table, he ate his meal in silence. The ever-present muffled sounds from the other flats were overtaken by the rattle of windowpanes from the buffeting wind hit them head on. The old glazing putty had dried out long ago, caking off in places, allowing the cool air to leak through the errant gaps.

Part of him wished Emi was coming. The day had proved to be a feat of endurance, and he realized how much he missed her welcome at the end of it. But she had used up her requisite number of excuses for not coming home that week. Another night away from the Stolzer household would have had her mother in a fitful state, and lead to questions that neither one of them wished to entertain.

Once he finished his meal and washed the dishes, he made his way into the study. He was about to reach for the familiar books when he noticed that one of the spines extended out further than the rest.

Merich had always ensured that the books were flush along their outer edge. It had been a force of habit, acquired back in the days leading to the counter-revolt. He was not unfamiliar with the workings of a dead drop, or concealments of a certain nature. He was not unfamiliar with the consequences of a poor execution either.

It was then he remembered that he would find an empty hole. The diary still lay on the floor, under his bed. Merich turned and made his way to the bedroom to retrieve it. Crooking his cane just under the edge of the bed, he placed the rubber end on top of the book, and slid it out into the open.

As he bent over and picked up the book, the pages splayed open. A couple of folded over sheets of paper dropped out on the floor.

Merich was surprised that he had not noticed the papers sooner. He thought that he had made a rather thorough review of the contents the day before.

Steadying himself against the bed, he took great care to lower himself onto his knees, one at a time. He picked up the book and laid it on the bed. He reached for the papers, then pulled himself up onto the bed and sat down. He opened the folded sheets and began to read.

"April 17, 1947 -

They tell me that is what today is, although I have no recollection. By my own count, I have been awake for ten days. How long I slept before that is based solely on the word of others.

I am told that I am in the Soviet Union, in a hospital in Leningrad. This seems to be true, as everyone here speaks Russian when they talk among themselves. They also tell me that my injuries were, and still are, extensive. The pain I feel is proof enough. It prevents me from doing much, including writing. I am grateful to Comrade Kalunin who is serving as my personal secretary, and by whose hand these words are being transcribed. I intend to add them to my journal when circumstances warrant.

The cause of my injuries, I am told, were the result of an assassination attempt two months ago. We had been heading to the theatre. The driver had stopped the car and opened the door immediately behind him, the one closest to Eva. Apparently, one of the men attached to my security detail exited the car following us, ran up and threw a grenade.

Eva took the full force of the blast. I am told she died instantly.

The driver was partially shielded by the car door and managed to live a week longer. It was explained to me that the angle from which the grenade was thrown, plus Eva being in the path of the blast are what likely saved my life.

My injuries hurt, but the fact I can only grieve her now pains me more. I feel shame for not having done so sooner, regardless of the circumstances.

Yesterday, I received a visit from our ambassador, Jiri Slotek. I have known him for years, but he seemed odd to me this time. To be honest, he is a mouse of a man, and avoids discomfort where he can. I presume that the extent of my injuries were off putting to him.

Jiri said that all was well, that Hugo had stepped into the breach, and that the conspirators had been dealt with. I told him that Hugo should be working with Nemeth. He apologized and said that is what he meant. I also asked him what he meant by 'dealt with.' He wouldn't elaborate on that, but it doesn't matter. I understood his meaning.

I did ask how my condition was being reported. Jiri said that Hugo has downplayed it, and that I would be resuming my duties shortly. I told him that I hoped that was true, but it would be better for the Central Committee to convene and discuss a possible succession. The Committee established a line of precedent for no other reason than to ensure the Party's leadership for the long term. I know that Hugo wasn't happy about it, but I was reluctant to force the issue. I think that Nemeth is a level-headed sort, and he has the presence in the Plenary not to be bulldozed. I was glad to see him named, and if I don't come back, the Party will be well served.

At this point, though, it doesn't matter. For the foreseeable future, I'm resigned to lie and wait, my pain and Comrade Kalunin my constant companions.

Merich examined the script. It had been a different hand that formed the letters, and one for whom both the language and the lettering were not second nature. Native Russian speakers had a

definite style of handwriting. He had seen it in some of the
correspondence his investigations at Nytriy had uncovered. The
letters did not have the same flow. They were stylized in a block
form, with some resemblance to their Cyrillic variants. He carefully
folded the papers and slipped them back into the book.

He remained perched on the side of the bed, staring out the
window. Then, turning back to the book, he ran his forefinger
slowly across the seam on the front cover where the supple leather
on the spine overlapped on its inner edge. His eyes trained their
intent focus on every scratch and dig in its surface, the pale tan
lines of raised hide that disturbed the otherwise smooth and
darkened patina. It was an asset and a liability, a key and a trap.

For a moment, Merich tried to run scenarios that would see
the diary somehow find its way to the Ministry. None proved to be
practical. If it were to show up anywhere other than Nytriy, people
were bound to start asking how. If it were to surface at the Palace,
they would end ask why now. Either his team missed it in their
sweep, or one of them had let it out. The path still led back to him.
Regardless of the approach, he was certain of a conversation with
Hartz he preferred not to have.

A frown crossed his face as he grabbed his cane and pulled
himself. Picking up the book, he walked out of the bedroom and
headed back to his study. He placed the diary back in the cubby
hole and duly covered it.

Answers were there – he knew it, felt it in his marrow. They
refused to relent their modesty. All Merich could think was that a
good night's sleep would burn the fog away. It was the one bit of
advice from Franz that he could always rely on.

CHAPTER 13

The University resembled a ghost town from some pulp novel about the American West, or so Merich thought. The buildings, the central courtyard with its ornate fountain - all were essentially intact, even if they showed obvious signs of neglect and indifference.

The lawns were left untended, save for portions where a modest flock of sheep had kept the grass short and flat. People needed to eat, and the animals were going to end up as a meal for someone - undernourished students left in the dormitories, or some family who had counted on the location being as fertile as it was obscure. Merich could make out a lone figure standing watch. The man and his rifle were a guarantee that none of the animals would leave for anywhere other than their intended destination. He was too far to see the man's features, but he knew that a suspicious set of eyes followed him at every labored step.

Merich remembered different days - different ways. The quad filled with students, while grass supported nothing more than the coloured blankets and picnic baskets of young lovers. The outer field had felt the steady, rhythmic trample of feet as men in their vigorous prime played football with a joyful abandon. The carved stone bordering the edge of the fountain pool held groups of keen minds who delighted in arguing the greater questions of the world, both visible and not seen.

His mind contemplated the lawn, now bereft of all but chattel. He turned to the base of the fountain. It held nothing more than a shallow pool of greenish brown liquid that gave off the fetid stench of decay.

The building that housed the Law Faculty felt as familiar as the back of his hand. He remembered the summer he turned ten. He would accompany his father to his office each day. In through the front doors and up a flight of stairs, then the fourth door on the left. There was the anteroom where Beate always greeted him with a chocolate, and where he would busy himself if Father was in a meeting. In between the steady parade of students and colleagues, he would manage to gain entry into the office.

The Merichs would sit in their appointed places - Franz behind the large oak desk, with Alex on the settee in the corner. Both passed the minutes and hours quietly reading, writing. Every so often, Merich broke the silence with a question, or some observation. Franz would drop his pen and assume the thoughtful pose before giving his reply, a contented smile that seemed welded to his words. The answer was given, and the two would resume their routine. Within a couple of minutes, Franz would take his turn and ask of his son. Back and forth, like a game of chess, it ended in a blissful stalemate when they left the office to join the picnickers on the quad with the lunch that Olga had attentively packed for them.

Merich stood alone in the middle of the lobby, his eyes transfixed on the staircase. His gaze moved up each step, careful not to miss one, until it reached the top. He noticed two figures standing short of the edge of the landing – one old and one young. Merich watched them talk. The older one began to laugh as he raised a hand to pat the young man's shoulder. They turned, then fell away from his sight. Quietly, he lowered his gaze, and continued on his way down the corridor that lay ahead.

The library had been the one part of the building that was *terra incognito*. His father spent a great deal of time there, but mostly on days when Merich did not come. On the occasions he did happen to be there, Beate managed to keep him preoccupied with one activity or another.

He first set foot in the cavernous hall shortly after the overthrow, certain that a clerkship with the Constitution Committee was imminent. He had spent a full day rummaging through what he could find on the subject. The call from Hartz a couple of days later negated any need for a return visit.

Beyond the door and to the right sat a reception desk. Behind it a bespectacled man was singularly preoccupied by his paperwork. His dress and demeanor fit the image that Merich had in his head before his arrival – the doddering recluse who found books preferable to people. He did not judge. He may not have ascribed to the aesthetic, but part of him appreciated it well, even envied it. He pushed out a shallow cough to garner attention.

The man raised his head, peering over the top of his wire frame edges. He rose to his feet. "Good afternoon, Herr Merich – it is such a pleasure to have you here."

"You know who I am?" asked Merich.

"No one outside of the library staff has been here in eight months, and you don't look like a student," explained the man.

"You get many of those?"

"Students?" laughed the man. "Haven't had one of those in nine!"

"At any rate," continued Merich, "I want to thank you, Mister…?"

"Goranevic. I'm the Chief Librarian here. I want to assure you that our staff have tried to see to your every request."

Merich had remembered specific mention of the gentleman by Hartz, that despite his eccentricities, he was a splendid researcher and documentarian. If you could get past his 'unique' personality, added the Minister, you would find a loyal and effective assistant. "I appreciate your help, Mister Goranevic," he answered. "I'm sure it wasn't easy."

Goranevic smiled broadly. "Well," he began, "some of the volumes have been damaged, but even those are fairly legible. Ironically enough, the best luck we had was with some of the oldest in our collection.

"You see; many had been stored in the underground vaults at the Museum. I suppose that no one thought enough of them to destroy them."

"Or maybe they had become something more than just a book?" volunteered Merich. "Anyway, I appreciate your help."

Goranevic looked at him with some curiosity. "You are not connected to Herr Doktor Merich?" he asked.

"My father," replied Merich.

Goranevic became awkwardly ebullient. "Ah, then it is a great honour indeed!" he said, attempting to shake Merich's hand. "You know; it was a great loss to this country!"

"Yes, thank you," he muttered. "It was also a great loss to my mother as well."

Goranevic's expression waned. "Of course, of course – forgive me…"

Merich raised his hand. "Please," he interrupted. "I understand what you meant…I'm afraid that I haven't been well."

"Let me send someone to the chemist for you…" volunteered the librarian.

"No – please – I'll be fine. I just need some time to do my work...I appreciate everything you've done here for me. All I need is the time to go through it all."

"Of course," nodded Goranevic. "Please - come this way. We have you set up in my office. I wanted to make sure that you were not disturbed."

"That's kind of you, but I can't do that. You must need that room more than I do."

"Please, Herr Merich," said Goranevic. "I insist. Believe me, this place is not what it once was. There are very few students reading the law, and most of them here are looking for a quiet place to do God knows what. You may be the only one in this building actually doing what it was intended for."

"You're a kind man, and I appreciate this...Again, I apologize if we got off on the wrong foot…"

"We didn't," smiled Goranevic, as he led Merich to the office located just behind the desk. "I respect what you are doing. It can't be easy, with what happened to the Doktor. For what it's worth, I think that he would approve of this."

"I hope he would," answered Merich with a friendly smile. "I get the feeling that you were fond of him."

"Yes, I remember him very well - very kind. Gentleman, he was," replied Goranevic as he opened the door to his office. "There are many men who've walked through this place in my time. They all talk about the law, they teach it. Very few, if any, ever lived it. Your father did, and I will always respect him for that."

Merich nodded, and proceeded into the room. It was small and plain, painted bright white in order to enhance the effect of the overhead light. The only access to the outside world was a small window along the top edge of the wall behind the desk. It appeared glazed by the dirt and cigarette smoke that he could still smell in the air. The tangle of long grass and thick weeds on the other side made the opening appear as black as night. The desk itself was heavy oak, where layers of dust and dirt stuck to the varnish and gave it a grey veneer. It held two stacks of books, each about a foot high.

"Well," he sighed, "it's a start." He hobbled around to the other side of the desk and lowered himself into the chair. "Were you able to find those volumes I ordered from London?"

"The Nuremburg transcripts? Yes, they arrived two days ago. Unfortunately, they're all in English. We haven't had the time to translate..."

"Don't worry. I'm fluent in English. I can take them as they are," assured Merich. He smiled and offered his thanks, as well as his firm assurance that he would promptly seek out the librarian should circumstance warrant.

Goranevic exited the office, shutting the door behind him. Left alone, Merich settled in to his task in earnest.

He took the volume from the top of the nearest stack and opened it. Musty damp had permeated everything his hands touched, everything his lungs drew in. The pages felt thick and heavy as he ran the index finger of his left hand along the lines. The ink from the script appeared as though it was beginning to lift up from the paper.

His finger ran through the lines quickly and steadily, like a locomotive steaming along a straight stretch of track. When it would stop – if it stopped – his right hand would spring to life, moving his fountain pen to perform the quickest of short hand transcription. It had been a talent that had served him well through his student days - one that he could thank Beate for as well.

The next three hours saw one of the stacks disappear with a page and a half of written notes to mark its brief life. Merich sighed as he considered the volumes that still remained.

He turned and stared out the window, its sepia tinged panes. He knew the statutes. As for precedent, where was that? Hitler did not make it to trial, and neither did Mussolini. Despite what his client believed, he was not a corpse just yet.

Merich bowed forward slightly, shaking his head. Licht was no Hitler or Mussolini. Certainly not an angel or an innocent, but not a psychopath. He mulled over his exchange with Bösek. Yes, a man could snap – that was true. The question was whether he could find his way back after all of that. Could a man unsnap? Could you lose what you held dear, including your life and still...

Merich stopped. He raised his head, his eyes narrowed to near slits. He dropped his pen on the desk. Reaching for his cane, he pried himself up out of the chair. The hours spent in the hard wooden chair brought an angry, resentful jolt of pain along his leg. He winced, as his knees buckled ever so slightly. Taking a deep breath, he pulled himself up straight, then made his way out of the office to where Goranevic had moved to work.

"Sorry," he interrupted. "I hate to bother you again...I have a strange request."

"I'll do what I can - what is it?"

"Well, I need to look at some film."

"We don't carry any in here, but the main library might be able to help. Is there one in particular."

"Unfortunately, no... see, what I want are newsreels - between 1946 and 1948."

"Not all of them," said Goranevic. "I don't even think that's possible."

"No... just one's with Johann Licht."

"Any particular subject?"

"No - could be anything - just so long as he is in them."

Goranevic frowned. "It can be done," he hesitated. "but it's going to take some time - a week at the least."

"At the least?"

"It depends - I might...Look, I'll have it done in a week. I promise."

Merich nodded, as he reached to shake hands on their understanding. "I wouldn't insist if it weren't important," he said.

"What is it you're looking for?"

"Evidence," he said.

CHAPTER 14

Despite the passage of a few days, the illness that had incapacitated Merich still had lingering effects. The dull headache and nausea were nowhere near the intensity of before, but they made their presence known all the same.

After leaving the library, he returned briefly to his office to pick up a few items. He would be leaving for the prison early the next morning and the earlier the departure, the earlier the return. He thought to call Emi from there, rather than use the communal telephone outside his flat. Dinner at the Klosters would have to wait until another day. He neglected to tell her his real motivation, that her company was the only redeeming part of those meals, and that he would much prefer a warmed over tin of soup in his own kitchen than to spend a couple of hours there.

Eventually he arrived home and set to work preparing his modest supper. The soup was a bland broth that he knew would be tolerated. That, some fresh bread he had purchased along the way home, and another pot of herbal tea was all that he craved. Placing the items on the table, he sat down and began to eat. Briefly, he glanced at the darkened study that lay just beyond the open doorway. All told, it had been a good day. It was not arrogance to know in your heart that somewhere, somehow the pieces would all begin to fit.

Merich stopped eating. Placing the spoon into the bowl, he raised himself from the chair. Within minutes, he had resumed his position, with the light in the study turned on, and the diary opened on the table to the left of his meal.

"July 9, 1940

It has been one of the worst days that I can remember. The Germans arrested a number of our key people - Klimsky included. Eva, Stern and I would have been among them too had we not been delayed. A man who saw the whole thing from across the street had told us that we had missed the last of the Gestapo by about fifteen minutes.

Such has been our luck to this point, but I can't help but feel that sooner or later it will run out.

A couple of weeks ago we met in the priory that Borsch opened to us. The Germans do not usually look in a place like that, but if they can't find what they are looking for elsewhere, they have no qualms about pushing their way in. Nevertheless, it is the closest thing that we have to a safe place.

We discussed whether it might be best for us to disband - to wait for better days. A few agreed with this sentiment, arguing that there was no valour in our current enterprise.

Stern opposed this, arguing that he could still get his contacts in Moscow to lend us help. Given the current pact that Stalin signed with Herr Hitler, I am skeptical of this.

Makuch voiced my concern, though, asking whether it was even a good idea to speak to the Russians, that they seemed more interested in carving up the continent between themselves and the Nazis, and they may be obliged to respect one another's areas of influence.

His reaction only confirmed my decision not to broach the subject. He let into Makuch in a way that even I didn't expect. It was only for some minor miracle that the two didn't end up coming to blows. Eva was hysterical, screaming for them to stop. She lit into Stern after - probably harder than she should.

Hugo quieted down after that and left. I'm not a stupid man - I know that he has feelings for Eva that go beyond friendship. If I thought that she shared them, I would be concerned, but my problem is just the opposite - that she hates him so passionately. Now, more than ever, we need to rely on one another. This fighting will surely be the death of us all if we don't get beyond it."

Merich gently closed the book, and continued with his meal. After placing his supper dishes in the kitchen sink, he returned the diary to its hiding place, and then prepared himself for bed.

Tomorrow was Shostoi. An early start meant that there would be a mercifully early finish as well. He drifted off to sleep quickly, too tired to even contemplate his day, or the one to follow.

CHAPTER 15

"You don't look well."

Merich shrugged as he placed his case on the table in Licht's cell. "It's nothing-just a cold."

The client stared at him with some sense of curiosity, as though he had seen a hair out of place, or some blemish. "It looks like more than that," he observed casually.

"Don't tell me you're concerned about my health," he muttered testily as he opened his case.

"Only where my own is concerned."

"You afraid you'll catch a bug?" asked Merich, as he continued to place his writing materials on the table.

"No - more like a case of rope burn."

Merich frowned as he shot his client a deadpan look. "Very droll. Now, can we get on with things?" he asked.

Licht's arms swept open in a broad gesture. "Of course...proceed," he declared.

"Have you come to any decision regarding what we talked about?"

"Concerning?"

Merich tossed his pen to the table. "The strategy!" he growled. "For God's sake, man, this is my third visit and we haven't even sorted this out!"

"I told you that I wouldn't sell out my comrades."

"Comrade. One - singular - and he's dead!"

"Or their memories," added Licht.

"At the rate we're going, he'll be able to thank you in person for being so gallant."

"That's the problem."

"With what?"

"With you - typical lawyer. Win at any cost. Kill my reputation to keep me alive."

"If anybody killed your reputation, it was that madman you want to protect. It was a mistake to have put him in charge of anything. If you can admit it maybe you can stop paying for it."

"I used to run this country!" shouted Licht. He glared with anger at Merich.

Merich kept his composure. "We all 'used' to do something else - be something else...," he replied in a low measured tone. "Now, we're not...You know, there is one thing that we both have in common."

"What's that?"

"It seems the world has let us both down."

Licht frowned, shaking his head ever so slightly. He gave a barely audible sigh of frustration.

Merich took his writing pad and turned it toward Licht, pointing to what he had jotted down from his time in Goranevic's office. "I've looked at almost everything the prosecution has collected for the trial so far. I've poured through all of the transcripts I could find for the Nuremburg Trials as well."

"And?"

"And I'm not particularly hopeful, to tell the truth."

"You're giving up."

"No - you're tying my hands. There's a difference...Look, we have very little room to maneuver. Some room, but not a hell of a lot."

"I don't understand."

"Okay, well they are using the Nuremburg Principles as the main instruction to the magistrates. There's roughly six of them."

"I'm not familiar with them."

The words brought an ironic smirk to Merich's face. He grimaced as he continued. "The first says that your regime is culpable for any acts committed against international law. The second says that a lack of penalty under domestic law is no excuse."

"Meaning?"

"Meaning that they consider what your government - what you did - is a crime, and there's no defense for that."

"So they're going to hang me on the advice of foreigners?"

"No - what they're saying is that just because you said it was the law doesn't make it so."

"It sounds like they're the ones who make it up as they go," grumbled Licht.

"They have to guarantee a fair trial," argued Merich. "Plus - and this is the only bright spot - they have three categories of crime that they can prosecute this way."

"Which are?"

"One is 'crimes against peace'. Since you didn't invade anybody, we can take that one off the table. There's also a category of 'war crimes'. Again, without a war, they won't act on that one either."

"That leaves one by my count."

"Crimes against humanity. That includes political and racial persecution. That's the one they're building their case around."

"Do we know this for certain, or is this more of your guesswork."

"I have the filing. One hundred and eighty-four counts between January 1947 and March 1948."

Licht removed his glasses and rubbed his eyes. "One hundred and eighty-four counts. You mean one hundred and eighty-four people - all their stories."

"I would view it as relatively good news," said Merich.

"Why on earth would you call this good news?!"

Merich paused to centre his thoughts. "Because," he declared, "the charges are confined - you know - to a relatively short timeframe."

"Well, of course. There was a threat to the government - to civil order. We had to act."

"That's not a defense," sighed Merich. "Most would see those actions as excessive at the very least. I might also point out the third principle."

"Being?"

"Being that a head of state has no immunity."

"That doesn't concern me," sniffed Licht. "I wouldn't hide behind a legal trick anyway."

Merich's leg started to ache. He shifted himself in the chair as to allow himself to flex it out fully. "Johann," he began, "I need to know - what was going through your mind during those months?"

Licht's eyes narrowed slightly. He reached into the breast pocket of his shirt and pulled out a package of cigarettes and a small box of matches. He extracted one from the pack and lit the end. He took a deep draw on the cigarette that made the tip glow like the window on a boiler door. "Are you asking me as a lawyer?" he said coolly.

"Yes - among other things."

"To be honest, I can't put it into words."

"They're going to ask you about it. You'll be expected to have an answer."

Licht took another heavy draw, the smoke curling out from his nostrils and the corner of his mouth. "I don't know if I can."

"You were badly injured. Your wife was killed. Surely you must have some thoughts on your situation - your state of mind."

"I wasn't crazy," he interrupted.

"I never said you were," defended Merich. He could feel the frustration welling up inside, and he pushed hard to keep it down. "I need to know what you were thinking though."

Licht stared at Merich and said nothing. His eyes glazed over as his attentions turned inward.

"The prosecutor," continued Merich, "is going to claim that you were so seized with grief and anger that you mounted a personal campaign of revenge. One hundred and eighty-four people died as a result."

Licht remained silent. He lowered his gaze, his mouth contorted into an agonized frown.

"More than a year of your life. For a man who has an opinion on everything, surely you have some thoughts."

"I'm sorry to disappoint you," he replied in a distant tone, "but I don't."

Merich grimaced as he watched his client draw into himself. "That scar," he said, pointing to Licht's hand. "I notice that it matches the one on your neck."

"It's the same one - runs down my side," he answered matter-of-factly.

"You got it when they tried to kill you?"

"Yes."

"Looks painful - does it still hurt?"

"Sometimes, but less so now. It just feels tight - not like my skin anymore."

"I know that feeling. My leg gets that way sometimes…You could have easily died."

"I suppose so. Not something I want to talk about – obvious reasons."

"Obvious…the first count against you - it's dated for three weeks after your injuries."

"Your point being?" frowned Licht.

"That you have a very hearty constitution."

"Yes…amazing, even," he said with caution in his voice.

"Hard to believe."

"The people depended on me."

"And you wouldn't have wanted to let them down – not with a dead wife and half your torso singed off."

Licht recovered his senses enough to shoot Merich a decidedly hostile glare. "Don't confuse crude with clever, Merich!" he snapped.

"And don't lie to me!" countered Merich with equal force. "You want me to stand up for you? Then you better come clean!"

"I'm not lying - I... I just have nothing to say about that time."

"I know - that part's true. Just don't expect me to believe you were in control."

"No one else questions it."

"Why would they? They want you dead – suits their purpose – but come on. Three weeks. Three weeks and you're back in the Palace, back to your job."

"You might not understand this, but when you have responsibilities to other people, you don't have the luxury of a private life. They come first."

Merich smiled politely. "That's quite admirable – really it is…I guess you did your job."

"I made good on my promises." Licht declared sarcastically.

Merich stopped writing. He leaned back in the chair, shoving his hands into his trouser pockets. "That's what you say."

"You sound more like a prosecutor than a defense council!"

"A defense counsel defends his client against the state. He doesn't have to fight with the man he's standing up for."

"I'm not fighting you, Merich. I'm sitting in this hole. I was here before you arrived. I'll still be here when you leave."

"Fine," said Merich. "I'll play your little game. What exactly did you do in the days after the attack?

Licht took another deep draw from the cigarette as he stared thoughtfully at Merich. "Not as interesting as you would think," he shrugged. "Mostly housekeeping."

"Housekeeping? What does that mean?"

"You ever have people work for you?"

"Well, sort of – maybe four or five at one time."

"All right – think about what you needed to do, lining up work, supervising, then imagine that for a hundred thousand people doing a list of things you can't fully comprehend."

"Be that as it may, I still want to understand – you know, the mechanics of it."

"Well, I suppose you're talking about the Plenary Committee."

"Plenary – what's that?"

"There were two committees in the Party. The Central Committee was made up of the regional administrators, village prefects. They met once a year to vote on new measures, review old ones…"

"So, where does the Plenary fit in?"

"It was like a Cabinet. There were Commissars named for various portfolios – agriculture, industrial production, mining…"

"Public Security?"

"Yes," sighed Licht. "That too. Anyway, the Plenary met every week to monitor the progress we were making, set some targets, come up with recommendations for the Central Committee…"

"And there were times when it got to be too much."

"What do you mean?"

"You missed a number of those meetings – busy, sick?"

"Never."

"Never?"

"Herr Merich, I don't think you understand. I fought most of my life for that revolution. If it failed, what would I have to show for it? Even if I was sick, I still showed up – with my doctor. If I was out in the provinces, the Commissars came by plane or train to meet me."

Merich frowned to suppress the impish smile that would have revealed itself. "Well, I admire that kind of dedication," he replied kindly.

Licht's expression, however, was deadpan and did not serve as a disguise. "You can be as sarcastic as you want," he cautioned, "but we did important work. We had directives to issue…"

"Directives?"

"Like minutes – the list of things we passed. They were printed and sent out to the various administrators, factory managers."

"They were official?"

"Of course – that's a foolish question."

"So they had a formal mark."

"There was a stamp, and two signatures – mine and the secretary."

"No one else."

"No," grumbled Licht. "Seriously, what are you driving at?'

"Back in my office, I have a copy of the Plenary Minutes for November 5, 1947."

"I'm sure you do."

"There are two signatures, just like you say."

"Naturally."

"Daniel Klimsky signed it."

"He was the Secretary. Like I told you, he signed all of them."

"This one also says Mihaly Németh."

Licht said nothing. He took what remained of his cigarette and drove it with a firm push into the ashtray to his side.

"Who's Németh?" continued Merich.

"Party Vice-Chairman," came the unaffected apply

"I took the liberty of reading your Party's Constitution. It covers these 'directives' of yours. A chap named Navratil was your Vice-Secretary. He signed when Klimsky wasn't about. Did I get that right?"

"Yes."

"And Németh was your second. He only signed when you missed a Plenary."

"*If* I were to miss a Plenary."

"Well, I saw his signature on the paper, and I didn't see yours."

"No instructions left Nytriy without my name on them," countered Licht. "You must have read it wrong."

Merich grinned. "Oh, I'm sure that's true. I saw one of those printed letters for that meeting, and it said 'Johann Licht.'"

"Well then, there's your answer."

"The original says Németh, but the circulated copies have your name on them. That's not an answer."

"My name's on it. If that's what went out, then that's all you need to know."

"Those notices were forgeries – every one of them. Tell me about Németh."

"He died with Stern at the armory. Is your whole strategy to blame dead people? Pretty pathetic move for someone who's supposed to be good at what he does!"

"They weren't always dead," countered Merich. "They were around long enough to sign papers – just not around long enough to burn them. Besides, if he died at the armory, that's all I need to know. He was in Stern's pocket, wasn't he?"

"I don't give a shit whose name is on that paper of yours," he said defiantly. "The ones that left Nytriy had my name on them. Thousands of copies. Every town and village, every Party official – It was my name they saw. What they did was on my orders."

"Really?" asked Merich. Grabbing his fountain pen, he pulled the writing pad back and quickly scribbled out a couple of lines. He turned the pad back around and pushed it in front of Licht. "Do you want to tell me that you stand by that?"

Licht lowered his gaze to read the note.

"Your name's on it," added Merich, "so I guess by your standard it must be true."

Licht's face became flush, his jaw clenched. "Guard! Guard!" he began to yell as he pounded his fist on the table. "Get this sonofabitch out of here! Now!"

Merich smiled calmly, nodding as he pulled himself to his feet. He set to work placing the tools of his trade back in the leather case. "You might remember that when we first met," he said calmly, "you made clear that you had certain expectations of me. Whether or not you believe me, I've tried very hard to meet them.

"The thing is that I only have one expectation of you, and that's not to lie to my face."

Closing the clasp on his case, he grabbed hold of the handle and hoisted it with his one free hand. By that time, the escort had arrived to see him out. "You talk about trust a lot," added Merich. "Is that all talk, or do you give as good as you take?"

"Just get out of my sight!" scowled Licht, as he reached for another cigarette. "Take your lawyer games and go to hell!"

"I would," he said with an impish smile, "but you Communists don't believe in either heaven or hell, so I'll just head home – if that's all right with you?"

Merich managed only a couple of feet past the cell door when he heard the sound of the ashtray shatter against the wall. For the first time, he got the feeling that he had a case worth fighting.

CHAPTER 16

The Havasy Sanatorium sat on a large, relatively unspoiled, campus adjacent to one of the capital's finer neighborhoods. Massive trees – oak and beech – had marked out their territory generations ago. Luckily, very few of them had succumbed to the diffidence of nature, or the brutality of man. Their reprieve from arbitrary punishment was likely due to the fact that such estates were the desired prize for those who dared. To raze them would be akin to a buccaneer throwing his newfound booty over the keel. Even madmen could be driven by a modicum of the logic that enlightened self-interest would often present.

The Sanatorium was not far from the Stolzer home, and Merich had passed by the grounds of the institution on many an occasion. Each time, he stared at the wrought iron gates that were perpetually propped back in a welcome pose. In a few instances, such as this, he made the conscious choice to have the driver turn in.

Like most hospitals in the country, Havasy had its beginnings as a monastery, and many nuns still resided on its campus. In the beginning, medical care consisted of comfort until the Almighty weighed the outcome. As the medical profession advanced and grew, pathology replaced prayer, and the sisters of that particular order took on the secondary roles such as housekeeping and nursing. They still held a nominal control over the institution, but this now took the form of weekly meetings where the Chief of Staff cordially informed the Mother Superior of decisions already made and implemented.

The hospital did have the odd accoutrements that seemed out of place for either its pedigree or its purpose. It had, in fact, a rather elegant - if not degraded - spa and Turkish bath in one of its wings. Almost one hundred years before, wealthy benefactors had sponsored the construction of the annex for the use of their family when circumstances would warrant. In those days, the facility served as a place of seclusion for that class for every reason ranging from tuberculosis to alcoholism to a place of 'rest' for young ladies who needed at least a year to recover sufficiently from their 'affliction.'

Havasy had lost much in the intervening years – most of her patronage and a great deal of her elegance - but she still retained her purpose. It remained a place for people to hide from the world, and vice versa.

Merich instructed the taxi to enter the grounds of the hospital. The car drove the thousand yards that extended from the front gates to the circular driveway bordered the building's front entrance. Presenting his driver with his fare, and a tip of a couple of crowns, he got out of the car and made his way through the large oak doors.

The foyer was dominated by a large, broad oak staircase that rose fifteen feet from the floor, and led to a large landing which Merich judged to be large enough to fit his entire flat. To either side of the landing were slightly narrower staircases that brought one fully into the upper wardrooms of the hospital.

To the left of the lower staircase was a reception desk, staffed by a couple of women in nurse's uniforms. Merich made his way over to the one who was making some notations on a patient chart.

"Excuse me, I was wondering if I could speak with Doctor Janousek."

"Is he expecting you."

"I believe so. I'm Alexander Merich. My mother, Olga Merich, is one of his patients."

"If you'll have a seat," she said politely, gesturing to a collection of chairs in the far corner of the room, "I'll call him and let him know you're here."

Merich nodded and thanked the nurse before he took his seat in the waiting area.

Within ten minutes, Janousek had arrived by way of the staircase. He nodded his acknowledgment to the nurse and he made his way to where Merich was.

"Herr Merich, it's good to see you again. I got your message, and the orderlies are making sure that your mother is ready for your visit," he said as he took his place in the lounge chair opposite.

"Is there something wrong?"

"Oh, no... no... We simply want to make sure that she is prepared to see you - physically, emotionally."

"She hasn't had another episode?"

"No... things have been fine for quite some time now. We've taken the precaution of moving her to another room. There are bars on the window, so we're sure that we won't have a repeat of that situation."

"That wouldn't necessarily rule out something else - I mean, if she tried something different."

"Our staff are taking every precaution. Also, I've increased the number of sessions we've had together, and I'm convinced that this is not going to be a problem so long as we have her in that spot." Merich shifted slightly in his seat to allow his leg some room and to work the kink he felt in his side. "About that, Herr Doktor - I presume that the new room will affect the amount of money needed for her living expenses..."

"Herr Merich, I understand your concern, and I wish to assure you that the new accommodations will not change our agreement. We will not be requiring any additional money."

"That's a relief," replied Merich, taken off guard by the answer. "Actually, I was about to say that I anticipate a change in my status with the Ministry, and that I would be in a better position to cover any extra costs."

"Quite alright," assured Janousek. "Your payments are more than sufficient to cover your mother's needs here."

"Are you sure? I mean, don't you have to place additional staff on this? I'm sure that the upgrades to her quarters are..."

"Herr Merich, I assure you that everything we are doing falls well within the remittance we receive on her behalf. If there were a need to change our arrangements, I would certainly contact you well in advance. Come with me. I'll take you her new room." Merich pulled himself to his feet as Janousek led him to the staircase.

"I'm sorry about this," said the doctor. "The lift is out of order. We can take our time..."

"That's fine," replied Merich, hugging against the thick railing attached to the outer wall. "Not every place even has a lift. It takes me a bit longer, but I get there."

Janousek nodded, and for the next couple of minutes he kept about three steps in front of Merich as they ascended to the second floor. "I'm so sorry about this, Herr Merich," he said.

Merich smiled. "Don't be," he replied. "You used to have her on the fourth floor, so you've done me a favour."

Janousek stopped at the second floor, waiting for Merich to complete the four steps needed to join him. "Again," he said, "I'm sorry that we have to go up this way. The lift…"

"That's fine," interrupted Merich. "Truth be told I don't like them much anyway. Can't trust that something won't go wrong when you're trapped inside."

"A lot of people feel that way," nodded the doctor. "Anyway, her room is just down here. Four doors to the right."

"Aren't you coming with me?"

"Your mother is calm. I trust that seeing you without me might be a nice change."

Merich shrugged as he nodded, then turned and headed slowly down the hall. The rubberized tip of his cane made a strange dull, tapping noise against the carpeted floor, like a finger flicking against a ripe melon. He came to the open door, stopping and staring for a moment before he cleared his throat and spoke.

"Mother…"

Olga Merich sat in a large padded chair adjacent to a window, and at such an angle as to allow her a view of the city beyond the heavily wooded grounds. No acknowledgment.

"Mother…it's me…Alex."

"You're late," came the soft rebuke.

"I didn't think you were expecting me," he said as he came fully into the room.

"I wasn't - until I saw you get out of the cab. It took you long enough to get up here."

Olga Merich suffered from the indignity that often occurs when time turns an asset into a liability. Youthful slenderness became aged frailty. Beautiful strands of golden hair became brittle shocks of coarse white, like the unkempt mane of a pony. Dimples no longer worked to the whims of flirtatious trifle. They stayed their ground, deepening their furrows ever further, and stealing her impish charms to the point where such manifestations became almost grotesque.

The nursing sisters were always there with a tactful turn. They offered to help her with her makeup and her hair. Time and again, they gave her assurances that all they wished to do was to reveal her true self to the world. They had sprayed her down with some perfume that embedded itself into everything its odour touched. It smelled like lilacs, pruned from the bush and boiled in a pot of water until their blooms had been reduced to a fibrous, translucent pulp. It smelled like trying too hard.

Merich found all of these well- meaning attempts to be mildly amusing. He may have been his father's son on a great many counts, but on the subject of physical affectations, he knew his mother's heart as well as he knew his own. Fashion did not qualify as even a passing interest.

"They moved you since the last time. I had a hard time finding you."

Olga laughed gently. "That's a relief. I thought the good doctor would have stopped you on the way in."

"Actually, I saw him on my way in."

"He's just relieved that I didn't kill myself before you came."

"He's concerned for your safety," insisted Merich, as he moved to take a seat on the edge of her bed.

"He's concerned about the damage to his precious asylum. He's trying to get the rich people back in here again, you know."

"I know you don't like him..."

"I don't dislike him," interrupted Olga. "You know, it's quite alright not to have an opinion on people...or anything."

"I can't see things that way."

"Yes - you have an opinion on everything...except for the one thing that counts."

"You're not going to pester me to go to confession again."

"Father Jaroslav does a regular service for us here. He comes to visit me every couple of days."

"I come when I can, mother."

"I'm not judging, but Father Jaroslav asks about you. He wonders why he doesn't ever see you here."

"I never met the man," stated Merich. "How does he know whether he's seen me or not?"

"You are sounding very impertinent."

"And Father Jaroslav sounds like an old gossip to me."

"You shouldn't talk like that," cautioned Olga. "He's a man of

God."

"He's a man - just that," argued Merich. "Besides, I don't see him on my visits either. Where is he right now? What does that prove?"

"Well, he's just concerned. He wants to know that everything is fine."

"Does he ask about your suicide attempt?"

Merich felt the awkward unease set in the moment the words left his lips. His mother stared at him with the look she used to register so many times when he was young. Olga let a moment pass, and then glanced back toward the window. "He knows the truth - and so do you," she said with a calm firmness.

"Yes...I know what you said, but it doesn't make any sense."

"Because, Alex, I slipped."

"Slipped."

"Yes, slipped," insisted Olga. "Didn't they tell you about the water on the floor?"

"No," muttered Merich. "They didn't say a word."

"Well, it's no wonder. I mean that horrid nurse who's always coming in here, she left the window open, and it all blew in."

"I'm sure that it was a mistake, and..."

"It wasn't a mistake, Alex! For God's sake, it's winter and they have the heat shut off! That woman means to have my jewelry! You need to take it somewhere safe!"

"The heat?"

"Yes - the heat! It was so cold that the water was already turned to ice! Horrible place... She knew that would happen."

"When was this?"

"Last week," Olga argued, the insistent tone of her voice growing stronger. "Aren't you listening to me? That nurse is out to finish me off!"

"Uh...yes...sorry."

"Anyway, I can't think that your father will be impressed!"

"No... I suppose not."

Neither Merich nor his mother said a word for the next couple of minutes. She turned her attentions back out the window, while he sat down at the foot of her bed. Beyond the sound of voices and footsteps in the hallway, the only thing that he could hear was the steady rhythmic clicking of the old mantle clock perched on a shelf. He had known the instrument his whole life, at different times and different places. It was a constant, and gave Merich the closest he had felt to normality.

Olga's sigh finally broke the quiet. "He's not coming home." Merich lowered his head, staring at his clasped hands. "No, mama - he's not."

Tears began to well up in her eyes. "I miss him so much. I truly do," she muttered.

Merich felt himself beginning to feel the melancholy spread. "I know," he acknowledged softly. For a moment, he felt an urge to make his way to her side, to place his arm around her shoulder. Part of him told him that was the thing to do – the expected thing. He remained in place, watching her from a more comfortable perspective.

Taking a handkerchief that lay on the salon table beside her chair, Olga began to dab at her eyes. "Please," she asked. "Could you put on the phonograph?"

"I'm not sure that they would want you to have that on."

"Nobody cares when the door's shut. Please. Just put it on." Dutifully, Merich got up from the bed and moved toward the old phonograph that sat in the corner a few feet from where Olga was. He looked at the stack of 78 rpm discs, all carefully placed in colorful jackets of tissue paper.

"There's already one on there."

Merich glanced at the label. "Why don't we try another, mama? Some Chopin, or even some jazz. You like that."

"No, just play what's there," she insisted.

He sighed as he turned on the switch. The player emitted a dull hum as the vacuum tubes received the spark. The turntable began to spin, and he dutifully, gently, placed the needle down on the outermost grooves of vinyl. For a few seconds, it crackled and spit like a fire at low ember. Then came the familiar performance in D flat major, the opening caress of the keys, the arpeggios.

Merich hated the song. Despite the beauty of the piece, it brought on a feeling as though each note pressed down the weight of the world on his shoulders. Every compression of the piano key felt like a single, fulsome teardrop streaking down a dappled cheek. It was possibly the saddest piece of music ever written. He knew where the music was taking his mother, but it was not somewhere he wanted to follow.

Merich continued to stand by the player, waiting patiently for the song to end. There was no point in sitting down just to struggle back up. There was even less point in speaking while his mother was so transfixed by the music.

Finally, the last plaintive, beckoning notes of Debussy echoed off into the scratchy crackle of amplified metal on vinyl. Without a word, he returned the needle arm to its cradle, and switched off the machine. It made a clicking sound as loud as the music itself. Merich hobbled back to his place on the edge of the bed. "Mama," he said gently, "I need to tell you something. It's why I came here…It's important."

Olga said nothing. She continued to stare out the window. He grimaced as he felt his resolve slowly dissipating. "Mama," he intoned, "I took on a case."

Still no reaction.

"Please," he pleaded. "I need to tell you this… I'm defending someone in court."

Olga turned her gaze toward Merich but remained silent.

Merich fought the desire to raise his voice. "People are going to talk, so I need to tell you what I'm doing - okay?" he insisted.

"You're a lawyer, just like papa. Why would people talk?" she asked.

"Trust me, mama – they'll talk. They're going to say things…"

"Who? Who are 'they'?"

"People – I don't know – everyone. Mama, you've got to let me talk."

Olga smiled gently and nodded.

"Okay," he said, as he drew a deep breath. "Georg Hartz asked me to take on a client - for the tribunals. He said that it was important for the trial to be done right. That's what papa used to say too."

Olga nodded her head and smiled. "Your father was very particular about that," she replied in a light, airy tone. "Everyone deserved justice, he used to say to us."

Merich swallowed as he considered his circumstance. "Yes, mama, please… my client is Johann Licht."

Olga turned to face her son. Her face turned tortured, angry.

"Mama…you heard what I said. My client is Johann…"

"Go!" interrupted Olga, with a firmness in her voice that he had not heard in years.

"Mother…"

"You need to leave and never come back," she added with cold resolve.

"Just hear me out..." he pleaded.

"Get the hell out before I have you thrown out!" she hissed.

"Mama, you need to calm down."

"Help! Help!" she screamed. She thrashed about as though attempting to fight off a swarm of wasps, even though her son was still a few feet away. "Somebody help me!"

It took no time for Doctor Janousek and a couple of orderlies to dash into the room. The doctor tactfully escorted Merich out into the hallway while the men did what they could to restore calm to the situation.

"Look, I'm sorry...," began Merich.

"I presume you told her about your work," said Janousek, looking past him and into the room.

"I don't know what you mean."

"It's in the papers – the tribunals. Your name shows up."

"You didn't say anything."

"Not my place," said Janousek. "My job is to care for your mother – full stop."

"I had to tell her," he explained. "It would've been worse if it came from somewhere else."

"I thought you might say something. We've been waiting in the hall the whole time."

"You didn't try to stop me?"

"Like you said – she was going to be told sooner or later. I couldn't guarantee I'd be there if it happened some other time."

"You...manipulated me?"

"I mitigated risk. You did what you felt you needed to do. All I've done is to make sure that I could control the situation – for the sake of your mother."

Merich seized Janousek by the arm as the doctor turned to walk back to the room. "You played me!" he snapped.

"Well, it's a shame you see it that way."

"I don't see how else you could see it!"

"We get newspapers; we get visitors – word spreads. Your mother will hear about this – from you, from one of the sisters, an orderly...I can't stop that. But she needed to hear it from you - not one of them – and I needed to be prepared for it."

Merich glowered at Janousek, his temper in a full simmer.

"You can be as angry as you like, Herr Merich," continued the doctor. "You must have known that she could act this way, but you still went ahead. I'm not going to judge you on that decision. I would hope that you won't judge me on mine."

A moment passed before Merich lowered his gaze. "Of course not," he sighed, rubbing his forehead. "It's just that I didn't want this to happen...I am grateful for the precautions."

"What's done is done," said Janousek. "Like I said, she was bound to learn at some point. Better it happens now when we can prepare."

"Thank you," replied Merich. "In light of this, I won't be visiting for some time to come. It's probably for the best."

"Of course. I was going to suggest as much."

"Yes...I'll be on my way."

Janousek nodded as Merich turned to leave. He ventured a few feet down the corridor before he stopped and turned back. "You didn't ask me why?" he said.

"I'm sorry," said the doctor. "Was I supposed to?"

CHAPTER 17

"December 15th, 1946

It has been a challenging day by anyone's measure.

We woke to a massive explosion in the south end of the city. The main power generating station in the Galadna district blew up – or at least part of it.

It was about three-thirty by my recollection. A loud boom, and rattling windows. Eva and I sprung from bed and grabbed for our dressing gowns. You never get used to such noises, and my head was swimming with all manner of thoughts.

The fireball was quite visible in the night sky, even from our vantage point. It was somewhat fortunate that it was in an industrial area, and that few people would have been present.

Needless to say, the day had been taken up by this situation. After breakfast, I met with Cdeno, who is in charge of infrastructure. There wasn't much he could say while the fire crews and reserve units were still trying to put the fire out. The whole plant was to be shut down for the foreseeable future, which means rolling blackouts – about three hours each day.

He also told me that the plant had five separate generators, and that it might be possible to bring some of them back into service if the damage were contained. I told him that I found it hard to believe that anything would be left after that blast, but he assured me that these things always look much worse than they actually are.

About an hour into it, Stern came in, yelling and carrying on about sabotage and criminal acts. Cdeno said that until the fire was put out they wouldn't know for sure. He added that the plant was getting older and had not been properly maintained for some time. Stern argued that if we waited too long the trail would go cold. He wanted to place the EBI and Vopos on alert.

I felt like a father trying to break up a fistfight between brothers. I told Stern that I understood, but I wasn't prepared to declare martial law over what might have been nothing more than a carelessly tossed cigarette, or some buildup of coal dust. I said that it was better to let a criminal go free than punish everyone in the city – assuming that there even was a criminal to begin with.

At this point things got worse. Stern turned his anger from Cdeno toward me. He yelled, banging his fist on the desk, cursing. I was firm – I told him to get a hold of himself. He proceeded to call me a coward, and accused me of sabotaging the revolution.

I asked Cdeno to leave, then launched into him myself. I caught him off guard, as I have never, to my memory, confronted him so. It was probably because I've held back for so long that it needed to be so harsh.

His face was flushed. Still angry, but he didn't respond. He just stood there and took it.

The whole situation left me feeling guilty for my part, so I attempted to assure him that if we found it was an act of sabotage, that he would be free to pursue whatever leads he found.

I found myself regretting those words even before I finished saying them."

Merich closed up the diary and returned it to the cubby. He then made his way to the large arm chair in the corner and lowered himself down. Stretching his leg out, he pointed his toes forward so as to feel the muscles in his calf tighten.

He leaned his head back and let out a deep sigh. The man in

the prison cell was hard to reconcile with the man who wrote the passages in the notebook. One made sense - the other did not. Merich considered what Bŏsek had said. Did Licht snap? He would have been naïve to believe the possibility did not exist. Everyone had their breaking point. Whether it was higher or lower did not mean that it would not – could not – happen.

It had been another long day, and the thoughts only served to remind him that his own physical limit had been reached. Lacking the energy to pull himself out of the chair, he drifted to sleep, warm in the glow of the coal fire.

CHAPTER 18

The central train station was the busiest that Merich had ever seen it. On occasion, his parents had taken him on trips - to visit relatives in the east, or to accompany his father on one of his conferences, usually in Prague or Vienna. There had always been a steady and rhythmic flow of people and freight. This occasion was clearly different, even if one were oblivious to the times.

The reception lobby consisted of a large, cavernous reception hall clad in art deco marble edifices. The support columns had been chiseled to resemble mythical titans who held sway over the elements of nature. Now, having been robbed of their divinity, they held no more than the support beams of the building's expansive roof. Above the ticketing windows and passenger lounges were plaster reliefs of industrial might - of men hammering raw ore into steel girders, of hardy women folk toiling in the fields among stacked sheaves of wheat, and of scientists manipulating all manner of chemicals in their labs.

Merich had noticed on a previous visit that the men in the reliefs had no eyes, and naturally it drew his attention from the moment they stepped out into the open. The steelworkers and scientists wore round safety goggles which made them seem slightly sinister. Only the women peered back, happy in their summer toil, bearing the grinning contentment of a life unencumbered by complication and convention. He wondered if progress was so wonderful, then why did its avatars appear to be so miserably transfixed by their tasks?

The travel party did not remain for long, only to garner the assistance of some uniformed men in ferrying the loaded contents of a couple of flat pull carts.

By this point, every platform was crowded at least ten deep, with porters vainly attempting to push their baggage carts through the mass, like a furrow being driven painfully slow and deep through the stubbornest of sod.

The Merichs and the Stolzers were eventually situated in a relatively calm part of the station, near the back. Beside them sat a passenger car that made no pretention about favoring quality over quantity.

Bruno Stolzer's father had been a prominent investor in the fledgling national railway system, which, in customary gratitude, conferred upon the family a private passenger carriage. Housing its own galley and servant's room, it also possessed a lavatory, sleeping quarters and a small, yet well-appointed seating area, paneled in the finest cuts of oak and inlaid mahogany. It sat dormant much of the time, pushed to a quiet corner of the station's vast switching yard, and was only pulled into service on those odd occasions when the Stolzers made the time for a family excursion to the mountains or to the west.

A couple of the porters had loaded much of the weightier items - steamer trunks and shipping crates - and had now begun to take aboard the smaller items that the party had carried with them. Franz had carried his son's modest suitcase, along with a bag of books he had selected for Alex's journey.

Stolzer took the items from Franz. "It's not too late," he remarked. "No one's checking visas along our route, and if they are, I can deal with it."

"I appreciate the offer, but Olga and I have made our choice. We're just grateful that you're taking Alex."

"I'd feel better if all of you came...Franz, I've seen what these people are like. I used to enjoy Berlin - not anymore. This charlatan Hitler has most of them feeding from his hand."

"People remember war," replied Franz." I can't see why they would ever go back to it."

Stolzer shook his head and sighed. "Every day I see people doing things that will put them in a prison, an asylum, or a grave if the Nazis have any say in it. You can't stop them - only step out of their way."

"I know - I suppose. That's why I'm grateful for anything you can do for the boy. He's the only thing that matters right now."

"He's my godson, Franz - probably the closest thing I'll ever have to a real one. I give you my word."

"Thank you, my friend. I'll always be in your debt."

"You are like family to me, and in my family there are no debts...Franz, for God's sake, just get on this train."

Franz shook his head. "No," he said calmly. "We'll be here to meet you when you return...I promise."

"I'll hold you to it," said Stolzer, as he held out his hand. The handshake became a brotherly embrace. He then moved back, nodded to Merich, then got on board the passenger carriage to join his wife and daughter.

Franz turned to his son. "You're almost sixteen," he remarked. "I know how tough this will be for your mother. You understand why she couldn't come."

"I know," said Merich. "She doesn't handle these sorts of things very well."

"She loves you," he volunteered. "You know that, don't you?"

"I know, papa. I love her too."

"Anyway," continued Franz, "I know this will be hard. You know why we're sending you away."

"Yes, I know. I just don't know why you're not coming as well. Herr Stolzer has offered places more than once - almost every time we've been in the same room with him."

"Alex, I would like to explain, but I can't. I can't sum it up."

"Just tell me why."

"Seriously, I can't. You're better off with no answer than a bad one. Just please trust me that it makes full sense in my head. "Merich paused, his face furrowing into a frown. "The Nazis could kill you," he said.

"Only if I get in front of their guns," smiled Franz. "I'm still too quick for that."

"I shouldn't go without you and mama - I should stay."

"You're leaving, and that's that. Trust me - if things get bad, we'll find a way to get to you somehow."

"Let me stay."

"No. No more about it. You'll be back before long. These kinds of people come and go for a time, but we're still here. We just need to wait them out."

With that, he gave Merich a fulsome embrace. "I love you, Alex, but I can't worry. I need you to be safe...Now, you better get aboard before they leave without you."

"I love you, too, papa. Please..."

"I will - we will. Promise."

Franz kissed his son's cheek, then let go. "When you get lonely, read the books," he said softly. "Just like we always have."

"Every night," assured Merich.

"Good, now get on the train."

Merich picked up his cases and turned to climb aboard the car. He passed Stolzer, who was engaged in an animated discussion with a man and his family who had made their way to that section of the platform.

"Seriously," the stranger shouted in panicked desperation. "I've got five thousand crowns – gold ones. You've got a big car, and we won't take up any more space…"

"I'm sorry – like I said, our car's full enough as it is."

"What are you talking about?! Four people?! These cars can fit up to thirty – even more!"

"I'm telling you it's full," Stolzer said firmly.

"Full of what?! Dresses?! Toys?! For God's sake, I'm offering you enough to buy more!"

"I'm sorry…I can't help."

The stranger began to sob uncontrollably as he got down on his knees. "Please," he croaked. "I'm begging you – you don't know what they do to our kind…"

"Get up!" ordered Stolzer. "Don't let your wife and child see you like this. Be a man!" The stranger attempted to compose himself as he helped him to his feet.

"You say you have five thousand gold crowns," intoned Stolzer. "You'll get passage. This isn't the last train, and the roads to the south are still clear. Make your arrangements and leave today…I wish you luck." With that, he turned to board the train.

Merich had stood at the top of the steps of the railcar, listening to the entire exchange. He made eye contact with Stolzer when he came aboard. "You said there was no room?" he asked.

"That's right."

"Then where were Mother and Father going to be if they took you up on your offer?"

"That's a completely different matter," said Stolzer.

Merich did not move. He stared at Stolzer, not saying a word.

"The man had money," continued Stolzer, "and he knew what was coming. If he loved his family, he would have made his plans a long time ago."

"You'd let him on if he were broke?"

Stolzer sighed as the consternation built up inside. "But he's not. He had options. Still does for that matter." He moved past Merich and reached to open the cabin door.

"He's Jewish, isn't he?" asked Merich.

Stolzer paused. "He didn't say," came the reply.

"He said 'his kind' – what else could he mean?"

Stolzer stood at the door for a moment, his hand still perched upon the handle. He bowed his head ever so slightly. "He didn't say," he repeated, this time in a low mutter. Then, without ceremony, he opened the door and walked through.

Merich stared at the stranger, his wife and child, who remained on the platform in front of the car. The noise of the steam valves connected to the train's braking system let out an angry hiss. He could not hear their words. All he could discern was a man attempting to reassure his family that all would be well, and a woman whose evident love and affection did not extend to unconditional faith. The scene was difficult to watch, and it made him feel awkward and self-conscious to view such private emotion. He turned and entered through the cabin door just as the train gave its first assertive pull against inertia.

Stolzer had removed himself to a small room that had been fashioned into a makeshift study. His wife and daughter were in one of the sleeping compartments, unpacking what they thought they would need while aboard.

The large sitting room was free to him for the moment. He looked around at the mahogany paneled section, with its lush, oversized chesterfields and settees, bordering a long and slender oak table, all of it perched comfortably upon a massive Axminster rug that appeared to be custom fitted for its purpose.

Merich walked over to the one chesterfield to his right that backed below a large window. He tucked himself in the one corner, his back against the padded arm. Bringing his left leg up and into a crook on the adjacent seat cushion, he began to stare out the window.

He continued to stare long after the station - his father - faded from view. Late fall had stripped the trees of their foliage, leaving jagged bony branches of a dull grey pallor. The early morning sun had not yet burned off the mist. It sat in the low apogee of the east like a low watt bulb. Frost put a dull glaze on dying grass, and water pooled in ditches and the occasional pond developed a brittle crust.

Already, the roads to the south were lined with cars and trucks. The desperate ingenuity of man managed to find ways of attaching crates and trunks in the most improbable of places. They lumbered slowly in their lines, easily outpaced by those who had filled duffle bags and, attaching them like rucksacks, made their conveyance on bicycles.

"What are you looking at?"

"Pardon?"

"I said what are you looking at? Out the window? Whatever it is, we must've passed it miles ago."

Merich turned away from the view. He had only met the girl a handful of times over the past few years. He did have a vague recollection of visiting the big house when she had been born, but he had been very young himself.

"I'm just looking," he sighed. "Doesn't have to be anything, does it?"

"My name's Emi," she volunteered, as she took a seat beside him.

"I know who you are," muttered Merich, returning to his interest beyond the window.

"Sorry," she giggled. "I didn't think you remembered me."

"Look…I'm not trying to be rude, but I'd really like to be left alone…"

"Miss your family?"

"What? No…just worried, that's all."

"Papa says they were foolish for staying behind."

"He has a lot of opinions, doesn't he?" he grumbled.

"They're usually right," asserted Emi. "He's met some of those Germans. He doesn't trust them one bit."

"Nobody wants a war – that's what my father says," countered Merich.

"That's why Papa says they'll be one. He says that people are so scared of war, they're letting Herr Hitler bully them. He says that sooner or later, they'll have to stand up and fight."

"If standing up is so important, then why is he leaving?"

"Papa says that we need to wait until people figure this out for themselves."

Merich stared at the girl a moment longer, then turned back toward the window. "Your father seems to have things all sorted out," he muttered. "I'm surprised he didn't take up that offer."

"What offer?"

"That man in the station – the one who offered him five thousand crowns for passage."

"Why would he? We have all the money we need," she answered matter-of-factly.

"Of course you do," he sighed.

"So, do you want to play chess, or something?"

"No…nothing…thank you."

"Suit yourself," she said airily as she walked out of the room. "We can play later."

"Brat…," muttered Merich, as the door closed behind her.

CHAPTER 19

The film repository was a small section of the University's archives, tucked away in the far corner of the building's basement. The elevator was out of service, so Merich was forced to navigate a narrow staircase devoid of a handrail. If it had been more than the two short spans and landing, he would have likely requested that the materials be delivered to the law library instead.

A dozen feet down a short hallway, he found an open door with a sign mounted on the wall beside it. *"Filmarchive / filmarchívumok"*. It led into a small waiting room, with a single desk, and some chairs along the wall. An older man sat quietly, pouring over a newspaper he had spread out fully over the surface.

"Excuse me," said Merich. "I'm looking for someone named Jerzy."

"I'm Jerzy. You must be Herr Merich. Goranevic told me to expect you."

"So you already know what I'm looking for?"

"Yes," replied the man as he slowly rose from his chair. "We couldn't locate them all. A lot of damage during the looting after the overthrow. We managed to get most of them, though."

Merich smiled and nodded. "I'm just glad to have whatever I can," he said. "So, where are we set up?"

"Down here," said Jerzy, gesturing down a narrow lit hallway. "I have the projector set up and loaded."

Merich followed the man down the corridor to a small room. He was told that it used to be used for graduate lectures, and looked as though it could hold twenty or so with relative comfort. That was then, and it appeared that for the longest time, it held nothing more than dust and stale air. The conference table had been pushed to one side, beneath a chalkboard partially obscured by a white canvas screen. A stack of metal film canisters sat on one of its leading corners.

In the centre of the room sat a large projector atop a trolley cart, and flanked by two large leather padded chairs. A thick black extension cord trailed out to the back wall.

"Please," said Jerzy. "Have a seat."

He flicked on the power switch to the projector as Merich took his place, then turned off the overhead lights.

The music blared as the title sequence flashed on the screen.

"Most of these are in Hungarian, some in Czech, but none in German," explained Jerzy. "I hope this isn't a problem."

"Not at all," assured Merich. "I've heard enough speeches in my life."

Jerzy gave him a confused look. "All there is, then, are the pictures?"

Merich looked up at him. "Do you know any English?" he asked.

"No... afraid not."

"The English, they have this saying about the value of images, that 'a picture is worth a thousand words'."

Jerzy thought for a moment, then smiled and nodded. "Then you won't mind if I turn off the sound?"

"Absolutely not."

Merich sat and watched as the familiar sight of Johann Licht appeared on the screen. No uniforms, no guns - just a rather unassuming figure, dressed in a wool overcoat and wearing a wide brimmed fedora. He walked effortlessly, happily along with his wife, arm in arm. His one hand, hidden in a coat pocket, grasped the end of a leash. A small puli, moved in front in a serpentine pattern, clearly excited by the attention as much as the stroll. A quick close up of the camera revealed happiness and contentment, love and hope.

"It almost makes him seem human. I mean not a monster," observed Jerzy. "What's he like - up close?"

Merich took a moment to ponder his response. He knew what Jerzy was looking for, what he wanted to hear. His eyes narrowed as he let a slight sniff leave his nostrils. "He's just a man - flesh and bone."

"I find that hard to believe. Following just a man - like that. I wouldn't do it"

"People don't follow men," he countered. "They follow the angels or devils already in them. Men just give their spirits the permission to do what they wanted all along."

Jerzy shook his head. "Well, I never did."

"Nobody did," observed Merich. "Nobody ever does...but there he is - father of the nation, friend to the worker...Somebody, somewhere, had to join on."

The archivist shrugged. "Well, he seems to love his wife," he observed. "My father used to say that if a man could find something in this world he could love, then there's hope."

Merich looked at the flickering images on the wall, the broad grins on the faces, and the casual air about them. Is that what happened, he thought to himself. Nothing left to love?

"Herr Merich...I need to ask you."

"Yes?"

"Why?"

Merich looked for a moment toward the disembodied voice, hidden in the shadows lurking beyond the bright yellow beam of the projector's light. Specks of dust danced about the beam as though they were drawn against their will to the light. "Why I took this case?" he asked. "That seems to be the question on everybody's mind."

"I'm sorry if I've..."

"No, no... It's all right. I don't mind...it's hard to explain, and I'm not sure I can do it justice."

"You know your own head and heart," volunteered Jerzy.

Merich was bemused at the observation. "You could say that," he intoned quietly. "At least I think I do."

For the next three hours, Merich and Jerzy reviewed the stack of newsreels - once, again, a third, and finally a fourth time. Intermittently, Merich would signal his need for a break, whenever the pain in his leg flared up, or when he needed to relieve himself. Jerzy took these moments to go to his office for a cigarette, and to catch up on any messages.

Through the continual viewing and reviewing of film stock, Merich had devised a numbering system that helped him keep track of what he saw. The first number was chronological, with all of the subsequent numbers representing particular aspects of the images - the style of dress, the physical surroundings, and the people present. All told, Merich's 'system' had twelve individual digits, each with at least a dozen separate possible values that took into account every possible factor he could imagine. In truth, it was a variation of the method he had worked out in his days as a law student in Bern, when he prepared for the Moot Court Examinations.

Depending on each film's score, they were stacked in particular places. Only the first number, which was unique to each film, was ignored in this sorting process. By the time they had completed the fourth run through, two canisters lay atop one another on the far right corner of the conference table.

"Those two over there," said Merich. "How many numbers did we match?"

Jerzy walked over to the table and examined the pieces of paper taped to each container. It took roughly five minutes of counting and recounting, before he turned back to Merich. "All but three, including the first number," he said.

"Which ones are they?"

Jerzy glanced at each of the tins. "Let's see...Number four from April 17th, 1946 and number eighteen - that one says February 22nd, 1948."

Merich shifted in his chair. He looked down at the floor, rolling the shaft of his cane between his hands. After about ten seconds, he looked up at Jerzy. "Do you have any equipment to edit film - you know - special things to look at stock?"

"Like the viewers that editors and directors use?"

"I guess...sorry, I don't know the technical term for them."

Jerzy frowned. "Unfortunately, this is as close to 'state of the art' as you'll find around here. What hasn't been smashed has been stolen. All I've got are four projectors."

Merich paused again. "Okay, then...what if...what if we used two projectors?"

"I'm sorry, Herr Merich - I don't follow."

"We place them side by side. We'll need two screens - on that wall over there. Anyway, if you and someone else ran the films together..."

"And we synchronize the places where they match?"

"Exactly. Can we get someone else in to help?"

"My colleague, Vaclav - he works down the hall. I'll try to grab him before he leaves for the day."

"Good," replied Merich. "I promise I'll have what I need in an hour."

"God willing," muttered Jerzy as he rushed out the door to catch his co-worker.

It was nearly two hours before Jerzy had been able to locate his colleague, and another forty-five minutes before the men had managed to set up the two machines in the right positions to allow the competing screens to align perfectly parallel to one another. Once Vaclav had threaded the film through the machine and wrapped the end around the spool, he gave a nod to Jerzy, who in turn reached for the light switch.

Side-by-side, the images flashed in their confined squares. Merich leaned in and watched intently, his eyes darting back and forth between the two newsreels. A couple of minutes into it and he could feel the effect of the steady concentration, the burning watering eyes, the nausea building in his stomach. Then he saw what he wanted, needed.

"Vaclav - freeze the film. Jerzy, keep it going," he said quickly. About thirty seconds later, he ordered Jerzy to stop his projector as well.

The men looked at the frozen images for a moment, pondering what they saw.

"Good!" exclaimed Merich, as he picked up his cane and pointed it at the wall. "See - there! There it is!"

CHAPTER 20

Merich arrived home at a quarter past seven. It had been a long day, but it could have been much longer. For the first time that he could remember he felt the tension bleed away from him. He was tired, but not exhausted, and for once, pleased to see the front door of his flat.

He opened the door just as Emi was carrying two dinner plates to his kitchen table.

"Well, well - what's all this?" he asked in a broad voice.

"Never mind what it is - you need to go wash up."

He smiled, and gave her a tender kiss on the cheek as he made his way to the washroom. When he returned, she had already lit a couple of candles and turned off the overhead light.

"So, what's the occasion?"

"A thank you...for taking me out tonight."

"Huh?"

"You know," said Emi with a knowing grin, "how you're taking me to a club tonight - some drinks, some jazz...some...you know?"

"You always want to dance."

"It's the gypsy in me," she laughed, repeating the same line that would drive her father to distraction. "I can even deal with two left feet."

"Yeah, but it's one left foot and a stick."

"We're still talking about dancing?" she said slyly.

Merich feigned surprise. "Why, Fraulein Stolzer," he exclaimed. "You have me confused with one of those bounders who troll for young ladies over on the Kriegsstrasse!"

"Oh, I have your number, pet. I'll take the lead."

"And maybe I'll let you."

"What?" she teased. "No argument? What did you do with that grump who just wants to sit in his drafty loft?"

"He's busy preying on helpless orphans and widows," he smirked. "I'm just filling in for tonight."

Emi walked up to Merich and, grabbing hold of the lapels of his suit jacket, pulled him forward. She moved her lips close to his ear. "You know...people will talk," she purred.

"They'll have even more to jaw about before the night's over." Emi giggled as she backed away. Grabbing a dish drying towel that was slung over the back of a nearby chair, she snapped it at him. "You sit down before you get into a real mess!"

Merich dutifully took his place, while Emi went back into the kitchen. After a couple of minutes, she returned with a couple of steaming plates. "I took the liberty of borrowing some things from mother's pantry," she explained as she set them down.

"I hope you don't get into trouble," he quipped. "You're far too young and pretty for prison."

"Frau Borchart complained. Said she was saving it for father's supper."

"I'm almost afraid to ask what you said."

Mockingly, Emi placed her hand on her hips. "I told the old trout that he could get a better meal at the Klosters, and that I was doing him a favour," she stated categorically.

Merich shook his head. "You're so cruel to that woman," he chortled.

She shook her head as she pulled the chair out to sit down. "When I was a little girl, she used to pinch me when I went into the kitchen. Really hard. Nobody believed me, so she kept on doing it...Anyway, I don't want to talk about that cow."

"Happy thoughts, my dear," replied Merich as he raised his wineglass in a toast. "Only happy thoughts."

Emi looked at him carefully. "I'm almost afraid to ask," she said.

"Ask what?"

"Your uncharacteristically good mood - I don't want a segue into you-know-what."

Merich took a gulp from his wineglass. "Neither do I," he said with a swallowing gasp, "so let's don't."

"You had some luck, though?"

"I think so. Hard to tell, but I think it's important."

"Improves your chances?" she volunteered.

"Maybe…"

"Alex, I think the best you can hope for is to avoid an execution."

"Actually," he said, "the best I'm hoping for is a night free of Brother Chairman. That's what you wanted, wasn't it?"

Emi smiled and nodded gently. "Eat up before it gets cold."

"By the way, are you still coming to the house for brunch?"

"When?"

"Day after tomorrow - after Mass. Really, we talked about this last week."

"Yes…sorry…of course, I'll be there."

"Well, you better be," she said mockingly. "Mother's counting on you."

"I know," sighed Merich. "It's just that she dotes a little too much. Makes me feel uncomfortable."

"That's her way. I would've thought you'd figured that out by now."

"I know she means well. I just thought it might tail off a bit. We're not children anymore."

"It's all she has right now. It's not like she has all of these parties to plan. I sort of feel sorry for her that way."

"You used to make fun of it."

"Only because I didn't want to do it myself," said Emi, raising her glass of wine for a sip. "I know that a wife has to support her husband, but why can't I have something of my own?"

Merich shrugged his shoulders. "I don't know," he said. "My mother lived for father. When he died, she disappeared too. To be honest, I don't know how healthy it is to be wholly dependent on another human being."

"Well, I wouldn't go that far. We all depend upon somebody from time to time."

"But not all the time. I won't do it, and quite frankly, I wouldn't want anyone else doing it to me - don't want the responsibility."

Emi took a swallow from her glass. She turned her head and stared into the darkened study, toward the window facing the city centre. The lights were beginning to come on, dotting each building, big and small alike. "It makes you wonder," she said thoughtfully.

"Wonder what?"

"If we should even bother...you know..."

"Getting married, you mean?" he asked.

"Marriages do involve give and take," she explained. "I mean; you can't help but be somewhat dependent on each other." Merich picked up the linen napkin from his lap, and wiped his hands before setting it down in a balled up pile beside his plate. "Yeah, but it's not all one-sided," he defended. "At least, it shouldn't."

"No... But maybe it's inevitable...you just fall into it naturally."

"Isn't marriage a sacrament? And you - good Catholic girl - you're questioning it?"

"Good Catholic girls don't come to jazz clubs with naughty boys, do they?"

"Well, that's a relief. For a minute, I thought our plans for the rest of the evening were off the table."

"Maybe they are...at least until you answer my question."

"What question? All I heard was a statement."

"The question was whether two people could get married without losing themselves in the bargain."

"You want a guarantee...I can't give you one...look, Emi, I can promise to love you and respect you, and I can try to not dominate you...Maybe I pull it off, maybe not...I can't give you more than that. To be honest, no man alive ever could."

"You think I'm being silly."

Merich smiled thoughtfully. "No... No, I don't," he answered. "You're scared - so am I. From everything I've seen, I think we should be."

"So... we shouldn't?"

"Life's scary. Getting up in the morning is the most frightening thing I do most times. Still manage to get up, though."

"Sometimes, I think you're mocking me," she said. "Like you think I'm flighty or frivolous..."

"I wouldn't do that...ever," he interrupted. "It's just that – well, you've always been the one pushing for marriage. Now, you're saying this. Just doesn't make any sense."

"Why wouldn't it? Any thinking person has a right to figure these things out before they move ahead."

Merich grabbed the napkin and placed it back on his lap. "Sure – reconsidering a commitment as you're serving a meal to them and planning a night out. Last meal for the condemned?"

"No – I mean I love you. No question in my mind. It's just the marriage part."

"Want to live in sin like those Parisian couples? What would your mother say about that?"

"Just shut up and eat," she chided. "We have a reservation to keep."

*　　*　　*

Club Django sat in the western fringe of what was known as the 'Austrian quarter.' Strictly speaking, it was not a 'quarter,' but merely that part of the capital in easy proximity to Nyitry. To mavens of architecture and history, it was the home of the capital's regal past, its palaces and ecclesiastic buildings. To sociologists, it was defined by the presence of the politicians and bankers. To everyone else, it was the part of the city that the police patrolled with any degree of efficient and effective regularity.

The nightclub had been established at the height of the craze for American Jazz music some twenty years before. The war and revolutions had not spared the establishment. Faded posters for Cinzano mockingly teased patrons with potables long since imbibed, and bottles whose last stubborn contents had been desiccated into a sticky amber resin that caught only light, dust and envious thirst.

Also long gone were the quartets and orchestras that used to take the stage every night. Gone were the itinerant bands of musicians who had perfected their syncopated patter in Louisiana brothels and Kansas City backrooms, whose only desire was not to see the world, but to play their heart's song and stand tall as men. In their place was a pale woman, waif like and tentative in her aspect. Two songs she knew with impeccable skill – 'Lily Marlene', which she dares not sing, and 'La Vie en Rose', which she tended to rely on too much. The rest of her repertoire was technically weak. Only the sense that she sang with a voice on the verge of tears made it feel soulful.

Emi thought that Merich appreciated the singer's skill. In truth, it was her barely concealed pain that he had felt some lurid attraction to, like the pity one felt for a circus animal put to the whip and the chain. After a couple of drinks, the warm glow of intoxicant washed over and through his sense of sordid guilt. Merich turned back to Emi. "You know, you're the most beautiful woman I've ever known," he said with a relaxed countenance.

A sly grin formed on her lips. "You didn't always think that."

"Well, you were a bit of a spoiled brat, but you grew out of that quite nicely," he quipped.

"I was - wasn't I," she blushed.

Merich leaned in toward the table, casually folding his arms on the edge. "If it's any consolation, I always thought you were cute."

"Not as cute as Liesl, though," she countered.

"That was a long time ago," he replied, running his index finger over the rim of his glass. "It doesn't even seem like it was me there."

Emi let forth a sigh as she cocked her head to one side. "I never liked her, you know."

"You were jealous," he laughed. "Didn't expect you to be friends."

"It's not that...I didn't trust her."

"Again, the jealousy..."

"Her eyes," interrupted Emi.

"What?"

"Her eyes. Something about her eyes."

"Beautiful blue eyes," teased Merich. "From what I recall."

"They looked fake."

"What are you talking about?"

"Fake. You know - they didn't look real."

"Well, if they weren't, it certainly fooled me!" he chided her.

"It wasn't as if she was bumping into things..."

"Make fun of me if you want," she protested.

"Well, it's not hard when you say something like that." Emi grimaced. "My grandfather had a hunting lodge in the east. When father took over the business, he went there to stay. We would go there to visit him a couple of times a year. Dreadful place."

"Leading us back to my romantic life..."

"Hush – let me finish... It was dreadful because he had all these trophies, these heads mounted on the walls. Some of them had this snarl, their fangs showing. That was bad enough, but it was their eyes – they bothered me the most."

"Don't they replace them with glass ones?" asked Merich.

"That's my point – those glass eyes - they looked so vacant. No expression. They looked dead."

"You're saying she had dead eyes?"

"Eyes are the windows to the soul," lectured Emi. "She had the blinds pulled down on hers."

Merich frowned like a headmaster calling out one of the children for what they called a 'failing of character'. "That's a cruel thing to say," he said. "Liesl did nothing to you."

"You still love her?"

"No – of course not. It's just a petty thing to say. Besides, she's back in Switzerland. I don't see what you gain from any of this."

"I'm sorry. It's what I feel. I can't help that."

The two sat quietly as the cabaret singer left the stage and headed to the bar. Merich watched as the woman nudged in beside one of her admirers who had already taken the liberty of purchasing a bottle of wine to share.

"Did you..."

Merich turned his attentions back to Emi. "Did I what?"

Emi began to fidget with the edge of the ashtray on the table. "You know ... you ... Liesl?"

"Us? Good God, no. Is that what you thought?"

"Well, you were together a long time. It only seemed natural."

"Timing was bad. Both of us were interested - just not at the same time."

"Or with the same people?" she volunteered.

"Maybe - I don't know...I think you give me too much credit."

"For what?"

"For knowing my own head," said Merich. "There isn't a man alive who knows that."

"Does that mean I should be worried?" she asked slyly.

"Not at all," he said. "I've learned to live with indecision."

"Yours or mine, councilor?"

Merich picked up his glass in a mock toast. "As I'm not under oath, and this drink has impaired my judgment, I politely decline to answer," he announced.

"I may have to treat you as a hostile witness."

"No... actually I'm quite friendly."

Emi smiled, offering the demure look that Merich recognized as a sign of comfort and ease. "I've missed you," she said thoughtfully.

"Me?" asked Merich. "I've been here all along."

"You would have thought so..."

"I realize...Look, I'm not an easy person at the best of times. It's just that life takes over."

"I'm sorry. I didn't mean to say that it was your fault. I'm no picnic either.... Actually, it's nobody's fault, and it's not fair for me to make you think that."

"It's fine, Emi. Really..."

"No - it's not fine. A lot happened when you came back. I don't have to have been there to know it was bad. I guess...I think about when we weren't here."

"I think about it too."

"Why did we ever come back? We didn't have to."

Merich's face took on a thoughtful pose. "No," he said slowly. "We did. Deep down, we know it - both of us."

"It's just - this place - it brings out things in people."

"In me, you mean?" he asked.

"No... not specifically...My parents are different too."

Emi paused for a moment, drawing her index finger over the outer rim of her glass. "Alex...I know we weren't going to talk about it – you know."

"The case? No, I'm happy to talk about it. It's the arguing that I'm not keen on."

"Well, for what it's worth, I don't want to argue either. It's just...Why?"

"Why what?"

"Why did you take it – honestly."

"Because...it's my job. I'm a lawyer. Lawyers try cases."

"Why this one? Why him?"

Merich took a healthy gulp from his glass, then raised his arm to beckon the waiter. "He has a name," he said calmly, firmly.

"You're avoiding the question," grimaced Emi.

"Look, Hartz asked me. I don't get to pick and choose. I take the ones I'm given."

"You've only been given the one," she observed.

"Have to start somewhere."

The waiter arrived at their table with refreshed drinks. Quietly, methodically, he placed them in front of Emi and Merich atop clean new squares of white paper napkin that already caught the cold sweat that pooled on the bottom. Merich pulled his loose as he took a fresh sip.

Emi smiled gratefully at the server. Her eyes continued to follow him as he began to make his way back to the bar. A few feet past their table, and she took her moment. "My point is," she continued, "that you didn't have to say yes."

"I thought we weren't going to argue?"

"Who said we're arguing? I just want to know why."

"I told you – I'll get appointed to the bench," explained Merich. "Isn't that reason enough?"

"That was going to happen sooner or later, and you're not that impatient. There had to be something else."

"Like what?"

"Don't know," she said. "You tell me."

Merich folded his hands around the glass on the table, as if he were lifting an enormous weight. "Look, I can barely remember what I did yesterday. You want me to tell you what was going through my head at that moment. I'm not sure what to say."

"You had to have a reason. That's all I'm saying."

"I thought I did – at the time...I don't know."

"Regrets?" she asked.

"Nothing but."

"About me?"

Merich smiled kindly. "Every rule has an exception – anyway, I made my choice."

"You could make another."

"So could you, for that matter."

Emi began to laugh as she shook her head. "Now I'm the one who's not sure of what's going on."

Merich raised his glass in a mock salute. "As the Americans like to say 'join the club'."

She watched him with a close intent. He could feel her eyes studying every movement, every twitch of a muscle. "So, answer me this," she said in a slow, purposeful drawl. "If Hartz were to ask you today, knowing what you do, would you still say yes?"

Merich shifted in his chair. "I think anything less than a categorical 'no' might get me into trouble," he observed.

"Anything less than the truth certainly will," she countered.

A young couple came up from behind Emi, making their way to the dance floor. Merich's eyes followed them as they passed near. He paused for a moment. "Okay - truth," he said. "I don't know. I might still have taken it."

"Well, you are honest," answered Emi wryly. "I'll give you that."

Merich frowned as he reached into the inside breast pocket of his jacket. "I think it's getting late," he said quietly. Extracting his billfold, he pulled out a couple of banknotes.

"I'll get Jaromir," she volunteered.

"Not for me," he said quickly. "It's not that far. I can walk."

"Night's not over yet," countered Emi.

"Isn't it?"

"No...it isn't," she said with firm confidence. She got up from the table. "You settle up - I'll get the car."

Little was said on the ride back to Merich's apartment. Emi held his hand tenderly, only giving it a slight squeeze when he seemed all too entranced by what lay beyond the window of the car door.

They arrived shortly before midnight. The building was silent, save for the sound of a persistent parakeet from the flat directly across the hall. With Emi clasping his left arm just above the elbow, he reached forward with his right to unlock the door.

Once inside, she flung her coat over the back of one of the chairs pushed up to the kitchen table. "Do you still have that bottle Father gave you?"

"Which one?" he asked. "He gives them to me faster than I can drink them. He must think I'm a lush!"

"People keep giving them to him. He has more than he'll ever use. Besides, who else is he going to give them to?"

"Well, don't these people ever give him money or something? He could throw the spare stuff my way."

"You'll get it all once we're married."

Merich paused for a moment. "What if I don't want it all," he sighed. "I mean, everything."

"What if I do? What if...our children do?"

"What if we can't have children?"

Emi walked over to Merich and placed a forefinger up against his lips. "All I asked for was a drink," she said softly.

"Sorry," he said haltingly. "I've got some plum brandy. How about that?"

"Pour me a little. Not too much, though – gives me a headache."

Merich entered the kitchen and reached into the cupboard

144

above the sink, extracting the bottle of liquor. He took two glasses that sat overturned in the wire drying rack and proceeded to pour.

"So why don't you see someone about it?" Emi called out from the other room.

"See about what?"

"About…you know. Doctor Reczek might be able to help, or know someone."

"He'll tell your father."

"I don't think so. He hasn't told him everything about me." Merich entered the room with the filled glasses. He handed one to Emi. "Maybe I don't want to be poked and prodded anymore, "he said before taking a sip.

"I thought I said a little brandy," she playfully admonished him. "Look…if it bothers you so much, it's worth a little hassle, isn't it?

"It's not a little hassle," argued Merich. "Look, I made a vow. No more surgeries. It's too hard."

"But if it's important to you."

"You have no idea how painful they are, and for what? I'm still a cripple."

Emi cocked her head to the side and displayed a look that Merich was all too familiar with. "That's a bit melodramatic, don't you think?" she pronounced. "You can still walk."

"I just don't want another surgery," he said firmly. "I wish you understood."

"Okay…look…I don't mean to sound…it's just that I can't let you go down. You know how you can get."

"I'm not down," defended Merich, gulping down another mouthful of brandy. "I'm just being realistic. I can't do the things I used to."

"Like running and jumping? Swimming? Alex, you never used to do them anyway. You walked, you talked, and you read."

"Not all the time."

"Trust me – you were more interested in a dusty book than anything else. Lord knows I tried to get your attention more than once."

"I don't remember that."

"Seriously?! Alexander Merich, I practically threw myself at you! I could have been laying naked on your bed and you'd still have your nose in a law book!"

"I'm not that oblivious," he laughed, as he started to feel the tension release its grip.

Emi smiled, as she turned to enter the study. "Actually," she said, "you really are."

She walked over to the record player. An album sat on the table beside it. Removing the disc from its tissue paper cover, she placed it gently on the turntable and turned on the switch. "You know," she said, placing the needle on the record, "you still owe me that dance."

"I'm a little tired..."

"Nonsense - you're tipsy. There's a difference."

Walking over to Merich, she took his hand and let him over to a clear spot in the room.

"I don't recognize this one."

"I just brought it. Father picked it up for me in London."

"Sounds like that American...Dorsey?"

"Close. It's one of his singers. Sinatra's his name. Anyway, enough talk. Just listen."

With that, Emi pulled Merich's left arm down to cradle the small of her back. He obliged, while moving his right hand just beyond her shoulder. The loss of his support made his waver slightly.

"Relax," she said reassuringly. "You don't need that crutch. Just follow me."

The room filled with lush orchestration, as the lyrics were delivered in soft and warm tones.

"What's it called," he asked.

"*I've Got a Crush On You*," she replied.

"I should've guessed..."

"Shh...If you talk through it, I'll make you do this again."

For the next few moments they stood in a close embrace, their feet shuffling back and forth in a slow sway to the music. Emi nuzzled her cheek against Merich's chest, moving only with each breath he took. "Better," she purred with contentment. "Much, much better."

Within a dozen seconds, the music suddenly stopped, and the room was plunged into darkness, save for the glowing embers from the hearth.

"You planned this, didn't you?" she teased.

"Wrong ministry. We don't shovel coal."

"No - you shovel something else!"

"Well, I'd like to take credit for it, but alas...look on the bright side. There are other things we can do - aside from dancing."

"Are you sure you didn't have a hand in this?"

Merich stepped back a pace and held his right hand over his chest. "On my word of honour...as a gentleman."

"If you were a gentleman, you wouldn't be suggesting what I think you are," she giggled.

"I'm wounded!" he laughed.

"Never mind," she said, taking his hand. "Let's go tend to your wounds."

"Be gentle."

"Of course - you've never complained about my bedside manner yet."

The two lovers laughed like they did before their homecoming as they made their way out of the room and down the moonlit hallway. For a time, the years, and the pain they brought, were left stranded by the silenced phonograph, its needle arm still caressing the grooved disc on the turntable.

CHAPTER 21

The Stolzers had recently moved back into the house on the Pedenstrasse. Generations of the family had resided there – before the revolution and the wars that had preceded it. Bruno Stolzer was the last to leave, only mere days before the first German soldiers entered the capital. He had returned from Bern in order to effect a last minute scouring of items before the occupation. The house, and what few items he had been unable to ship to Switzerland, were to be left in the possession of a Waffen SS Colonel named Hoeninger, and remained so until they, in turn, made way for the approaching Red Army. It had sat dormant for a short period, and then was taken up by the Socialist Republic's new Commissar for Agriculture, a dour and dyspeptic man named Ferenczy.

Now, more than a year beyond the counter-revolution, and the Stolzers had reclaimed their lost possessions. Ferenczy now lived in a much more modest situation at Shostoi, among those housed in its southern annex. It was an honour bestowed upon those who the Provisional Government had deemed to be a low level security threat.

By the time Merich had reached the front door, Nadia Stolzer was waiting to greet him.

"Alex – do come in," she insisted warmly, if not anxiously. "The food is already served. You must have lost track of time again."

Living in Bern with the Stolzers had made Merich accustomed to the mannerisms and eccentricities of the household, and its matron in particular. She had always chided him, and the others, for being perpetually tardy. In truth, they all tended to be generally punctual on such occasions. He had concluded that Nadia Stolzer was pathologically rushed and thus always early.

"I'm sorry, Mama Stolzer," he said affectionately, giving her a gentle kiss on the cheek. "I was stuck at the University…but I did find time to get these." He presented the modest bouquet of partially wilted roses to his hostess.

Out of courtly convention, she raised the bundle of faded flowers to her nose to drink in the memory of their fragrance. "Really, Alex," she said, "I know you can't afford these – why do you insist?"

"My mother taught me never to come empty handed."

Nadia smiled thoughtfully. "How is Olga," she asked warmly.

"Same as ever, really," he explained.

"Does she…know you?"

Asking about his mother was the customs of the ritual. Nadia asked as a reflex, and he would give his perfunctory response. None of his skill or training lent him the ability to answer her without some degree of discomfort. It was all too innocent, too well meaning, to deserve a strategy. "Half the time she doesn't know who she is," he remarked. "It's no matter, though. She's calm, and reasonably comfortable at the hospital. I'm hard pressed to do it myself anyway."

"You are a good son, Alex, and a good man. I think that she knows that – even if she can't show it."

"Perhaps," he sighed, trying to block out the memory of his last visit. "I try to do what father would do under the circumstances."

She placed a gentle hand on his shoulder. "I'm sure he would approve…Anyway, they'll be time for all that later. Come." Nadia led Merich through the large reception room to the left of the foyer. Along the back wall were a series of French doors that led out to a terrace. It was there that the Stolzers would have their customary brunch immediately after Sunday Mass. "There's still a bit of a chill, but it's the best day we've had so far. I thought this would be a nice change," she declared.

He walked over to the table where the others had already taken their places. Draped in bright white linen, its leading edges gently ruffled and swayed with the errant breezes that cut through the dense shrubs and brush that fenced the property. The bone china, the silver flatware that gleamed with the afternoon sun, and the vase of roses that marked the centre of the surface were the accoutrements that Nadia insisted were necessary to proper dining and civilized discourse. Merich knew that his hostess was fastidious about these details to the point of obsession. He fought his natural urge to make some observation on this trait mostly out of love and gratitude for this woman, but also out of some trepidation over the likely consequence of a remark.

The man at the table gave a broad grin at the sight of the rest of the party. Dressed in a light tan coloured suit, and a brushed eggshell oxford shirt, he looked as though he had just had time to remove his necktie from their prior visit to the Cathedral. His hair was mostly grey, but still maintained a healthy measure of its youthful hue of dark brown. He rose from his seat.

"Alex - glad you could make it," said Bruno Stolzer in his typical fashion, gregarious without seeming too ebullient. He extended his slender but firm hand to Merich and they shook cordially. Bruno smelled of sandalwood and pomade. It was the first thing Merich could ever recall about him. It was as though his sweat glands secreted the sickly sweet odour. Never could he detect the smell of perspiration, of salty musk whetted down by humid air. He once held a private jealousy of this perfection. That was long ago, though, before he began to mistrust anything that did not feel real.

"My apologies - I've been trying to prepare for the case, and..."

"And Hartz won't give you a continuance," volunteered Stolzer.

"Not exactly. Nagy has been named as the presiding magistrate for the case."

"Sure, sure, but that old buzzard pulls his strings too. Don't let him tell you otherwise," declared Stolzer, as he gestured for him to sit down next to Emi. "Have I ever told you about what he was like back when your father and I were in his class?"

"Actually, yes. You told me that he was a miserable sonofabitch..."

"Really!" exclaimed Nadia. "You two know better than that! It's the Sabbath, and I'll have none of that language in this house." She promptly crossed herself as if to emphasize her point, as well as her resolve.

Merich leaned over and gave Emi a kiss on the cheek, then turned to Nadia. "I'm sorry, mama. Sometimes I forget myself," he said with the look he used to display after he had done something particularly impudent.

"Let's start again," she declared. "Alex, you seem to be getting around a little better these days."

"It's the weather, mama. The dampness is starting to go."

"You know, it would be better if you just gave up that awful flat and moved here. There's plenty of room."

"The boy wants his own place," interrupted Stolzer. "He needs privacy, *ja*?" The knowing look he gave Merich and Emi managed to escape Nadia's notice.

"I appreciate the offer, but Bruno's right," added Merich. "I need to work on my case, and it's the perfect place..."

"It's a tenement...I'm sorry, but that place isn't fit for you," declared Nadia. "You're still sick. I know - I can see."

"You just said he looked better, mama," chimed in Emi, as she took a sip of her orange juice.

"Well, what about you?" countered Nadia. "You visit him there. Don't tell me you feel safe."

"Actually, it's not so bad," laughed Emi. "I'm used to the rats, and the gypsies always make extra beet soup."

Nadia shook her head. "All of you are absolutely dreadful. You all make fun of me for caring...Now can we just enjoy a nice family meal?"

Meals at the Stolzer table were a solemn occasion. Conversation occurred before the blessing and after dessert, and not in-between. Anything beyond asking for the salt and pepper, or excusing oneself from the table, met with looks of incredulity. Merich thought it to be a peculiar ritual. Neither Franz nor Olga was particularly quiet at supper. Most times, the senior Merich encouraged him to speak up.

It was not as though there was some formal convention or rule. Nadia was determined that her guests to eat before the food went cold, and showed immediate displeasure at anything - or anyone - who detracted from that objective. Bruno did not wish to speak of his business dealings, which comprised almost the full extent of his conversational interests. As for Emi, she was not inclined to discuss her work - which they did not understand - or her personal affairs - of which they would not approve. The silence seemed to suit their agendas, and Merich learned to oblige.

After they had finished, Bruno retired to his study as Nadia began to marshal her household staff to clean up the table. Emi and Merich made their way to the terraced garden that sat at the back edge of the property. Perennials were beginning to bear their buds in eager anticipation. As plain as it all looked, within a few weeks it would be alive with colours and textures. Splashes of pale pastels would meld with vivid tones to overwhelm and intoxicate. Honeybees would swarm activity, as frenetic as a factory gate when the shift change sounded. But that would be later. It gave Merich a strange sense of satisfaction. Everything he encountered seemed to have the promise of something better - why should this be any different?

"I hope that mother hasn't bothered you too much about...you know."

"No, not at all," he replied. "She means well. I think I could forgive her most anything. She reminds me of my own mother...back in the day."

"You don't have to talk about it if you don't want," she said, gently placing her hand over his.

"Then I won't," he smiled. "It's far too nice a day for all that."

They made their way to the concrete bench near the back of the grounds, as they were wont to do, and took their customary places.

"Well, there is the question of a wedding," began Emi.

"I didn't think that was an issue?"

"Well, you said you didn't want to be married in a church."

"And you said that you didn't want to get married."

"I said not right now," corrected Emi. "Someday - of course - but not now."

"But you're thinking about it."

"I guess," she sighed. "Maybe - I don't know. It's always in the back of my mind."

Merich looked down at his shoes, then glanced at the leading edge of his cane. "You're not worried, then."

"About what?"

"You know. We've talked about this before."

Emi gave Merich a look that reminded him of what his mother displayed when he brought her news of a grade he had received on a test. "And you know what my answer is, don't you," she declared in a calm, gentle voice.

"Your father has expectations..."

152

"Yes. Yes, he does, but you're not marrying him, are you? Maybe I don't want any."

"But that is a choice you get to make. What if it's already been made for us?"

"Then it's been made. Seriously, if you're just saying this to get yourself out of our engagement..."

"You know me better than that," defended Merich.

"Sometimes...I'm not so sure."

"You mean the case, don't you?"

"Among other things...Look, Alex, I don't want to fight about this, but I've thought about what we said to each other at the Atrium. I might not have said things the right way, but I wasn't wrong."

"Meaning?"

Emi sighed as she looked to the top of the oak tree a few feet in front of them. "Meaning that if we are going to have a life together, we really need to discuss these kinds of decisions," she said. "We need to choose a path that works for us together, for our future."

"And that applies to you as well?"

"Of course it does. Alex, if we're serious about this, then we need to start acting it. No lies, no hiding - everything all together." Merich shrugged. "Honestly, I thought that was what I was doing. Being a magistrate gives me some security - a good salary and lifetime tenure. It's also a pretty acceptable profession for people in certain circles."

"That's the last thing you should be worried about. Those circles are orbits, and they go around my father. One day they'll go around you."

"You know how I feel about that," he said intently. "That's reason enough not to get married."

"But not enough reason for you?"

"It's the cross I'll have to bear. At least I can throw those dilettantes out when I want."

"If I don't beat you to it!" laughed Emi. "I can't stand them any more than you. Unfortunately, Father will invite every one of them to the wedding."

"Speaking of - you want to talk about it?"

"Actually...yes. I would like us to talk to the priest at Saint Michael's about him performing the ceremony – when we're ready."

"Saint Michael's is a bit grand isn't it?"

"You've never set foot in the place."

"Well, I have walked past it...Look, I have no idea what's involved. I wouldn't know where to begin."

"Well, first you actually have to come to Sunday Mass. Look, we'll meet Father Borsch and find out what we need to do..."

"What?" interrupted Merich.

"The sacraments...you know...confession?"

"No. I mean who is this Father Borsch?"

Emi shook her head. "The priest at Saint Michael's, which you would have known if you ever bothered to come to Mass," she scolded.

Merich refocused his mind on the conversation at hand. "I would," he began tentatively, "but confession would take up a week, and I have work to do."

"Well, it's not going to get any easier putting it off. Do you want me to talk to him?"

"No. Not right now...maybe after the case."

"That's a long wait."

"It'll be over by August - not so long."

"I suppose not," she sighed. "At least it gives Mother time to make her plans - and you know she will."

"I know. They say the wedding is more for the families than the couple."

"Speaking of...I ...is she going to be okay?"

Merich gave a slight frown as he shrugged. "It doesn't matter. Even if Janousek had her medicated, she wouldn't understand what was going on, and quite frankly, it would just remind me of things. I might not be big on this wedding business, but if we are going to do it, I want it to be a good day. No tension, no guilt..."

"And no remorse?"

"No remorse."

"There's something else that we haven't really talked about," she said.

"What's that?"

"My career - I've worked very hard to be good at what I do. I don't want to throw it away."

Merich shook his head. "Who said anything about throwing it away?" he asked.

"Nobody...yet...but I know that a woman's career is looked at as what you do until you get a husband."

"I don't doubt that there'll be times when I'll need you to support me, but I'd like to think that I'll be there for you the same way."

Emi looked directly into Merich's eyes, veering neither to the left or the right. He had always been somewhat envious of how effective her stare could be when there was a point to be made. "I hope so, but people change, and I'm afraid I won't be more than a judge's wife," she explained.

"Look...it's hard to explain, but I really don't have that kind of expectation for us."

"I want to get married, but I also want to make sure that we understand each other…"

"Emi – you know how I feel about my work. I can only imagine you feel the same way about yours…I'm not saying that situations might not happen. Hell, we're in one right now…I guess what I'm saying is that we'll figure it out."

"That's easy to say right now," she remarked.

Merich smiled kindly, as he placed his hand on her knee. "I'm not saying that we won't disagree," he began. "I mean; I know how you feel about my case. At the end of the day, we have to trust each other. I have to believe that you wouldn't do anything to hurt our relationship, and I hope you would feel the same."

Emi stared at his hand for a moment. "After this case, Alex."

"I promise…After this case."

CHAPTER 22

Merich sat in the corner of the Café Schweidner that had become his usual spot by default. It was a secluded part of the establishment that was in close proximity to the lavatories. On occasion, his physical limitations made it difficult to reach a facility in enough time. Beyond the obvious damage to his tibia, some pellets had entered his lower abdomen. While he had been assured that there had been no lasting damage, he suffered from an urgent bladder, as well as the occasional episode of sharp, stabbing pains just below his belly. The same physicians had assured him about his leg, and Merich knew how well those prognostications had fared.

The café's toilet was clean and well kept – hot water, towels and toilet paper. Beyond the Klosters, it had been the only place in the city he had found where the facilities were maintained. He appreciated the effort. People had taken to walking about with balled up wads of tissue stuffed in their pockets and purses. At least here he would not have to waste his reserve.

He had found the establishment shortly after his return to the city. While it was a diminished facsimile of the cafes in Bern, it felt inviting to him. Staff and patrons alike appeared somewhat happy to be there.

Cups with imperfect bottoms rattled on saucers, making a gentle tinkling noise like the discrete wave of a dinner service bell. The large espresso boiler on one end of the counter gurgled and belched with anger until it directed its wrath in a cloud of scalding mist.

The waiter recognized him as he came in the door, and was ready to place the cup of coffee in front of him as he was readying to sit down. The acidic bite of the thick Turkish blend became both sweet and salty to his tongue, mixing with his saliva as it trickled down the back of his throat.

He looked past the other patrons, past the din of banter, polite and otherwise, through the plate glass and out into the street. This was his moment, and he guarded it as jealously as anything in his possession.

The gusts of wind that rolled through the narrow lane darted and weaved around every obstacle, every lamp post and awning like a drunk attempting to navigate his way home. The green and white fringes of canvas that hung over the front of the café flicked and snapped in spasmodic convulsions. Beyond, the fine rivulets of rain, illuminated by the pallid glow of the nearby gas lamps, spun to and fro like a sabre dancer working themselves into a frenzy.

Merich looked at the wall sconce closest to him. The frosted glass of the fixture was caked with dust that had been mortared to the surface by the sweat of the steam. It housed a light bulb that flickered and burned low, low enough that he could discern the shape of the tungsten filament without hurting his eyes. To him, it resembled one of the cut lilies they left on a grave days after the mourners took their sorrows elsewhere.

Merich took a moment to try and remember what he looked like. The idea of not being able to recall made him feel a momentary panic, as though something had just been stolen. It had been a long time, and he could not recollect where he had stored his family's heirlooms, such as they were. His was a mind that could not recount a name or a face without some context. To remember one thing, he needed to remember it all.

*   *   *

"Alex, your father's ready to go. Hurry up!"

Merich had been busy putting the finishing touches on his latest article. He hurried to place it in his usual hiding place – a small hole in the wall that lie behind the steam register in his room. In the other room, he could hear the gentle admonishment from his father to her, telling her not to worry, that being a few minutes late was hardly the end of the world, and that nothing would begin without them anyway.

Merich smiled and laughed to himself. For as many years as he could remember – before and after his time in Bern – it had always played out this way. A few gentle, yet firm, words could place Olga Merich at ease for a time. He admired how his father could do this – for her and for others. It was a gift that he was both proud and somewhat envious of.

He had been back in the country for a little over six months – much to his mother's outright disapproval. Life was only marginally better with the new regime, she cautioned. It was still not fit to return. While she could not say exactly when he should come back, now was certainly not the time.

Franz Merich was far more sanguine about the issue. He shared his wife's concerns and apprehensions, but he was nevertheless happy to see his son after such a prolonged separation. He had not regretted his decision to send Alex away, but he could not shake the sense that he had somehow abdicated his responsibilities. Often, he wondered whether Alex was more Bruno's son than his.

"I'm ready," Merich announced to his parents as he entered the room. He walked over to the foyer and reached for his overcoat that sat perched on a peg behind the front door.

Olga reached for the woolen scarf that her son had once again neglected. She draped it around his neck and proceeded to tuck the loose ends into the top of his coat. "Seriously, boy, when are you going to learn to take care of yourself! I can't imagine Nadia ever let you leave the house undressed!"

"No, she had the servants dress me," chided Merich.

"You fuss too much, mother," interjected his father, placing his hand on Merich's shoulder. "He does well enough for himself."

"As much as anyone can in this godforsaken country," she countered. "Really, Alex. I can't fathom why you would possibly want to come back to this?"

"Who else would remember my scarf?" he joked, leaning in to kiss his mother's cheek.

"It's time. Best that we be on our way," interrupted Franz.

The two men left the flat and made their way down the hall to the elevator. Merich's father pressed the button, and they stood waiting for the lift to arrive. "Don't let her bother you," he said. "It's just her way."

"I know," replied Merich. "I thought I remembered, but it's taken some time to get used to."

"For all of us. It's a bit of an adjustment. Sometimes I forget too."

As the elevator car arrived. Merich pulled the cage door open and gestured for his father to go in. Merich shut the gate. It had been freshly lubricated by the superintendent, causing a streak of grease to smear across the palm of his hand. He sighed, and started to rub his hands on his coat.

"If you use the inside of your pocket, your mother won't see it," offered Franz.

The car gave a jerk as it began its descent.

"I had to come back…I can't explain why," said Merich.

Franz remained staring forward. He raised his head to watch the light above the door count off each passing floor in sequence. "Alex," he began thoughtfully, "most of my life I've been driven by one thing or another – most of which I couldn't explain either. I'm not going to pretend to know why you came back, but there's a selfish part of me that's glad you did."

"You're not angry, then?"

Franz grinned. "I'd prefer to call it 'concerned'," he said slowly.

"I understand, especially with the EBI rounding up everyone in sight."

The Public Security Directorate was known by many names throughout the country. German speakers called it the SMD – short for *Die Sicherheit der Menschen Direktion*. The minority Czech population referred to it as the LBR, or *Lidé je Bezpečnostní ředitelství*, while the Hungarian speakers called it the *Emberek Biztonsági Igazgatóság*, or EBI. Given the still enduring hostility toward all things German since the war, even traditionally Teutonic families like the Merichs took to calling it by that particular variant.

"They're scared," explained Franz. "Ever since the attack on Licht and his wife they've been watching everyone and everywhere."

"But…they haven't bothered you?"

"That's due more to dumb luck than anything else…You know, when the Russians left and the socialists took over, it did get better – at least a little bit for a little while. There had always been a dark side to them, but not like now…Now, it's different."

"That's a difference far too subtle for me to notice," said the younger Merich.

Franz shrugged. "It's hard to explain," he said," but in the beginning, there was a sort of logic to it – to what they did. Of course, I never agreed with any of it…but I could still see the rationale behind what they did. It's easy to function in those circumstances. Moves and countermoves, they follow patterns. They have a pretext."

The son shook his head. "I'm still not sure I follow," he sighed.

Franz lowered his gaze from the top of the door and turned to his son. "Let me put it this way," be began thoughtfully, "you're walking in the forest and come across a wolf, all alone. You know he won't hunt without a pack, and you know he can't climb a tree – that dictates what you do. You don't challenge or threaten, and if he gets aggressive, you climb a tree and wait for him to tire. You know the animal's motivation, and his tactics. Work within that, you survive."

"And now?" asked Alex.

"No pattern, no logic," shrugged Franz. "People get rounded up and never come back. Some are scientists and some are ditch diggers – none of them likely have a head for politics."

"So, why take them?"

"Fear – nothing more than primal fear. It will seize you up, make you do things that you could never contemplate…It makes men do things that God would never intend."

"Yes, but whose fear – theirs or ours?" asked the son.

"Doesn't really matter. Theirs makes them aggressive. Ours makes us timid. In the end, it's the same result."

"And that's what the EBI is doing?"

Franz turned back to the door of the lift. "It's the only think that makes any sense to me. God knows I've tried to understand…"

A bell signaled their arrival at the lobby. The inner door slowly opened to reveal three men.

"Franz Merich – come with us," ordered the lead man, as he grasped the gate with his thick fingers and pulled it open. Franz grimaced. His face became sallow. He turned to Merich. "Go back to your mother," he said calmly.

Merich felt the blood drain from his face. "I'm coming with you," he insisted.

"No," said Franz, fighting to maintain his composure. His voice became more calm, his words becoming monotone. "You need to go to your mother…now."

The two men who had remained silent to this point lurched forward, each grabbing one of Franz's arms, pulling him out of the lift. The lead man gave Merich a mocking smirk as he pressed the button that would send the elevator back up, then slid the gate shut.

Merich felt faint, his stomach churning in a dull ache. He quickly pressed the lobby button. He paced back and forth, like a caged animal seized with a rush of adrenaline fueled by fear. He smashed his fist against one of the wood panels in the car. His knuckles ached and bled in a momentary rush of release.

A muffled bang echoed in the shaft. He worried that the old lift was about to stop, leaving him stranded between floors. It continued to shimmy and shudder, but kept on its moderate pace.

The doors finally, mercifully opened. Merich pushed open the cage and ran down the hallway. The door to the family's flat was ajar. He pushed it open hard enough to embed the doorknob into the lathe and plaster wall behind. He stopped.

Olga Merich stood with her back to him. She stood at the open window, the wind blowing fine sharp pellets of snow and rain against her face, coarse like Sahara sand

"Mother," said Merich.

No movement, no reply.

"Mother!" he repeated, as he moved closer to her. Still nothing.

He stood beside her, looked at her intently. Her skin was flushed and wet.

She still did not acknowledge his presence. She continued to stare out the window, eliciting no other sound but the shallow movement of air from her breath.

Merich slowly turned from her to see for himself.

The figure of a man was haphazardly splayed on the street below, a few yards from the front entrance of the building. The arms and legs were distorted like the limbs of a marionette without a guiding hand. A large deep crimson stain, illuminated by a nearby lamp post, surrounded the figure's head, like a halo. It slowly consumed the snow around it, then tapered at one side, where the flow of fluid made its way along the gutter and into a storm drain nearby. A dozen or so people had already gathered from the vicinity to survey the scene at close range.

Merich closed his eyes tightly, trying to squeeze out the world. Nothing remained except the final strains of Debussy's 'Clair du lune' on the photograph, and the wet sting of the cold snow.

*　　*　　*

Another sip of coffee brought Merich back to the café. By now, the rain had abated and a number of the other patrons had taken the opportunity that this respite offered to make their way home, or wherever. He had not noticed their departure, and their absences caught him off guard.

"Another coffee, sir?" asked the waiter.

Merich placed his hand over the cup and politely shook his head. "No…thank you…I need to go."

He grabbed his cane and pulled himself to his feet while the waiter began to clear the table. He reached into his pocket and extracted a bill and some small coins – an amount sufficient to induce a fulsome expression of gratitude from his server.

Poor bastard, thought Merich. *That amount of gratuity laid on the table at Bern would have generated nothing less than a contemptuous sneer. Have we fallen that far?*

Fixing his overcoat and hat, he plodded out the door and in the direction of his apartment.

The cobblestones of the sidewalk held small pools of water on the sunken edges. Merich tred slowly and carefully. He could feel the moisture coming up through the soles of his shoes, and by the time he had reached the halfway point of his journey, his socks were soaked through.

Merich remembered the name of the man who had led the reception party for his father – the one who had pushed the elevator button - Zhukov, Dmitri Zhukov. Most people had simply referred to him as "the Cossack." He had read the reports of that final stand at the former barracks, that Zhukov had stood by Hugo Stern's side during the worst of the assault. He learned how Zhukov had been apprehended by one of the militias, and that he had been defiant as ever. He had been reported as yelling that the nation was a 'godforsaken shithole' and that his heart remained in Mother Russia.

Merich had heard that the militia commander was not without compassion, and that within a couple of weeks the Soviet Embassy had received an anonymous package with particularly grisly contents, as well as some terse instructions on where the item had been meant to remain.

Within a few minutes, he reached the front door to his building. Extracting the key from his coat pocket, he reached to unlock the door latch. He turned to his right, a reflexive action, finding a solitary figure about twenty yards away. The person immediately moved to the adjacent alleyway, which Merich knew was a dead end and devoid of an open passage. Whoever it was, they were not going far.

He hurried himself inside and quickly shut the door. Rushing up the staircase as quickly as his leg would allow, he gained entry to his flat and slid the deadbolt behind him.

CHAPTER 23

Even after having travelled half the distance out to Shostoi, Merich was not convinced that another interview was the best use of his time. He may not have had extensive experience with clients, but he knew that dealing with Licht was something out of the ordinary. The mood swings – from defiance to resignation – had not made things easy. He hoped that, in the course of the banter and hyperbole, the man might slip up and let go of a useful fact.

He had become somewhat acclimatized to the prison, its people and its routines. The attitudes and demeanor of the guards had not changed demonstrably, but neither did they hold the surprise they had the first time. He still harbored concerns about the place, but knew that it could have been much worse. He knew what worse looked like.

As he entered through the cell door he found Licht already sitting at the table. "Good morning, Johann," he said pleasantly. "You look well today."

"I'll take that in the spirit it's given," came the reply, neutral in inflection and delivery.

Merich offered a weak smile that looked more like a grimace. He set his case on top of the table and unfastened the clasp. "I'm hoping that we can wrap things up early today," he answered, as his hand reached in to pull out the intended contents. "I'm sure you'd prefer that too."

Licht leaned back in his chair, folding his arms across his chest. "Take your time," he yawned. "I find my schedule suddenly open."

After extracting the contents, Merich managed to maneuver himself down into the seat opposite. He took the items and spread them out with great care, each one in its intended place and order.

"What are you staring at?" asked Licht.

"Pardon."

"You're staring straight at me. Is there something on my glasses?"

"No...not that I can see."

"Well, you're looking me straight in the eye. You could at least blink a couple of times. It's very disconcerting."

"Sorry..." hesitated Merich. "Didn't mean to..."

"Am I allowed to ask why?"

"Why what?"

"Why you're distracted. You're the one constantly talking about wasted time. I should think that applies to you as well."

"It's nothing. I apologize. Let's get on with it..."

Licht extended the index finger of his right hand and began to tap on the table. "This is my defense – my life. I deserve to know if there's something affecting it."

Merich shook his head, and continued to slide papers around the surface like a croupier at a baccarat table. "Seriously, it's nothing," he dismissed. "I was thinking of something someone said the other day."

"About the case?"

"No – it might surprise you to know that I have a life outside this case, although you wouldn't know it to see."

"I'm sorry," sneered Licht. "Are you just spouting off, or are you looking for sympathy?"

Merich opened the folder on the table. He extracted a large glossy photograph and slid it across.

"Was is it?"

"I'm told that it's the change of command ceremony. The one where the Russians began their pullout."

Licht removed his glasses and picked up the photograph. He examined it like a master jeweler, attempting to find the flaw in a gem that would receive the sharp wedge of his chisel. "Yes, that looks like it," he said as he handed it back.

"You sure?"

"Of course," he huffed. "I can see General Fetisov standing in it. He oversaw the handover personally."

"When did you see him again - after that?"

Licht took a moment to ponder the question. "It would have to be...maybe two weeks later. He met me at Nytriy- to sign the final agreement."

"That the withdrawal was complete."

"Of course."

"And that all Soviet troops were gone."

"With the obvious exception of those in their embassy compound, but that was less than twenty."

"But no others?"

"No – none...Really, what is the point of this? I told you the truth."

Merich leaned forward. His right hand moved toward the photograph, which he tapped with his index finger. "What if I told you that Fetisov and his forces didn't leave - that they were here as late as February 1948."

"Impossible," sneered Licht. "They were gone. I saw to it myself."

"That picture was taken from a still from a newsreel dated February 22, 1948. Why are there Russian soldiers?"

"There weren't any. You're mistaken."

Merich pulled the photograph back toward him. "I spent hours poring over newsreels – hours," he began. "I had two archivists at the University in the capital – professional archivists – helping me. There are very few things I'd bet my life on."

"I don't give a damn what your film says!" snapped Licht.

"That was in late 1946! I should bloody well remember that!"

"But you don't seem to remember most of 1947 and a good part of 1948. Perfect recall one minute, amnesia the next."

"It was 1946! I'll stake my life and anything else you've got to add on it!"

"I know," smiled Merich. "I know you're telling the truth. I can see your hand in the picture. No scar."

The client leaned back in his chair, extending his arms upward in triumph. "See - I told you!" he exclaimed.

"That still doesn't explain why this was shown more than a year later."

"How the hell should I know?"

Merich felt his moment come His extended hand quickly balled up into a tight fist, and smashed against the table. "Because – as you're so fond of reminding me - you were the head of the party!" he yelled back. "You were the head of the country! All this time you've put conditions on me - now it's your turn! You start to level with me right here, right now, or I walk!"

Licht sighed as he looked about the cell. His eyes went back to the photograph before honing in on Merich. "You know," he began in a slow drawl, "despite what I say, you still don't get it…What I remember, don't remember - that doesn't matter. I was in charge."

"I don't think you were," asserted Merich.

Licht leaned in, reaching forward with his right hand. The index finger was extended, tapping against the photograph. "I think you wanted to find this," he said, "I think it took a long time, *ja?* Well, most people don't ask. They see, and they react. They saw me, and they acted on it."

"They were wrong."

"I asked them to help me - to believe in something bigger than themselves. That is precisely what they did. Where they wrong for doing that, or me for asking?"

Merich shook his head. "You don't think I understand what you're doing," he began. "Well, let me tell you what I really think. You started out simple enough. Organize a group of people around some ideas, and make it grow. When it took root, it emboldened you - made you want more. When it stalled, you were desperate to do anything to keep it alive. You made choices you knew were dangerous, but you figured that the risk was worth the reward. But it wasn't, and you started to lose control. Problem was that Johann Licht was dead. You were First Secretary; you were the regime.

"You're delusional."

"And you're in denial. Every act done in your name was you. Every time a clerk filed a paper, or a Vopo stopped a man on the street, if they did it in your name, it was as good as you being right there."

"See, you know it yourself!"

"It's all bullshit," said Merich. "You don't believe in God, but you think you have all this power."

"I'm not a god," defended Licht. "I just believe that you're responsible for what you get people to do."

"Not for what Stern made them do."

"I made Stern!" yelled Licht.

"You didn't make Stern!" Merich snapped back. "I don't even think the devil's willing to take credit! You know full well – he was bent before you ever laid eyes on him!"

Licht bowed his head, back to staring at the photograph "Hugo Stern was the third son of a sheep farmer in the eastern provinces," he said. "He never attended school beyond the mud shack in his village. At one point, every intelligence officer, every policeman, in the country reported to him. You think it was fate that put him there? Divine destiny?"

"I think that you overstate your own importance," argued Merich. "I think that even with your glowing recommendation, somebody else – anybody else - could have stopped them if they wanted to. Besides, that doesn't change the fact that he knew what he was doing."

Licht raised his head, and leaned back in his chair. His left hand rose to rub the back of his neck. "That's all hypothetical – me or him. Doesn't matter."

"And yet, you don't mind taking responsibility for all of it. The things you did, and the things you didn't. If it doesn't matter, then don't do it."

"You don't understand anything. I lead by example," declared Licht, summoning some of the air of his former self. "You inspire those around you to work hard, to sacrifice…to be better."

Merich shook his head. "Examples are worthless if no one follows them," he countered. "You realize none of your party friends are owning up to what they did. Either you ran the country by yourself, or there are a few comrades who want to pass everything on to you. Nice to see you've been such a moral influence on them."

"Circumstances challenge people. Sometimes they fail."

"Not much of a challenge if you ask me. They're sitting in cells with windows to look out, not more than a hundred meters from here. They get to eat in the mess hall. They get visitors. They get mail. They stabbed you in the back for a plea bargain. They weren't tortured, and the only threat was a longer prison sentence."

"That's your interpretation."

"You're the one talking about loyalty and example," argued Merich. "All I see are a bunch of your friends willing to let you hang if it means shortening their sentence by a couple of years…Come on – tell me that it doesn't piss you off!"

Licht became even more subdued, his words carefully clipped for content and tone. "What is it you want from me, Herr Merich?"

he asked. "I realize that we're both new to this lawyer-client relationship, but I can't help thinking that this isn't the way it's supposed to work."

"You're absolutely right," replied Merich. "The way it's supposed to go is that you are completely honest and open with me, and that you are willing to do anything I ask in order to win. My job is to do everything that the law will allow to make that happen."

"You want trust."

"Yes – I want trust. I need trust."

"You – son of the great Herr Doktor Merich. Yes – I know who you are. Dragging your bum leg around like a loose piece of meat. I'm supposed to trust you?"

"I agreed to take this case," replied Merich. "I'm sitting right here, right now."

"That doesn't prove anything. You could tell me anything right now, and then sell me out in front of the judges. Let them sentence me so you don't have to get your hands dirty."

"You think I'm someone who lets others do my dirty work for me?"

"Is that remark supposed to make me feel better? How the hell am I supposed to know?""

"It's not in my best interest to lose."

Licht gave Merich a considered look, and then smiled. "I would trust an ulterior motive more than some sense of duty. You're not that stupid, and neither am I."

"Well, then."

"Well, nothing."

"We have an understanding," said Merich.

"We have nothing of the sort."

"I told you…"

"That you have a motivation," interrupted Licht. "You didn't say what it was. Anybody can imply anything."

"And a liar can make up anything to fit a story."

"True, but even if you're full of shit, at least you're making an effort," said Licht, leaning back in his chair. "You're not insulting my intelligence."

Merich paused. His index finger casually drew a circle on top of the photograph. Then, it pressed down hard. He pulled it back toward him, picked it up and slipped it back into the folder.

"Judge," he finally said. "They promised to make me a judge if I win."

"Like your father."

"My father was never a judge."

Licht smiled for a moment, and then brought his open hand forward. "We start anew," he said.

Merich hesitated briefly, but raised his own hand to shake on the truce.

CHAPTER 24

If Merich had been honest with himself, he never intended to come. The Stolzers were loyal devotees, even in Bern, and as their charge he had been compelled to attend with them each week. On occasion, he had been able to extricate himself from this solemn duty. He would employ any one of a number of reasons and rationales that were routinely shuffled like a deck of cards, lest their repetitive nature become all too obvious.

He did not hate any of it – not the church, not the priests, nor the Creator. There was nothing inherently wrong with the Mass, and he did not begrudge it to anyone who needed it. He could readily name a dozen or so employed in the Ministry who he thought might benefit from that sort of edification.

What bothered him was when the priest would routinely ask all the congregants to offer thanks for their many blessings. The Swiss could be thankful for having been spared the ravages of war and separation. Emi could be thankful for having her family safe and sound, while Bruno and Nadia could give pious praise for having all of that, and their money too. Merich could never understand why he was required to be just as grateful for far less grace. Surely just being in one piece was not as great a gift as the others had been bestowed. He came to the conclusion that as his benefit received was far more modest, the level of gratitude he was expected to show could be less exacting as well.

Merich crossed the Stanislaus Bridge which connected to the south-eastern section of the city – part gypsy and Jewish ghetto, and part bohemian enclave. Although similar in architecture, style and symmetry to other quarters, one developed the immediate sense that they had crossed more than a stone span over a river.

Since the war, it had changed a great deal. The once common sight of Orthodox men, their wide brimmed hats and generously full beards, had been supplanted by poor peasant families from the East. So, too, had the joy and fellowship that community brings. Merich felt sympathy for their plight, but still looked at them as squatters who had taken in the most opportunistic of ways.

He had been told that the priest had taken many from the gypsy community into his protection during the war, and in the subsequent rise of the Commissariat. Despite the ideological differences between the Nazis, the Soviets, and the Commissars, none seemed to have much use or toleration for the Roma.

St. Michael's Cathedral was a large and imposing gothic tower that hovered over the quarter, like some immovable emissary of the Almighty. Small by the standards of other holy shrines in other places, its grandeur came partly through how it dominated its surroundings. It was the focal point of attention for those who happened to find themselves near at hand for one purpose or another.

To be impressed, however, was to be an interloper, a foreigner in this land. Those who lived in its shadow were people who saw nothing good from institutions – monarchy, fascism, or the people's state. And there was little one could say or do to convince them that the newly crowned and anointed would be any fairer, or kinder, than their predecessors. As far as the Church went, the same applied, but they were practical enough to make one exception. They would not pray to a God in Rome, but they were willing to pay some fealty to its disciple who had stood between them and the Angel of Death.

Priests made Merich uncomfortable. No matter how kind or gentle, their very demeanor implied guilt. He reasoned that a clergy so schooled in the dictum of 'original sin' could not help but see a flawed vessel in every soul it encountered. His training, in contrast, told him that one had some right to a presumption of innocence and a right to be defended. That innate knowledge somehow made the task at hand feel less daunting.

Merich entered the sanctuary and slowly walked the length of the nave, his cane making a dull thump each time it made contact with the polished marble. Once he reached the chancel, he crossed himself, then moved forward to light one of the many candles placed to the side of the altar. As the flame took hold of the wick, he looked to his right. Noticing a young priest speaking with an older woman, he made his way over to them.

"Excuse me," he interrupted. "I'm sorry to bother. I'm looking for Father Christoph. Would he happen to be here?"

"And you are?" asked the priest, in a tone far more conciliatory than the words he used.

"Alex Merich. I wanted to discuss something of a private nature with him."

"I am Father Tadeusz. Father Christoph is in the confessional for the next hour. If what you wish to say is private, you can wait for him in the vestry. I'll take you there in a moment."

Merich looked past the priest and noticed the small ornate booth that stood along the wall. "Thank you," he replied. "I will."

As soon as the priest had directed his attentions back to the woman, Merich quietly made his way to the booth. It was empty. He went inside and, after shutting the door, he took his place on the stool that sat in the corner. The sliding door between the compartments opened, and he crossed himself.

"Bless me, Father, for I have sinned."

"How long has it been since your last confession?" came the voice.

"During the war, when I was abroad."

"That would have been quite some time ago," observed the priest. "Why have you decided to come now?"

"I have an ulterior motive, Father Christoph. I came here to talk to you. I need your help."

"Many people come to me looking for help. What is it that you need?"

"I am a defense counsel for the government's Tribunal. I believe that you know my client, and that you may have information of use to him."

"Who is your client?"

"Johann Licht."

The voice on the other side of the divide wet silent, although Merich could still hear his breathing. "I'm sorry," he finally said. "I don't think that I can help you..."

"Father, I just want to talk. I know you're are a cautious man. You can choose to tell me what you feel comfortable with. I'll respect your wishes, but it's important that we talk."

Another moment of silence passed before Christoph spoke.

"I must hear confessional for a while longer. If you wish to speak with me, you may do so after I finish."

"Thank you, Father," replied Merich. "I appreciate this very much." He rose from the stool, about to leave, when Christoph stopped him.

"Where are you going?" he asked.

"Out...To wait for you."

"Do you not want to confess your sins?" asked the priest.

"Well..."

"I will speak only if you stay to confess," he insisted.

Merich hesitated for a moment.

"Are you ready to confess?"

"Fair enough," Merich sighed as he sat back down on the stool. "I'm not sure where to begin."

"Begin at the beginning."

"Well, I have known a woman outside the bonds of marriage," sighed Merich. "Beyond that, I really don't think I have much to say."

"You've committed sins of the flesh and neglected the confessional," declared the priest. "I think that's a great deal. I'd tell you to say one hundred Hail Marys, but I doubt that you'd even remember how...Wait for me in my quarters. Tadeusz will take you there. I'll be along in a while."

"Thank you, Father," said Merich. He then left the booth and sought the assistance of the younger priest. Father Tadeusz, who had spent the last couple of minutes looking for Merich, verified what instructions had passed on to him.

The living quarters were located in a small cottage on the larger grounds of the cathedral, behind the sanctuary, separated by a dozen or so yards. Between the two stretched a cobblestone path, bordered on either side by gardens which, at this particular time of year, were still barren, save for some oak trees that dominated the courtyard.

"It must be pleasant here in the summer," remarked Merich.

"Yes. Father Christoph spends a great deal of time tending to it. It is his passion."

"Passion?" asked Merich. "That's not a word I readily associate with your kind."

"Yes, passion," affirmed Tadeusz. "We are priests, but we are also men. Sometimes we need to partake of earthly beauty."

"Is that how you get your release?" quipped Merich, not realizing the impertinence of the remark until it had already been made.

"That is a very crass way of putting it," replied Tadeusz, in a calm, yet unimpressed fashion. "But, yes, in a way, that is true. Beauty, this natural beauty, is a reminder of God's love. We honor Him by tending it. With all the pain and suffering we have had, it is no less a duty than the formal ones we must observe."

"Forgive me, but it sounds like a means of avoiding the world, not changing it."

"No less than those who wrap themselves up in rules and institutions, or seek pleasure in indulgence," the priest countered.

"You presume to know me, sir," said Merich.

"No more than you presume about us," replied Tadeusz. "I wasn't even talking about you. It was a general observation of the world. I apologize if you took it personally."

The young priest smiled as he turned away from him. *A smug grin, thought Merich. They are around God so much they begin to think that they are God, all holier than thou.* But he knew deep inside that he would not have been so bothered had the comments been that outrageous or implausible.

Tadeusz led Merich into a stone cottage where the clergy resided. A modest two-storey structure, it, like so many other places about, was showing clear signs of neglect. On the ground, Merich noticed fragments of slate roofing that had broken off, as well as bits of rock and mortar.

The floors were hewn of thick oak planks which, after years of waxing and wear, had developed a rich patina. Despite its condition, the dwelling was clean and kept in the order that one would have expected.

"It looks very comfortable," remarked Merich.

"Actually, it is," answered Tadeusz. "It lacks certain luxuries, but it provides us all that we need. Please, you can wait for Father Christoph here in the parlor. May I offer you something to drink."

"No, thank you. I'll be fine."

"Very well. I have to attend to some matters, so you'll excuse me."

"Yes, thank you for your help, Father."

The young priest left Merich alone. Alone to sort through not only what he planned to ask Christoph, but why he had come in the first place. Licht had never mentioned the priest in their conversations. If he were to agree to provide witness before the tribunal, there would be the need to explain how Christoph came to be involved. More important, there would be the need to do so without mentioning the diary. By now it had less to do with Licht's reaction to this revelation than the court's reaction to the withholding of evidence. Rather than getting Licht's sentence commuted, he would end up with one of his own. He sighed as he rubbed his eyes. *Just what am I doing here*, he thought to himself.

In a moment that seemed to last hours, Merich sat there, alone, silent. The more he thought about his situation, the less his mind was resolved to this predicament. In defending the indefensible, he could not help but think this might be a fool's errand.

"Father Tadeusz has told me that you are an inquisitive fellow, Herr Merich," came the voice from the hallway. "But I had sensed as much."

Merich stood up to greet his host. "I almost certainly have to be, given my line of work," he replied.

Father Christoph entered the room and gestured for Merich to sit. "I'm about to have a sip of wine. Do you care to join me?"

"No, thank you. I still have a great deal to do today."

"Yes, Johann's hearing. And you are his solicitor?"

"I'm serving as defense counsel for Herr Licht, if that is what you mean."

Father Christoph nodded, then paused a moment before he spoke. "How did this all come about?" he finally asked.

"I was approached by the Justice...," began Merich.

"That's not what I meant," interrupted the priest.

"I'm not sure that I understand you."

The priest walked over to a large sideboard cabinet. A skeleton key was protruding from one of the locked panels. He gently turned it and pulled on the end to open the door. Then, he gently reached in and extracted a decanter of cut crystal. The light from overhead hit the carved facets, making the liquid in the half full container appear both purple and red simultaneously.

Taking the stopper from the bottle, he poured a healthy amount of wine into one of the glasses that sat atop the sideboard. After replacing the decanter in the cupboard, he returned with his wine and sat in a chair adjacent to Merich. "Very few people knew that I was acquainted with Johann," he explained. "Beyond you, him and I, the rest are dead, in exile, or know the value of discretion enough not to discuss this with me. The only reason I agreed to speak with you is because I knew who you were already – from the newspapers."

"Then you know the answer for yourself."

"Johann would never have mentioned me to you. He may be a lot of things, but I know him to be a man of his word. So, I am asking you again – how did this all come about?"

Merich stared at Father Christoph, attempting to get some sense of the priest, some sliver of elemental emotion that belied the man that was hiding under the frock. Either the Almighty had succeeded in removing it, or the man had managed to conceal it well. "I'll tell you…but I expect that your desire for discretion to extend to this," he replied cautiously.

"I may know of you, but I know nothing of the man you really are. I'm not prepared to make that kind of promise." Merich grimaced. "Then I suggest that we go back to the Church," he sighed.

"What for?"

"I'll tell you in the confessional," he explained. "I know you can keep my confidence there."

"I'm not going to have you cheapen the act of contrition!" said Father Christoph firmly.

"Well, I need a guarantee. This appears to be the only way," he replied. "Believe me. It is in everyone's interest to keep this between us."

"If it's so obvious that silence is needed, then go ahead," countered the priest. "I'll hear what you have to say. We can dispense with all of these theatrics,"

Merich shook his head. "Humour me, Father," he sighed. "I would prefer that we do it this way. I've been betrayed before."

"We all have, Herr Merich. The only thing that keeps me from losing my mind is my faith. You mock it when you mock the sanctity of the confessional."

"Then let me ask you again, Father. Do I have your word?" Christoph paused for a moment. "Fine," he sighed. "You have my word."

"Good," said Merich. "The answer to your question is no – Licht told me nothing. I found his diary in the Palace, so I'm aware of your relationship."

"His diary."

"Yes."

"You...found it."

"Yes, I found it."

"But he knows you have it."

"Actually, no."

The priest's mood took a turn for the worse. "It's bad enough you've made a mockery of a sacrament, but you lied..."

"I never lied," defended Merich. "I told you I found the diary. Yes, he doesn't know. You didn't ask and I didn't volunteer." Father Christoph got up from his chair and began to walk away. "You can show yourself out," he said firmly as he gestured to the door.

"Please wait, Father..."

"You've misrepresented yourself to me. Unless you can convince me you're sincere, we have nothing to talk about." Merich remained in his chair. he clasped his hands and lowered his head. "Bless me, Father, for I have sinned..."

"No," said the priest, his tone becoming increasingly terse. "I told you I wouldn't do this."

"I'm confessing - no strings attached - here and now. If you still want to send me away, then I won't bother you again."

"Confessions are meant to free the soul - not win court cases!" Merich sensed the answer he had been searching for since he had entered the room had now come to him. It would lead the way if he surrendered to it. "At this point, there's no difference," he said solemnly.

Father Christoph stood over Merich, whose hands remained clasped tightly together. His eyes widened, his jaw clenched. Then, he closed his eyes in a slow blink. "Fine," he sighed. "This isn't a formal confession. Say your piece."

"No, Licht has no idea I have the diary. Nobody does, except for you. I found it at Nytriy on Ministry business. I should've turned it in, but I didn't. Now it's too late. They can disbar me and throw me in prison for it."

"Why do it then? To win the case?"

"No - I found it before the case was offered to me... I don't know. Morbid curiosity, maybe."

The priest frowned. "I think you do," he said. "Most of the

people I speak with, they don't have a clue what drives them. They lack self-awareness. It's not their fault. When you're busy trying to stay alive, there's not much time for big thoughts. You're not like that. I know that much."

Merich paused for a few moments, then picked up his cane and gently placed it on the table. "My leg," he began, "is a piece of mangled meat. I need this to walk more than three paces. It has caused me pain every waking hour for almost two years. Not as much now as it used to, but it's still there.

"My father...my father's lying in a pauper's grave somewhere with a revolver slug still in his skull. Half the reason I took the job with the Ministry was because I thought I might find out where he was buried. My mother's in a sanatorium. I try to visit, but if I don't end up upsetting her, she upsets me.

"I used to be angry - probably still am - but now I need to know why. I did turn to the Church, but all I got were fairy tales. No reasons.

"I wanted to understand why all of this happened. Then, there I was, alone with the book - his book, his private thoughts. I was going to read it, then bring it back to Nytriy - toss it in a pile somewhere, let some guard find it and turn it in. Then I got pulled to do the case. Too late then."

The priest took a sip of wine from his glass, then cradled his chin in his left hand, the elbow firmly pressed against the table. "I'm a priest," he said. "I don't deal in a world of 'too late'."

"Then you won't cut it in the courts," observed Merich.

"Render unto Caesar...," came the priest's reply.

"I guess."

"But you agreed to this case, *ja?*"

"I wasn't forced, if that's what you mean."

"I have a hard time believing that no one has questioned why you did."

"Nothing but, it seems," sighed Merich. "Every hour, every day."

"And the answer?"

"Sorry, Father. It just is. You're in the business of taking things on faith."

"I have faith that God knows why," answered the priest. "If you don't know your own heart and head, that's a different matter...But why even bother with me if I can't go public. You can't call me as a witness. You can't even use me to corroborate testimony."

"You can still help me a great deal."

"I don't understand."

"Look," explained Merich, "Licht is going to be found guilty. That is a foregone conclusion. No lawyer in this country, no matter how good, could ever get him off. My job isn't to get the charges dismissed. No disrespect, but I think even God Almighty would have a hard time of it. What I can do – what I know I can do - is keep him alive. Life sentence – maybe exile in some neutral country – I don't know. But what I do know for certain is that I can't make any of it happen unless I can convince those judges that Johann Licht is not evil incarnate."

"Again, Herr Merich, while I appreciate what you are saying, I still do not see what role that I play in all of this?"

"He's a very guarded man. Talks a lot without saying anything. Most of the time, I feel as though I am the one on trial. He clearly doesn't trust me...I need to know the real Johann Licht – not the biography, and certainly not any of the propaganda. I need to know Johann Licht, the man – flesh and bone human being. I could interview him for a million years and still end up no closer than I am now...But you know him, and he did trust you."

"So you want me to testify," said Christoph, still not convinced that Merich was not trying to lure him into a hearing.

"Only to me," reassured Merich. "Here and now. I need to understand my client if I am going to represent his interests."

"I'm not sure that my insights would be of any help. People change. The Johann Licht I knew was an idealist. He thought he was doing right. I'm not certain that he would view matters in quite the same way."

"Then, tell me about the idealist," said Merich.

The priest paused for a moment, turning to look out a window. He took a heavy breath. "A gentle man," he sighed. "As I remember - possibly a little naïve about the ways of the world. He didn't believe in God, but there were many times when he displayed a Christian heart. I thought that I could change him, rather than the other way around."

"He changed you?"

"Of course. Life - everything in it - it changes you. You're changing me right now, as we speak. I'll stop changing when I am ready to be with my Lord."

"You're still a priest. You still believe in God," observed Merich.

Christoph laughed a little and shook his head. "I said that he changed me, but I never said that he shook my faith. Understand that when we begin to love, we love as children. Age and wisdom don't take love away. They make them deeper, and, I would argue, more lasting."

"Love sometimes disappears altogether," observed Merich.

"Sometimes it does," the priest conceded. "Although, one could argue that every passion must be able to withstand such whims of fate in order to truly be real. Even our Saviour spent all those days in the desert, alone, with nothing but the temptations of Satan before he could emerge as he did."

Merich raised his eyebrows. "You seem to imply that Licht did not pass his test?" he said.

The priest smiled. "Ah, well, he is just a man, you see," he remarked.

"And he listened to temptation?"

"Yes," sighed Christoph, "and he appointed him to his government as well."

"It sounds as though he surrendered himself to his demons."

"No, I wouldn't say that. There was Eva, after all."

"His wife."

"Yes…He loved Eva – that was plain to see. I know she felt the same, probably more so. But it really was more than that. They seemed to fit one another, like pieces of a puzzle. Believe me, I would be so pleased if every couple that I married were so committed to one another."

"You married them?" said Merich, not wishing to divulge the specifics of what he knew from the diary.

"Yes. Mind you, it was really Eva's idea. Johann wanted a civil ceremony, but he wanted her happiness even more. They went to her family's place in the country with a few friends, and I performed the sacrament…Yes, she was very beautiful."

"Sounds perfect, if not a little Bohemian."

"Not perfect," corrected the priest. "No, I had my misgivings. Please understand."

"I'm not sure that I follow?"

"Stern. He wanted Eva for himself. She had confided that to

me – not in the confessional, though. Anyway, Johann never knew of this. He was so much in love with her, but he was intensely loyal to his friends. It made him blind to a lot."

"Stern loved Eva, then?" volunteered Merich.

"Oh, no," answered the priest, shaking his head emphatically. "I doubt that very much. He was jealous of Johann and wanted everything for himself. He was a very ugly man."

"Obviously you and Stern must have had an interesting relationship," mused Merich.

"Actually, I never did let him know how I really felt about him. It's not a secret that he was very volatile. He antagonized easily. I have no doubt that I'd be dead right now had I ever spoken my mind."

"I don't understand. Why did Licht keep company with someone that…unstable?"

"You have to go back to Johann's sense of loyalty. Trust did not come easily to him. I think you know that already. Anyway, in the early days, the Gestapo – and the Secret Police before them – they used to plant people close to him. So, once he found someone he could rely upon, he held on to them tight.

"But it was more than just that. Stern lacked much of what Johann possessed, but the reverse was also true. Johann was not a violent man by nature, but it became quite clear early on that someone better have the stomach for such things."

"Nature abhors a vacuum," observed Merich.

"You understand the dilemma," replied Christoph.

"The dilemma, yes, but certainly not the choice he made. You say it as though he had no other alternative. As far as I am concerned, excuses are the domain of cowards."

The priest frowned. "I hope you are saying that as a legal tactic, and not as a point of personal conviction. I don't think that your client would be well served if it were the latter."
Merich said nothing.

"They were mounting a revolution," continued Christoph. "What did you expect? That they would write a letter, make a formal request – please, sir, may we have some freedom?"

"So that justifies everything?" countered Merich.

"No - of course not. On the other hand, it's more than a little naïve to assume that when a person is hit that they will not feel the need to retaliate."

"Whatever happened to 'turn the other cheek'?"

"Our Lord Jesus was God incarnate. We are merely pale copies, fraught with all the shortcomings and frailties that it implies. Believe me, I have seen many of them in my life.

"Someday, we may become perfect beings – free of sin and pride – but there's a long way to travel before we get there, and much work to be done. Being a priest is not just about seeing paradise; it is about charting a course to get there. For that, the journey must begin somewhere."

"A lot of people died on that journey to the 'New Jerusalem'," countered Merich.

"This collar and these frocks don't make me infallible. In the end, I am a man – flawed like the rest. *Mea culpa.*"

Merich gave a thoughtful look. He took his cane off the table and proceeded to lift himself from the chair. He extended his free hand to the priest. "Thank you, Father. I appreciate your time...and your candor. I might not be wholly convinced, but I think that I'm beginning to understand."

"I'm relieved to hear you say that. To be honest, Herr Merich, for a moment, I wasn't sure what side of this you were on."

Merich looked down to the floor, to the tip of his cane pushing against the carpet. "As his counsel, I'm in his corner," he said. "As for the rest of me, to be honest, I'm still not certain."

CHAPTER 25

Despite having spent the last nine hours rummaging through the archives at the Ministry, Merich felt no closer to a solution than when he began. Having catalogued much of it himself, he had an ever slight advantage in his quest. Unfortunately, it also meant knowing that any search for evidence on Stern was going to be a largely unrewarding experience. Either by accident or mercenary means, the vast majority had been destroyed. There was really only one piece of evidence that truly supported his case, and so far it had done nothing more than frustrate him.

He returned home around the supper hour, eager to arrive before Emi came. He counted on a solid twenty minutes or so to quickly scan through the diary, to find something that might put him back on track. Merich knew that the entries about Stern could have made his case – if they had been admissible. But they were not, and all of his searching thus far had not uncovered an iota of information to back it up. He thought about losing the case, about the possibility that it would be lost not on Licht's stonewalling, but possibly his own deception.

He opened the door of his flat to find that another change in plan would be necessary.

"You're back early," came the cheerful greeting.

Trying not to appear surprised, Merich nodded as he removed his hat and hung up his coat. "Not much reason to stay," he sighed. "I think that man could give you lessons in stubbornness."

"I thought you saw him yesterday?"

"That's how frustrating he is."

"It's called being assertive, you grump," she countered.

"Maybe for you, but it's goddamn annoying from where I sit...Honestly, I don't know what his game is - fight hard, roll over - it doesn't make any sense."

"Maybe it's not supposed to?"

"When did the world decide talk in riddles?" he sighed. "I swear there isn't a man alive in this country that can just come out and say what they mean?"

Emi walked over to him and gave him a tender kiss on the cheek. "Then it's a good thing I'm a woman."

Merich smiled. "You are that, aren't you," he said, placing his free hand on her waist and drawing her forward.

"Settle down, tiger," she purred, placing her hand gently against his chest. "You need to clean yourself up. Remember?"

"Oh, yeah," he replied. "The picture."

"The painting," corrected Emi. "Seriously, I've been working on this restoration for months. Even Papa is coming to see it."

"So will your pompous patrons."

"They've all been nice to you."

"Because of both our fathers. Without them, they wouldn't look at me any differently than the people they walk over in the street."

Emi gave him a scolding look. "You're tired - I get that, but can't you just do this for me?" she asked.

"I'd do anything for you - you know that."

"Then get ready!" she scolded playfully. "I brought you a nice suit to wear. It's lying on your bed."

"In a minute," he replied. "I just need to check on something before I forget."

"I'll lay your things out. Do hurry. I have to meet people when they arrive."

"Just a minute or two," Merich assured her. "I promise."

With that, Emi smiled and headed down the hallway to the bedroom. Merich, in turn, went to his study.

Removing the volumes of books from the shelf that hid the cubby hole, he reached down inside to extract the diary.

It was not there.

A quick jolt of anxious energy shot through his body. Did it fall down into the wall? He glanced at the stack of books he had removed. Ibsen was on top. Why was Ibsen on top? He started to panic, as he counted the books off again. Three books to the left, which made Ibsen the fourth – but it was not the fourth. The order was clearly wrong.

The diary had not dropped down. It was gone. Merich's mind began to race as a thousand possibilities began to flood in.

His hands trembling, he began to replace the books on the shelf when Emi entered the room. "What are you doing?" she asked. "We're going to be late."

"Uh, nothing…just looking for something that I misplaced," he muttered.

"Well, what is it? Maybe I can help you look for it."

Merich froze for a moment. "I... It's something for work," his voice trailing off.

"Can't it wait then? We have to be out of here in twenty-five minutes," she insisted.

"No! I need it now!" he snapped. "Have you been here alone?!"

Emi's face registered the immediate surprise from his turn of mood. "Of course I have - really, Alex, what are you saying? You think I took something?"

"Were you here alone?!" he repeated. His expression turning from agitation to deliberate determination.

"Jaromir walked me to the door," she said quietly. "He went back down to the car - what is wrong with you?"

"Where's your handbag?" he demanded.

"What?!"

"Where's your handbag?! Let me see!" he snapped.

"I most certainly not!" she barked back. "What the hell is wrong with you?"

A torrent of angry fear washed over Merich. "You took it, didn't you!" he yelled. "You won't show me because you took it!"

"Took what?! What?!"

"Give me your purse!" he ordered.

"Go to hell!" she screamed, as she picked up your bag and headed toward the door.

Merich hobbled quickly after her, lunging forward to grab the bag. "Show me!" he yelled. He knocked the purse out of Emi's hand and onto the floor. The contents of the bag spilled out.

Emi crouched down and started to frantically grab the items and shove them back in. Merich stood over her, his eyes frantically scanning for evidence of the leather book. It was not there.

"Are you satisfied?!" she snapped. "Are you?!"

"I'm..."

"A sonofabitch! Yes, yes you are! If you didn't want to go with me, you should have said so!" yelled Emi.

"No... no... I did..." he muttered, as he reached forward to help her with her belongings.

"Stay the hell away from me!" she cried, moving her hand up as if to strike him across the face.

Merich pulled back, his body shuddering as his mind caught up with his emotion. "Please...," he whimpered.

Emi rose from the floor. "Goodbye, Alex," she said firmly, as she strung the strap of the bag over her shoulder. She headed out the door, leaving it ajar. Merich heard her footsteps trail down the hall, down the staircase, then finally, the opening and closing of the door to the street. He walked over and closed the apartment door. He shuffled over to an armchair in his study and collapsed into it. This time there were no answers, no cunning strategies. The question that was foremost in his mind was no longer what should he do – it was what was going to be done to him.

Eventually, he pulled himself up and went to the kitchen, where he poured himself a large tumbler of whisky. He nursed the first couple of sips, then resolved to swallow down the rest to bring on that familiar warm feeling. He returned to the chair with the bottle and the glass.

Merich felt the unease tighten his stomach even more. After a few more minutes of drinking, and staring at the now exposed hole in the bookshelf, he could only think of leaving. Leaving the flat, leaving the case - leaving everything completely.

He could return to Bern. Better still, he could move elsewhere, maybe even America - somewhere where he could live in obscurity. His English was not perfect, but it was passable, and it would improve over time and with practice.

Liberty. A woman and her torch. It was the last almost pleasant thought he had before the alcohol had brought him to an uncomfortable slumber.

CHAPTER 26

Exhaustion and emotion had caught up with him. Little by little, his alertness, his acumen, had dulled. All around him life took on the quality of a poorly filmed motion picture – detached activities performed by strangers within a grainy subtext. Somewhere along the line, a moment of clarity would awaken his mind to the circumstances at hand. Then, a good night's rest, followed by a hearty meal, would set him right once again.

This was not the luxury to be afforded to him presently. Licht's stonewalling had cost him valuable time. That had left him with a diary that he could never use at trial, and witnesses that could not be called without allowing the journal's existence to be known. Now, he did not even have that.

He thought about thumbing through the pages of the leather-bound ledger, the random scanning the collection of words, sentences, and ordered paragraphs. He racked his brain to remember even a casual sentence or word. The only thing that sprang to mind was Emi, and the events of the evening before. Like the case, he was powerless to do anything about that either.

Propping his head on his left hand, his elbow firmly anchored on the desk, he attempted to scribble ideas for his opening statement. The trial was scheduled to begin in a couple of weeks, and he was no further ahead than when he began. The knock on the door mercifully startled him out of his thoughts.

"I hope I'm not disturbing you... Mind if I come in?"

Hartz stood in the doorway, looking relaxed. Merich felt a mix of anxiety and resentment, which he swallowed hard to keep down.

"No…please," he said, rubbing his eyes from the strain.

"Come in. I could use a bit of a break."

"You look like hell, Alex," observed Hartz, taking his place in the chair facing Merich's desk. "This has been a tough job, but I think I might have something that will change things."

Of course you do, you bastard, thought Merich. *You have the diary, and you know where it has been.*

Merich had noticed that Hartz had not arrived empty-handed. A thick file folder was placed on the desk and gently slid toward him. Relieved by the apparent absence of the book, he regained his equilibrium. "No offense, but I'm very tired," he explained, "and I have a lot to do before we go to trial. I'd just as soon you tell me exactly what it is."

"It's a reprieve – for Licht, and for you."

Merich slowly blinked and sighed, "Please – no riddles. Just tell me what you mean."

"They're files from the old Public Security Directorate," said Hartz. "The things that Commissar Stern didn't have the time to destroy. A lot to sort through, but we managed to come up with this."

"Where did you find them?" he asked.

"Basement of an old town house on the Frederickplatz. EBI had used it in the past. A bit of a hunch."

Merich slowly opened the folder and began to glance over the neatly typed summary on the top. "So, what does it mean?" he asked.

"Come now," chided Hartz. "You're a lawyer. You know very well what it means."

"Maybe I want to hear it from you?"

Hartz laughed. "Very good - I like that. Of course it's proof that Stern was the architect of the May massacre. It appears that Licht never sanctioned it."

"Licht was head of state," Merich pointed out. "Ultimately every decision, or action, is going to fall on him."

"You sound more like a prosecutor than a defender," observed Hartz.

"Well, I can't defend a man if I don't consider what's going to be thrown at him."

"Very true, but…" said Hartz, as he pointed at the opened brief, "as you can see, the whole matter is much more nuanced than that. Licht declared a general state of emergency when the assassination attempt was made, right?"

189

"The one where his wife was killed."

"The same. Well, it seems that Stern had a much freer hand to deal with the situation than we had thought."

"How free a hand are we talking?" asked Merich.

"Well, how much has Licht told you about that time?"

Merich felt a rush of blood to his cheeks. He clenched his jaw to keep his face frozen in expression. "Less than you've told me since you sat down," he said in an efficient voice.

"It appears that Brother Chairman was not quite in charge at the time."

"Go on."

"Based on this information, it seems as though Licht was quite badly injured by the blast. The reports state that he had sustained severe burns to much of his body."

Merich shrugged. "That's pretty common knowledge, though. I mean, I see the scaring on his face and hands when I'm with him."

"Yes, but the three broken ribs, punctured lung, and the sub-cranial bleeding?"

"He won't talk about it…"

"They managed to stabilize him," interrupted Hartz, "then sent him by a private train to Moscow. No less than Stalin's own medical team was put on the case. He was in hospital for five months, and another two in a dacha on the Caspian."

"So he was out of the country for seven months," observed Merich, trying to appear surprised by the news.

"Not just seven months, but the seven months that covered the May massacre and the mass arrests…"

"…and executions," added Merich.

"Yes, and the executions, but even beyond that. I suspect that once Licht was out of the picture, he never really came back. They propped him up for parades and photographs, but that was about it. Stern ran the show - to protect Licht and the regime, of course."

"Well, it does fit… if it's true."

"It's true. All of this, of course, to get to the bottom of the assassination plot, and everyone that was behind it. Mind you…" said Hartz, as he flipped a couple of pages, and pointed at the middle of the exposed section, "he didn't need to look very far, did he."

Merich read the paragraph pointed out to him, the looked up

at Hartz. "How reliable is this?" he asked.

"Very," replied Hartz. "The British uncovered some interesting intelligence from an anarchist group in Greece. It seems as though our friend contracted their services in exchange for a shipment of weapons."

Merich frowned. "It seems to be a bit too cloak-and-dagger."

"Not really," answered Hartz. "He couldn't go to the Soviets, or any of their allies. They liked Licht and would have stopped him cold. He couldn't go to the west either – they knew what kind of beast he was. No, he needed to secure an independent party for this one."

Merich leaned back in his chair. "Stern hired some Greek anarchists to kill Licht in exchange for a place to train. They blow up his car, kill his wife - almost kill him. Licht gets dispatched to Moscow and spends more than half a year hidden away, while Stern, under the pretense of going after the plotters, jails or murders any person who has ever crossed him."

"I didn't say that it was a pretty or elegant plan," defended Hartz. "Neither is Stern."

Merich shook his head. "Well, that's all well and good, but you can't try a ghost."

"And we won't have to."

"I don't follow," said Merich.

"A couple of months ago, our American friends let us know that Stern and some of his entourage might be hiding somewhere in Ecuador. We contacted the local authorities who began their own investigation.

"Three weeks ago, the authorities raided an underground political newspaper outside of Quito – violent overthrow, Marxist revolution – the usual stuff. That's where they found our friend. He claimed he was a German who arrived before the war, but they saw through that pretty quickly.

"We sent a couple of our people there, and they made a positive identification."

"Where is he now?" asked Merich.

"On a BOAC flight to London – probably refueling in Newfoundland as we speak. We have already seen to chartering a plane to get him in Geneva when he gets that far."

Merich became silent. He stared at the type print on the page until it began to resemble something other than letters and words.

"It's good news, Alex," volunteered Hartz.

Merich's face bore a slight grimace. "Is it?" he asked. "He's a sonofabitch, to be sure, but that doesn't change things. I still have a case to defend."

Hartz paused, and looked at his protégé thoughtfully. "Your case," he began, "well, that is what I wanted to discuss with you. I will be amending the charges."

"But nothing's changed," said Merich. "Whether or not Stern is in custody doesn't change the fact that Licht was Head of State. Inevitably, it lies at his feet."

Shaking his head, Hartz remarked, "If I didn't know better, I'd swear you want to lose this case?"

"It was lost the moment I took it. I understood that, but I've got an obligation to fight for the best terms that I can. If I don't prepare for a hard fight, I won't be prepared."

"There won't be a hard fight if you don't want one," replied Hartz.

"What is the catch?" asked Merich.

"No catch. Licht just needs to testify against Stern. Pure and simple."

"He won't do it."

"Fine, then he doesn't say a word about Stern. He only needs to answer where he was for the weeks and months immediately after the assassination attempt – the magistrates can draw their own conclusions from there. Reasonable doubt."

"That is all well and good, but…"

"I want Stern's head. I'll give your boy a pass, but only if he helps me get it."

Merich leaned back in his chair and clasped his hands thoughtfully. "I suppose he will agree to this based on his desire to do the right thing. After all, he's such a civic minded fellow to begin with."

Hartz looked nonplussed. "If your client accepts, he'll get life in prison – possibly exile in another jurisdiction. If not, he'll hang. Now, Counsellor, are you going to tell him or not?"

"That depends."

"On?"

"On the real reason why you're doing this. I know you want Stern, but don't tell me you don't want Licht as well. You have both, and you hold all of the cards. Why make a deal?"

Hartz shook his head. "Is it too much to accept this proposal at face value?" he asked.

"You would never have hired me to work here if I were the kind of lawyer that took the bait that easily," stated Merich. "I believe the sincerity of the offer – I truly do – but I need to know why, and don't tell me that you're doing me a favour."

Hartz stared at Merich for a moment, pondering his next move. "You weren't here yet – in '45, I mean," he said.

"Not for want of trying. My father got word to Stolzer one time – had me picked up on the train platform by the Bern police."

"Regardless, I don't think you know what went on."

"I know the Soviets pushed for early elections," said Merich.

"Seemed odd that they'd even bother with the formality."

"It was a little more complicated than that. They didn't have the free hand everyone thinks they did."

"The Red Army had troops all over the place. Pretty free hand if you ask me."

"They never went past the Magyets frontier, did they?"

Merich shrugged. "Hell if I know – I'll take your word for it," he said.

"Trust me, they didn't. They stayed in their zone."

"What zone?"

"The Soviet zone of occupation," explained Hartz. "Coming out of Yalta, the Allies started working out how each country was going to be handled. You know the arrangement over Austria?"

"Sort of."

"Well they agreed on that plan for us as well. Three zones, one American, one British and one Soviet."

"Never saw an American or British soldier, at least not here," replied Merich.

"Just like Austria, the Soviets tried for a power grab. They got Renner elected, so they thought they could do the same here with Licht."

"Can't quibble with success, I suppose," observed Merich dryly.

"The Soviets wanted Licht," continued Hartz. "He appeared reasonable enough, so the Yanks and the Brits held back. No percentage in a fight."

"That doesn't explain how we end up here."

"Okay, so things are quiet at first. The Soviets are happy, so they do nothing. The Americans are not exactly happy, but not so unhappy that they want to start another war over it. The Brits have their own problems at home and elsewhere. They're not spoiling for a fight either.

"Everything's good until someone tries to kill Licht. Wife's dead, and he's nearly there too. Stern fills the vacuum and starts doing all the things he couldn't do before.

"The Soviets found out that Stern tried to take out their golden boy – not good. He's also starting to steam-roller his enemies – even worse. At the same time, they're getting pressure from the Americans and the Brits. They get told that some Brigadier named Weilland – a real hawk, like Patton – was going to come in across the border with a task force straight through to the Magyets, and nose to nose with the Reds if they didn't get their house in order."

"But they didn't, did they?"

"Not that simple. I mean, come on, Alex, use your head. Why didn't the Reds stream back in to stop us? Besides, where the hell do you think all of those Webleys and Brens came from. How did we end up with truckloads of Bangalores?"

"I always assumed that Bruno had something to do with it," he said wryly.

"He did," answered Hartz. "He's a prick, but a patriotic one. The Russians promised not to lift a finger to help. So did the Yanks. The Brits would provide the arms through an intermediary. Stolzer made sure they got into the right hands from there."

Merich nodded. "That's all well and good," he said, "but I'm not clear why the Red Army shouldn't roll in anyway. They don't give a shit about either Licht or Stern. It's a chess game, and they're not going to forfeit a pawn for no reason. Even I know that."

Hartz's face contorted into a pained frown. He combed his left hand over his head, the fingers picking up lengths of hair in its furrow. "You know, more than this damn job, that is the thing that gives me indigestion. I'm going to fill you in on some things – things you're going to forget the moment I leave."

Merich paused before nodding his compliance. "I've got my own problems without taking on yours," he cautioned.

Hartz shrugged. "So," he continued, "about five weeks before the big offensive in the city, the coalition committee received a message."

"From?"

"From the Red Star Brigade," answered Hartz.

"They're all dead?"

"Not the ones that got into Russia," he replied. "They were always well connected. Anyway, they laid low for a time, but they didn't disappear.

"One of the Commissars, a fellow named Kalunin, he watched over them – especially when some EBI agents took out a couple of Red Star operatives in Kiev. Messy affair. Some bystanders got caught, and one ended up dying of their injuries. Locals were used to not asking a lot of questions, so they wrote if off as business as usual. KGB knew better. So, when Licht was hurt, Kalunin took charge, and every EBI operative they could find in Russia got sent to the camps – if they were lucky.

"The Soviets didn't like Stern for putting a hit on Licht, but they hated him for running agents in their own backyard. Problem was that by the time Licht returned, Stern had everything locked up.

"Cagey fellow. He left Licht in place, so the Russians would stand down. Moscow wasn't about to unseat a socialist government run by their man – not with the Yanks and Brits standing on the border.

"Early on, though, the Red Star cells started coming back to organize a coup. Leave Licht, but clean out the Politburo. They learned the hard way that it wasn't going to happen. Not enough men, not enough means. In the meantime, Washington and London were making noise about all of the refugees coming their way.

"So, they made the decision. Red Star would help us where they could, surveillance, sabotage…"

"Sabotage?" asked Merich.

"The main power plant in the city – that was their handiwork," explained Hartz. "None of them made it out, though. Got to admire their commitment."

"What was the deal?"

"Pardon?"

"The deal," repeated Merich. "What did you promise in return?"

"Three things," answered Hartz. "One, we wouldn't outlaw the Communists – at least their version; second, we wouldn't take sides; and third, no foreign troops."

"Neutrality?"

"Sort of, for the time being. It's been trickier than a lot of my colleagues thought. This doesn't go any further, understand?"

"You're my boss," pointed out Merich.

"Bombings, killings – we don't have the resources to shut it down. We could ask the Yanks or the Brits for help, but then we would have Soviet tanks in the square. We won't ask them, but what if we did? How would the Americans react? No, we can get all of the grain and Red Cross relief we need, but what good is it if we can't stop it from getting stolen?"

"You're training more police, *ja*?"

"You know it's not enough," said Hartz. "You've said it yourself. Besides, any one of the three sides is better armed than the government."

"Three sides?"

"Our old militia friends, the Red Star cells, and the old EBI loyalists of Stern's."

"Can't you negotiate something?"

Hartz began to laugh. "Now you're really being naïve," he remarked. "It's a proxy war – our friends versus their friends. The only thing that they can both agree on is killing off the EBI, but they're too busy rubbing each other out to do that right."

Merich raised his hand, rubbing his strained eyes. "Georg, I know you well enough," he sighed. "You don't tell me anything without a reason. All I'm hearing is your problem – not mine."

"If you plan on staying in this country, it's your problem too…The only people who want Licht to hang are the EBI. Red Star – the Russians – they want him free. Our friends? They couldn't care less either way.

"On the other hand, if we shift the focus to Stern, then everyone's reasonably happy. Everyone except the EBI, and who gives a shit about them."

"You told Bŏsek that he's going to shift his case?"

"Not yet," answered Hartz. "I'll talk to him next. I thought I'd pay you the courtesy of knowing first."

Merich rolled his eyes. "You know," he began, "all that makes me wonder something."

"What's that?"

"It makes me wonder why you gave me this case in the first

place."

"We've already been through all that," answered Hartz. "That's a closed conversation."

"Despite what you said, I know there are better lawyers. You didn't have to use me – and you definitely didn't have to agree to my terms. On the other hand, Franz Merich only had one son. That would be the same Franz Merich you're all so busy turning into a martyr. That's not a coincidence."

"That's pretty cynical – even for you."

"Doesn't mean I'm wrong," stated Merich. "I wanted this on my own merits."

"You wouldn't have got it on your own merits," countered Hartz. "Besides, you'll win or lose on your own – isn't that enough?"

"Not really."

Hartz shook his head derisively. "Then get used to being miserable. You're Franz Merich's son. Soon, you'll be Stolzer's son-in-law. Add to that your fancy Swiss education. If people think you're spoiled, there's nothing you can do about it.

"Half the people in this building feel sorry for you, and the other half think you're a brat. They felt that way before you even set foot through the front door. You haven't changed them yet."

"Well, you haven't helped matters either," argued Merich.

"Not my job," countered Hartz. "I've got a ministry to rebuild – brick by brick. I don't have time to hold your hand. I made an assessment of the situation and I called it. Honestly, Alex, did you think I'd give you a bench appointment for nothing? You don't want to ride on anyone's coattails, but you think I should make you a judge for nothing?"

"I didn't say that."

"You either earn it or you don't. I'll make you a judge because you helped me sort this out – not for Stolzer, and not for Franz. That's what you say you want, so leave it at that."

"Not that simple," argued Merich.

"You're angry because you feel like you've been played," stated Hartz. "Get over it – we all get played sometime. The world moves. We move with it. I have my job and you have yours. Get your client to cooperate and everything turns out, *ja?*"

"Then what?"

"What do you mean?"

"Say we do it," said Merich. "Stern's in and Licht's out. Let's even say that you manage to round up every last EBI thug. Then what?"

"A clean start."

"A civil war," corrected Merich. "The Americans and British arm and train the militias while the Soviets do the same for Red Star. I'll wager you a thousand crowns that they'll be back at each other's throats within a year. And who's going to stop them? You? Your teenagers? A quarter of them don't have guns and half of them don't know how to use them. Most haven't been paid in weeks – yes, I know all about that. I heard them talk at the Palace."

"I'm too busy fixing today," countered Hartz. "Tomorrow has to wait."

"Not going to wait long."

"No, I'll tell you what's not going to wait – an answer on your client. You need to forget what your professors told you. Politics isn't about months and years – it's about minutes and days.

Hartz got up from the chair. He placed his hands firmly on the edge of Merich's desk and leaned in. "You need to get this straight," he began, "because I don't plan on having this conversation with you again. If we don't survive this, there's no long term, no civil war in a year. There's Soviet tanks parked in front of Nytriy, and all of us hiding in caves. That's the alternative. This isn't some classroom. The sooner you clue into that the better."

"You're playing with fire, Georg."

"Fine," sighed Hartz, pulling himself back. "So be it. That's what we're all doing. When the time comes, I'll round up a bucket brigade."

With that, he started to walk out of Merich's office. He stopped short of the doorway, then turned back. "Oh, that reminds me. One of my men came across a rather rare find from some black marketer. Would you believe your client's personal diary? To be honest, it was that that helped us corroborate what we found in this file. I'm surprised that you didn't come across it yourself." Merich summoned his best poker face. "Maybe I would have had I not been pulled away for this damned case," he muttered.

"Perhaps…" said Hartz, in a slow and methodical drawl. "Anyway, this fellow came across it from someone else. I mean there is no way that he would have been allowed within a hundred meters of the palace. We'll find out who his source was."

"Poor fellow, whoever it is," he added. "I bet he doesn't have a father-in-law who'll end up owning half the factories in this damned country, and could keep him out of Shostoi…anyway, I've kept you far too long. Goodnight, Alex."

"Wait," said Merich. "Tell me something."

"What do you need to know?"

"You said that they had found Stern over a month ago – that means you knew that he was alive – where he was – when you assigned me this case."

Hartz said nothing. He smiled and with an easy gesture he closed the door behind him.

CHAPTER 27

Merich had felt a nagging unease from the moment he left the Ministry. He usually felt this way after a fight, or when he was especially fatigued. The fact that he had dealt with both instances in less than a day made it all the more draining. Adding to it all the fate of the diary and the reappearance of Stern, it was nothing short of overwhelming. He felt his brain slowly shutting down.

Entering his building, he made his slow and strained climb up the staircase. The unease seemed to increase with every step, every tap of the cane. Once on his floor, he plodded over to the door of his flat. Pulling the key from his coat pocket, he attempted to shove it into the lock. His trembling hand caused the sharp jagged piece of metal to scrape and tear small grooves into the brass finish.

Peering over his left shoulder to the side, he could see the shadow along the wall over the staircase. It became smaller as its source neared. Another larger, ill-shaped figure followed it in tandem.

Merich's heart began to race as he finally managed to open the lock. He turned back again to catch sight of the man.

The solitary figure slowly, methodically, opened the front of his overcoat to reveal the preferred tool of his craft. The luster of oiled gun metal flickered under the dull flame of the gaslight. Merich felt numb, his stomach nauseated with intense tension under the assassin's aim.

The man smiled ghoulishly as he raised his weapon level to Merich's chest.

Merich closed his eyes and said a Hail Mary under his breath. He felt the rush of hot air rush past him as he felt his legs collapse, ending with a thud into the wall behind him, and then a louder crash.

He opened his eyes and saw his would-be executioner laying on the floor in front of him, his hand still gripping the Ruger, the smell of expended gunpowder wafting from the end of the silencer. The man's eyes remained open in the blank glassy stare that comes from viewing one's eternity. The queer orientation of his head gave evidence of a neck well snapped.

Standing over his quarry, the second figure Merich thought he had seen finally moved forward into the light.

"Get up!" snapped Jaromir. "Go in now!"

Still stunned, Merich shook himself to sense. Grabbing his cane, he pulled himself up and moved as quickly as he could inside the flat.

Jaromir rushed in behind him, shutting the door as carefully as he could. He shoved past Merich and went straight to the pantry in the kitchen. He grabbed the half-empty bottle of whiskey and a large tumbler that sat on the counter. He filled the tumbler and thrust it at Merich. "Drink it now!" he ordered.

"No," muttered Merich, still unsure of himself and his situation.

"I said drink it now!"

Merich's hand trembled as he took the glass and carefully sipped from it.

"Drink it all! Faster!" snapped Jaromir, as he made a hand gesture to indicate a healthy imbibing.

"Go to hell!" spat back Merich, gagging from the bitter, pungent tang.

"You are drunk. Your lover refuses you. You drink to forget, and you pass out. No man - no gun...*ja*?" explained Jaromir, in a softer, yet still deliberate tone.

"Screw you! There's a dead man in the hall! You killed him!"

"Before he shoots you, *ja*? He will be gone, and you will pass out. You were too drunk to see anything...Now, drink more!"

Merich's eyes began to narrow, and a quiet began to settle upon him. He acquiesced and took a large spiteful swallow. The intense fire down his throat made him cough and wretch.

"Good," said Jaromir, taking the glass from his hand, and tossing the remaining drops in Merich's face. "Now go to bed. You saw nothing. No man - no gun. Now, go!"

With that, he grabbed Merich by the shoulders, spun him in the direction of the bedroom, and gave him a firm shove forward.

"Hey," croaked Merich, as he turned to face him, "you - you took...".

There was no reply. Jaromir had already made his way out. Merich stood quietly - long enough to gain his bearings. The adrenaline began to steadily succumb to the alcohol. Slowly, he hobbled to the door, opening it just a crack. The hall was empty, save for the faint edge of a large deformed silhouette moving out of range, down to the lobby. Closing the door tight, he turned the deadbolt, and gasped for breath.

Dropping his cane, Merich got down on his hands and knees. He crawled to the kitchen and opened one of the lower cupboard doors. He extracted a large tin pot, and with a slow spasmodic lurch, he continued on all fours, down the hall, to his bedroom.

He tossed the pot up over his head onto the top of the bed, near to his pillow. Then, with a painful groan, he summoned all of his upper body strength to pull himself up on his knees.

From that position, Merich managed to lift himself onto the bed. He wriggled like a worm evading a bird until he was able to place his head firmly on the pillow, mercifully cool to the touch. For the next hour, he lay still, and fighting - the welling nausea, the throbbing in his skull, and the temptation to go back into the hallway.

CHAPTER 28

They had found the small cabin on the outskirts of the city only a few weeks before, long abandoned and left to the fickle ravages of nature and time. The roof had largely disappeared, leaving little but a few errant timbers clinging stubbornly to rough hewn supporting beams. While the structure was of little utility, it covered a cellar that was uniquely large and contained enough to suit their purposes. The floor was solid, and a thin covering of moss covered over those gaps in the planks that decades of dirt and grease had not sealed up. The only place where light shone through was the thin seam around a trap door that hid the only access. One would have been hard-pressed to find it from more than a couple of feet away.

There were no more than a dozen of them attending, but each represented a larger group who, in turn, possessed cells that could be called upon in a moment's notice. The chain of command had evolved over time. Of those who had led the effort when the Socialist Republic was declared, only a dozen or so were left. Virtually all of them were the political face of the movement. Anyone earning their seat at the table on the trigger end of a gun tended not to stay long.

Merich knew his choice to join had not been a popular one – not with his mother, with Emi, or with Bruno. If he had been honest with himself, it was not his first choice either. After Franz had died, when Olga had gone to stay with a cousin in the western province, he tried lending his talents to the political arm of the movement. For three weeks, he had gone to meetings, where every topic imaginable had been debated and discussed, from the new executive to how dispossessed property owners were to be compensated. Every codicil, every punctuation mark, was a bone of contention, or so it seemed. Old men who reeked of cigarette

smoke and cheap brandy yelled and screamed over whether
something needed a two-thirds vote or if a simple majority would
suffice.

The only time, it seemed to him, when they would stop their
bickering was when there was news of an EBI station getting
bombed, or a power station being knocked off line for a day or
two. Merich watched them get up, clap and cheer, then shake
hands and pat shoulders as if their incessant nattering had
somehow caused the enemy to burst into flame or fall upon his
own sword. He wondered if any of them were willing to do what it
took to bring about the change they clamored for.

Annoyed and disillusioned, he sought out Hartz and aired his
frustrations. The old man was reluctant to entertain any dramatic
actions. When pressed, though, he did effect an introduction to
Anton Korovny, an ex-artillery officer who knew the old professor
from the Italian campaigns of the Great War. Korovny, in turn,
brought him into a cell run by one of his former junior officers.
Merich could not recall his name. The man had been killed shortly
after the introduction had been made.

He had expected some sort of formal training, some stripped
down version of a military academy. Instead, he was issued an old
Lee Enfield rifle, and sent to a town in the western province where
he was to practice for a couple of days. Then the rifle was taken
back and he was told to go home and wait for word, which he
obediently did for a month.

Merich proved his value not as a fighter, but in having a keen
eye for detail. His training as a lawyer seemed to compliment the
task at hand, and the strategic tactics tailored for the courtroom
translated well in the field – anticipation, prescience. After a couple
of small raids, his commander decided to better use his skills as a
sounding board for planning operations. It was in this role that he
found himself invited to attend.

He arrived early to find one of the militia leaders already there,
lighting a coal oil lamp to add to the two kerosene lanterns already
ablaze. "Hello, Vlahovic," he said to the man. "How long have you
been here?"

"Not long," came the matter-of-fact reply. "Spent the last two
hours scouting the area for EBI."

Merich did not know much about Vlahovic – not even his
Christian name. He was a large, barrel chested man from the east,

and it was obvious that nothing had come easy for him. He did know that it was not in the man's character to do anything by half measures. His gregarious nature was off-putting at first. Merich had never felt at ease with such displays, but more so when it came from such a physically dominant presence. But Vlahovic was a man lacking in pretention and agenda. Over time, Merich found himself more at ease with the man. "Well, I seriously doubt that they would bother us here," he observed.

"You don't think so?" asked Vlahovic, setting the lamp on the large table in the centre of the cellar. "They picked up a couple of my men three days ago - just four kilometers from here."

"That may be, but they can't be hiding under every rock and tree, now can they?"

"They don't have to," he said, smoothly rubbing the forefingers of his right hand against his thumb. "They pay enough to get the locals to do it for them."

"I don't know how you can possibly stop that sort of thing, then," said Merich. "We can't afford to shell out bags of crowns to every peasant farmer we meet."

"Don't have to," came the reply. "There are things that work much better than money."

"Such as?"

Vlahovic smiled knowingly at Merich, the interplay of shadow and flickering lamplight making his face appear contorted. "Some rope...a castration tool."

Merich's face registered his disgust. "Then you're no different than Stern," he declared. "For God's sake, we're supposed to be better than that!"

"And we will be," assured Vlahovic in a calm, deliberate voice. "Once this war is over and we put the run to these Bolsheviks, then you and your kind can write your laws and give your little speeches. Until then, we get our hands dirty."

"I'm sure that Licht and Stern said something similar at one time."

"I have more reasons for stopping than to fight...Once upon a time I was a shopkeeper. I was happy then. I want to be happy again - even if I have to be miserable now."

"You won't be happy – ever," countered Merich. "You'll open your shop early every morning because the nightmares keep you up and you'll need to do something to occupy your mind."

Vlahovic shook his head and let out a laugh that seemed to travel up from his gut. It shook the man as it made its way out and into the room. "You know, Merich," he chortled, "I'm nothing like you. It doesn't take all that much to make me happy. Give me food, drink, a warm bed and the occasional screw and I'm happy. But see, that's the difference - I don't want to change the world, and you do. You'll end up the miserable one."

Merich shrugged. "If that's the way you feel," he said, "then I have no idea why you even signed on for the cause?"

"I didn't sign on for your cause," came the reply. "I signed up for my own. They just happen to fit."

"I suppose I shouldn't ask what would've happened if they didn't."

The shopkeeper continued to laugh. He took a hand and patted it on Merich's shoulder, just as the other men began to arrive. He leaned in and said in a low voice "I think you know the answer to that. Now, we talk about tomorrow."

* * *

The first of the streetcars began to leave the central yard a couple of blocks east of the Koenigsplatz just after four o'clock that morning. The first to depart were the ones that serviced what was known as the 'Outer Ring' – a mixed collection of suburbs of the city that included leafy boulevards to the north and west, the hard scrabble neighborhoods to the east, and the industrial zones in the south. The cars of the 'Inner Ring' were the next, timed to reach their furthest point when the Outer Ring routes met them with their first loads of transfer passengers.

The workers along the city railway did what was expected of them, and when it was expected. It was not that they failed to notice the unusually high number of passengers – they did, of course – but they had their jobs to do. Unless someone were to flash an EBI badge and ask them questions, they felt no compulsion other than to move on. By half past five, the Inner Ring routes began to disembark their first – and only – passengers that day.

The advance team were with about their instructions, and duly waited for a good twenty minutes before they set to work. Starting with the lines that serviced the main travel corridors of the city, and working their way out to the industrial and residential neighborhoods, they began to cut the electrical cables that kept them all in motion. Within the hour, most of the transit system had ground to a halt. Some of the cars sat like dead weights in the middle of intersections, where passengers attempted to push their carriage out of the way of a growing line of motor vehicles and horse-drawn wagons.

Another fifteen minutes saw members of Vlahovic's militia begin to construct barricades at each of the key locations that had been identified and scouted weeks before. Each man and woman knew where they must be, and what they needed to bring - arms and obstructions alike. By seven that morning, there were twenty hastily assembled, but well-constructed, defense points. Each was a pell-mell agglomeration of overturned cars and carts, furniture and lumber, adorned atop with garlands of razor wire.

Korovny's loyalists, consisting mostly of former career army officers, had snipers in and around the top floors of buildings that lined the main thoroughfare that connected the Nyitny Palace to the Central Armories. Partisans attached to Klements, in the meantime, would move in and around this route at street level. Armed mostly with sidearms and grenades, it would be their job to harangue and harass the soldiers as they moved in, then make for a quick exit.

Merich was part of another group whose job was, arguably, the most challenging. They would defend the barricades against the government troops when they came. Mounted Bren guns and Bangalore rockets smuggled in from the Adriatic were among the tools of their trade.

He lay on the inner side of the barricade, his stomach and knees pushing into an old wooden door that had been positioned flat against the slope. His responsibility lay with the Bren gun that was perched immediately before him, along the crest of the blockade, the long barrel cradled between a piece of wood and a porcelain glazed wash basin. Korin, the teenager to his right, kept watch on the boxes of ammunition that sat near his feet. He fought to stay still, but the smooth surface of the door forced him to dig the toes of his boots into the pile of scrap that extended just beyond the wooden edge.

Hold steady! Don't shoot until they open up from the sides," came the command from down the line.

"They'll be too close!" Korin blurted loudly, his face growing pale with the ever closer phalanx of soldiers nearing their position.

Merich twisted onto his side to turn and face the young man. "Shut up and do your job!" he growled "I'm going to need bullets and lots of them - got it?!"

Korin snapped himself back from the scolding. Nodding obediently, he crouched ever closer to the pavement.

For a split second, Merich felt pity for the boy as he acknowledged the pit forming deep in his own stomach.

The government troops were a block away, and their individual features were now easily discerned. A dozen or so infantry led a convoy of a tank, three armored cars, and five trucks each carrying at least ten soldiers apiece. Merich knew that each of the checkpoints were likely to face a similar show of strength. He imagined Vlahovic saying that it could be worse, although it was hard for him to believe so. He curled his finger gently around the trigger of the gun and took a deep breath.

The signal came as the front line of the convoy stood about twenty meters from the barricade. Men about three stories up from either side of the street began to lob grenades and Molotov cocktails on the soldiers below.

The squad leader yelled out above the chaos. "Now! Fire now!"

Merich squeezed on the trigger. The gun shook and shuddered as it spit bullets at a frenetic rate. "Get ready!" he yelled over his shoulder. "They're going fast!"

The troops at the front of the column scattered to find cover among the vehicles they were escorting. Merich could hear screams and yelling coming from a two-ton truck about twenty meters behind the lead tank. He saw the rag-stuffed bottles being hurled from overhead, leaving a trail of black smoke to mark their trajectory.

The barrel of the T4 began to move, adjusting to a slight incline upward, and to the right. A few seconds elapsed, and then the shot rang out. The loud explosion rocked the tank in recoil, emitting a shockwave that gave Merich the sensation of being bludgeoned with a club. He pressed his face hard into the door.

Behind him, and to the side, the front facade of a building, from the third to the sixth floor, blew out and onto the street below. Most of the defenders' weapons cache, and the men guarding it, were now caught in the hellish hail of brick, wood and glass. Those at the edge of the collapse who managed to escape the debris staggered out like ghostly specters, coated in plaster dust.

"They're cutting us off!" screamed Korin. "They're trapping us in!"

"Shut up and give me more!" yelled back Merich.

The soldiers, having recovered the initiative, began to come away from their shelter. Merich, along with the three other remaining gunners, continued to spray the oncoming phalanx. Immediately, a dozen of them dropped to the pavement, never to rise again. The T4 responded in kind by spewing forth its own torrent of bullets. Within moments, half of his compatriots were gone. The armored column began to creak forward once again.

The acrid smoke of expended munitions began to smother the street – cordite, black powder fuses, and the discharge of guns. Grey ghosts danced about above the rubble, embracing, kissing the collected with their filthy mouths. The unfortunate ones would consummate the union today.

Merich's eyes began to water from the thick chemical mist. Men became formless blotches of colour that scurried to and fro. His accuracy had been lost. One shot kills needed two or three bursts before the shapes stopped moving. Losing no time, he wiped the wet from his eyes and started aiming for the top of each blur than sprang forth. The stock of the rifle pounded into his shoulder with each rapid recoil, like the frenetic beating of a snare drum to announce an execution.

He could tell from his vantage point that most of the force had been successfully sectioned off. That still left two troop carriers and the formidable T4 to deal with - more than enough of a challenge to their barricade.

"Grab the guns! Move! Move!" came the command from behind the position.

Merich pulled the Bren gun down from its perch, and turned to Korin. "Grab as many of the boxes as you can!"

The teenager grabbed an ammunition box with each hand and stood to turn to the rear. A single shot tore into his lower back, to the left of his spine. He collapsed to the ground. "Oh God! Oh God!" he screamed hysterically, rolling onto his side.

Merich dropped the gun and rushed forward. "Hang on!" he yelled, as he grabbed Korin by the wrists and attempted to drag him back from the line. "Just hang on, for Chrissakes!"

One of the government soldiers mounted the crest of the barricade, just an arm's length from where Merich was perched. He caught sight of the two and raised his weapon. The first shot took Korin dead center in the chest, silencing the boy's voice in mid scream.

Merich's eyes widened. Fear overtook the adrenaline. He let go of Korin's lifeless arms, and turned to run when another shot rang out. Almost instantly he could feel something hot and sharp penetrate the upper thigh of his right leg. The force of the hit knocked him to the ground.

He lay still atop scattered debris, now facing his young comrade, whose icy blank stare still beckoned to Merich for salvation. Just over Korin's head, he could see his assailant, positioning his gun for the final coup.

More gunfire, this time from behind, pounded out rapidly like the beats of a snare drum. Merich saw his would-be executioner jerk violently to and fro as the bullets met their target. He fell back, and out of sight from behind the barricade.

He closed his eyes, ready to join his father. He fell effortlessly into the clouded haze before hands stronger and steadier than his own took control over his fate.

* * *

The makeshift litter made its way to an apartment building three blocks to the west of the Charlesstrasse. Two men led the party, kicking in the front door when it did not readily oblige. They quickly set to work searching the lobby for signs of activity, then for a ready access to the cellar door.

"Here! In here!" barked the one man, as he spotted the passage. The heavy door was stubborn to open, and the man leaned in strong with his shoulder to pry it open. The party quickly passed with their fallen comrade, making their careful procession down the steps in an awkward, halting fashion.

As the men's eyesight adjusted to the dimly lit gloom of the basement, they could to discern a large rectangular surface with a few random items scattered about. A workbench, no doubt for the landlord of the building to effect repairs.

"How bad is it?" asked Vlahovic.

"I don't know," grunted the doctor, as he swept his arm over the large wooden workbench to clear it of objects. "Here - put him up here! Gently! Make sure the sheet stays underneath! I don't need to deal with whatever's on this table!"

The men placed Merich as carefully as they could on its surface. Despite their obvious diligence, Merich groaned in deep agony with every movement they made.

The doctor turned to and fro among the gathering. "You!" he barked at one man. "Get me a light - any light!" To another, he yelled for him to find a knife, easily provided from the man's pocket.

The doctor leaned in toward Merich. "I need you to stay with me - do you understand?" he said to him with a calm firmness. "Now, I need to tighten the belt. It's going to hurt, so you need to brace yourself, *ja*?"

Merich whimpered as he nodded his acknowledgment. He lowered his arms and grabbed the edges of the bench top, his fingers pressing hard into the wood. He felt a couple of errant splinters, whose sharp jabs gave a partial tonic against the doctor's actions.

The doctor pulled at the leather belt a notch tighter. Merich felt the vicious stab of pain, which gave itself over to an intense burning sensation. He let out an agonized yell.

The first of the men had located a kerosene lantern, and managed to light it. He brought it close to the bench. "For Chrissakes, somebody shut him up!" he snapped. "He's going to get us killed!"

Vlahovic unhooked the shoulder strap of his rifle, then placed it to Merich's lips. "Bite down on this," he ordered. "Don't scream – bite!"

"Easier to just leave him here," continued the man with the lantern. "He's dead weight."

"He comes," said Vlahovic.

"He'll be dead before nightfall! Look at him! He's bleeding out like a stuck pig!"

Vlahovic turned away from Merich and pivoted toward him. He stood his bulk within inches of the man, the flicker and glow of the flame contorting his face. "He comes," he spat.

"Okay - the knife!" ordered the doctor, holding out his hand toward the other man. "And get the hell out of my light!" Taking the blade, he began to cut away at the fabric that covered much of the wound. The material was now a deep crimson - almost black - heavy with blood that had already begun to congeal.

The doctor sighed heavily as he surveyed the wound. He looked at the man who had brought the blade. "Get me a sheet and some hot water!" he barked.

"Where?"

"For Chrissakes, we're in an apartment building!" bellowed the doctor. "Go to one of the flats! Kick in a door if you have to - just go!"

As the man made his way up the staircase, Vlahovic turned to the third, and remaining, man who was standing near the base of the steps. "Whatever place he goes, you stay. If the people there try to leave or call for help, you shoot. No one gives us away, *ja*?"

The man nodded. Grabbing his AK-47, he quickly followed his compatriot up the stairs in pursuit.

"Is he going to die?" asked Vlahovic.

"Not if I can help it," came the distracted reply. "I need to clean this mess before I can tell."

"Tell what?"

"Whether the femoral artery is severed. If it is, then I can't help him. Even if it isn't, I don't know. We can't move him, but we can't leave him here either. He needs a hospital."

"Out of the question."

"Don't you think I know that?! Over there - grab my kit!"

Vlahovic reached over and grabbed the canvas bag by its shoulder strap. He handed it to the doctor, who peeled back the top flap and began to rifle through its contents.

"Your men better make it quick! I can't dress the wound until I clean it!"

"What about the bullets?" asked Vlahovic.

"I can't take them out - not now. We need to patch him up enough to keep him alive. Maybe in a day or two, when he's stronger, and we can get him out of the city. My brother practices in a small village in the west. That's his best chance - provided those bastards of yours hurry up!"

Within moments, two of the men returned, one balancing a large washing basin that held steaming water. A large white flannel sheet was draped over his left shoulder.

"Good - now you - hold the light over his leg - not too close!

And you, put the water there. Start tearing strips off the sheet!"

The two makeshift medics set to work carrying out their orders. The doctor sat his canvas bag beside Merich's head. "Bite down hard," he instructed. "I'm going to have to cut."

Tears welled up in Merich's eyes as he clamped his teeth down hard on the sinewy fabric. He could taste the sweat and grime of the strap mix with his own salty saliva.

The doctor extracted a syringe and a small vial of clear liquid. Jabbing the needle into the container, he held it upside down in front of the lantern. Slowly, methodically, he drew back the plunger, before taking it out of the bottle. He let fly a small stream of fluid. "Morphine," he announced. "It's all I have, but it should help."

Carefully, he rolled back the sleeve of Merich's left arm. He flicked the fleshy inner joint of the elbow, which brought forth a large bluish artery. With as much care as he could summon, he gently pierced the skin and depressed the plunger. Merich could feel the warm sensation of the drug dull his agony. His clenched jaw relaxed, his fingers loosened their grip.

The doctor placed the needle and the vial in his bag, then quickly turned his attention back to his patient. "Vlahovic - find me a soldering iron, if you can," he said, still examining the extent of Merich's wound. "There's got to be one around here somewhere." Merich lay still on the bench, unable to do little more than open and close his eyes. The combination of the opiate and his own exhaustion made the next hour a jumble of random sights and sounds - of poking and prodding, voices in the ether, the occasional flashes of light amid the dim of the cellar. He fought to make sense of his surroundings until he could fight no longer.

Merich drifted into a trance of colour and amorphous shapes shifting in and out of form. His mind was fascinated by this spectacle, and in no particular hurry to leave. Occasional moments of lucidity did not last long enough to do more than ask whether this was the gateway to heaven or hell. They did not even linger long enough to wait for an answer.

When he finally won the right to open his eyes, he found himself on a stretcher, its ends balanced upon ammunition boxes. It was a large truck - that much he could tell. He stared at the heavy canvas cover that hid him and his fellow passengers from sight. The errant holes in the fabric let through flickers of reddish gold light, like fiery stars fixed in the firmament. It was nearly night. The day had surreptitiously bled away, making Merich overly conscious of his situation.

"Calm down," said a familiar voice. "We're out of the city - heading west."

"It's...done then," muttered Merich, still lost in his foggy haze.

"It's just started," corrected Vlahovic. "We seized the western province. Two army divisions have defected, and they are heading there too. We're travelling with General Mrozek's command."

"They're still fighting?"

"It's a goddamn mess! Practically door to door, like when the Reds went after the Nazis! Mrozek and Paperny pulled their commands out and came to us. Brought us some T4's and Katyushas. It's a fair fight now!"

"I... I don't..."

"We have a place to regroup. No EBI, no Vopos - just us in charge. The bastards are in the east, and nobody behind us but Yanks, Brits and Austrians. We're in it for the long haul, Alex!"

Merich began to groan. "I'm tired...just want to sleep..."

Vlahovic placed a hand on his shoulder "Sleep - get some rest!" he chortled. "We'll have you up and ready for a scrap in no time!"

Merich nodded, then closed his eyes again.

CHAPTER 29

The knock on the door did not take Merich by surprise, but it did engender more than a little trepidation. Only two people ever knocked on the door. Emi would do so as she was in the act of unlocking the door and swinging it open. The only other person, Frau Fischer, always accessorized her loud wrap with a throaty "Herr Merich." Neither of these things occurred, and so he considered what other options there might be. Not far from the top of the list was that someone had come to complete the task that his last unexpected visitor had failed to accomplish.

He walked up to the door. No peephole to peer through and no chain to buy him some time. Placing his hand carefully on the doorknob, he swallowed hard, then clenched and turned.

Nothing.

Merich pulled the door open to reveal his visitor.

"I didn't expect to see you again," he said with evident relief. "You seemed quite clear about that."

"I was," replied Father Christoph, taking a quick step forward. "Things change...Look, I'd prefer to do this in private if we could."

Merich gestured for the priest to enter the flat. "Yes – of course. Please come in. Can I take your coat?"

"I'm not staying. I'd rather not be here long. The sooner I get back the better."

After taking a quick glance down the hall, Merich closed the door. "Forgive me for asking, then, but why are you here?" he remarked.

"A friend – he asked me to talk to you."

"Let me guess - One of your parishioners? Someone named Stolzer?"

"Heavens, no!" declared the priest. "Believe me, I know all about you and the Stolzers. That's why I came here instead of asking you to see me."

"Aren't you afraid of running into one of them here?"

Christoph gave Merich a knowing look. "We won't be disturbed," he replied. "I'm pretty sure of that. Anyway, I came to give you something." He pulled out a package he had kept tucked inside the left breast of his coat. "I've been holding onto this for a long time. I don't mind telling you I'm glad to be rid of it."

"What is it?"

Christoph held it out to Merich. "Read it for yourself."

Merich did not reach for the package. His hands remained firmly in place. "Humour me," he said. "What does it say?"

"A police report. July 14, 1937 to be exact."

"That's about ten years off of anything my client's charged with," observed Merich. "I appreciate you taking the time, but..."

The priest waved the package at Merich. "I'm not an idiot," he declared. "I know the when and where, and so do you. This is the why."

Merich sighed, then reached to take it. "All right, I'll play," he said. "Tell me why it matters."

Christoph stepped forward, past Merich, toward the kitchen table. "I got a call that night – late," he explained. "A young woman who I had known for years, she was in trouble."

"What kind of trouble?"

"She was admitted to the hospital – roughed up rather badly. The doctor insisted that someone be called, and she didn't want her parents to know. When he said he wanted to call her 'father' that's when she thought of me.

"I came and saw her. Hurt so badly."

"She was raped?" asked Merich.

The priest nodded. "I came to the hospital," he continued. "It broke my heart, what happened to her. That sort of thing should never happen to anyone, but it seems worse when it's such a gentle soul."

Merich moved toward Christoph, laying the package on the table. Loosening the flap, he pulled out the folder and opened it. "Eva Kreutzer," he read aloud, before flipping over the top page to reveal the victims picture. "Licht's wife."

"My family's known the Kreutzers for years," explained Christoph. "She sought me out when she moved here for her school. Came to Mass every Sunday. Didn't miss a week until she got wrapped up in politics."

Merich's eyes remained fixed on the contents of the folder. "Friends or not, that doesn't explain why a priest has an old police report he's been hiding," he muttered. "You didn't get it from her either."

"She was afraid. She just wanted me to get her discharged - nothing else. I insisted that she press charges, and it took a lot to convince her.

"I called a detective I knew, asked him to take care of things. He came to the hospital and took her statement, took the photos as well."

"Did they make an arrest?" asked Merich.

"They brought the man in. Photographs, fingerprints, but she wouldn't press charges. They held him overnight, then let him go. It's on page three."

Merich flipped to the third page and began to quickly scan the typewritten notes which ended in the signature of Eva Kreutzer. He closed the folder. "Why are you giving me this? Why now?"

"Isn't it obvious?"

"Actually, no. No, it's not."

"Really," chided Christoph. "This country - this city - it doesn't run on crowns, or dollars or rubles. Secrets are the real currency. Everyone has them. Most people spend half their time exposing other people's secrets, and the rest of it hiding their own."

"And you hear all of them."

"I'm a priest. I'm familiar with the concept of resurrection. I believe that such a case happened recently."

Merich raised his gaze from the papers. "I only found out a day ago. How long have you known?"

"Longer than that."

"Obviously. Well, you can resurrect a person easier than a charge... How did you get this?"

The priest nodded to the folder on the table. "When the Socialists took over, my friend, he understood what he had. Before the police were put under the Public Security Directorate, he resigned. Took the file with him."

"Clever, but he'd still be a marked man," shrugged Merich.

"He left me the file and headed to the west with his family. He was over the border before they even got orders to arrest him. EBI's been on his trail for years, so he's had to move around. Every so often, he'd get word to me – check if I was still alive too, I suppose."

"I suppose…and he agreed to this – giving it to me?"

"He would."

"But did he?" asked Merich.

"He left it to my discretion," answered Christoph. "If I thought it was the right time."

"Like now?"

"Like now…Look, you're a smart man. You'll find a use for it."

"Not as evidence, I won't," argued Merich.

"You couldn't use that little find of yours for evidence either," countered the priest. "Still had its uses, though."

"Four all the good it did," replied Merich. He glanced down, running his index finger across the cover of the folder. "Death penalty's on the table for both of them. This won't change anything, except maybe his attitude."

Father Christoph stared at Merich as he fastened the top button of his coat. "Sometimes the truth is an end in itself," he said. "Sometimes we have to know whether a shadow is just a trick of the light or something else. He needs to know, and this is the time to do it."

Merich's mouth pulled to a tight frown. "I'll show it to him," he replied in a slow, considerate drawl. "Then I'll take it to the Ministry."

"Is that such a good idea? Can't you just tell him?"

"His diary was nothing but trouble," he explained. "I don't repeat my mistakes if I can help it."

Christoph shook his head. "My friend's still in hiding," he said. "If you file it, someone will find out…"

Merich rubbed his eyes. He paused, taking the measure of Christoph, then the folder. "Nothing's going to happen to your friend," he finally said with a heavy sigh. "Stern's as good as dead…but I can do something else."

"Like what?"

"I can make your friend's name disappear," he sighed. Silence passed between the two. The priest adopted a contemplative pose. Merich had seen it before – in Bruno, in his father. It always happened to the men who were predisposed to being quick of tongue and foot, the ones who relied on position and personality to power through almost anything. They had to dig down deeper into their bag of tricks.

"That's a serious thing, if I understand you correctly," the priest finally said.

"I'd be dismissed, disbarred," Merich agreed. "Most likely, I'd end up in Shostoi myself."

Christoph lowered his gaze, like one of the more penitent of his flock. "I can't tell you what to do," he sighed. "This time, I'm in your hands."

The words made Merich feel ill at ease. It was far easier to be the one begging than the one who was expected to answer the plea. The objective of the beggar was singly minded – mercy, forgiveness, relief. The one who granted clemency was the one who had to reconcile revenge with justice. They were the ones who had to live with the possibility that the exchange would be one-sided. For a brief moment, he realized that life as a judge would be nothing but that from now on.

"Then tell me that you can keep a confidence," he answered.

"Tell me that it would do some good."

The priest shrugged. "I can tell you that if you were to do this, a little girl will get to grow up with her father in her life," he said thoughtfully, glancing back at the folder. "I don't know if that's the kind of thing you're looking for."

Merich's face softened to a smile. Nodding his assent, he reached out to shake Christoph's hand. "It's a better excuse than I've had for anything I've done up to now."

CHAPTER 30

It was early evening, just after the supper hour, when Merich arrived at Shostoi. Despite the hour, the prison staff had, with some reluctance, obliged his request, including a place to stay for the night for himself and his escorts. The incursions along the road had increased considerably in the past few days. What had been dangerous was now becoming nothing less than suicidal. Merich reasoned that the intensity would increase as the Tribunals drew nearer – especially with Stern in custody. It was likely that the EBI holdouts knew a great deal and were hoping for a chance to rescue him on his way to the prison.

He found Licht in the exercise yard, the lone inmate and under heavy guard. From the first moment he had been brought to the prison, it had been decided to segregate him from the rest of the population. As a matter of practicality, there were not enough guards or money to isolate all fourteen Politburo members individually. The decision had fallen to Hartz, who did not think the measure to be necessary. He had told Merich once that the cabal had 'no balls and no imagination' as they so easily transitioned from unquestioning loyalty to Licht to unflinching support for Stern. If they did not have the guts to make a move when they were free with power, why would they even try now? They needed a catalyst, and removing Brother Chairman from the equation seemed a basic prerequisite for keeping order.

For a half-hour every evening, as the others were being sent back to their cells, he was permitted a brief stint outside. As Licht perambulated the yard, he never fell out of the gaze of the armed guards along the top of the wall, or the one that was never more than a half dozen paces behind.

"Counselor, my friend!" exclaimed Licht. "Come, walk with me...Guard! Give my friend a cigarette!"

"No...thank you," replied Merich, gently raising his hand in a prohibitive motion to the guard. "You're in a particularly good mood."

"Twilight. Fresh air. Why wouldn't I be? So why are you here? Shouldn't you be home doing whatever you do in your spare time?"

"This is what I do," answered Merich, "at least for now."

Licht gave a slight shrug. "I'm curious about one thing," he said. "How soon do you think that they'll take?"

"Right to the point."

"We're friends. At least, I'd like to think we are. Friends can be candid."

"If you mean to deliberate, I would expect a week or two after we conclude our defense. They're obligated to go through all of the documents...Since we're moving closer to the trial, I could see about a transfer into the city. They're going to have to move you anyway. We could make it sooner."

Licht smiled kindly at him. "I wouldn't bother. One way or another, I won't be here much longer."

Merich began to shake his head. "Every day's a surprise with you," he remarked. "I can't tell where you'll be from one day to the next."

"You seem to have had luck finding me here so far."

"You know exactly what I mean."

Licht shrugged as he pulled a cigarette out of his lapel pocket and beckoned to his minder for a light. A small gust of wind almost blew out the match as he cupped his hands around the contact tip. The shredded shards of tobacco turned a fiery orange red as he took his first deep draw. "I guess," he said, "I guess it's because you're the only person I talk to. Any other time, I'm alone. Guards don't say anything.

"Long ago, I had friends...I had Eva. I'd say something, and they'd say something back. Wasn't always pleasant, but it was something. I also kept a diary. Eva got me started on that. I found that for the things I couldn't say out loud, I could put them there.

"Now...everything happens in my head – nowhere else. I guess I just need to think out loud to know the difference anymore...Maybe to know it ever happened in the first place. I suppose you think that sounds crazy."

Merich smiled. "Actually, no – I don't."

"Don't get me wrong," Licht continued. "I'm not looking for immortality. I just…I just want to know that I exist, that it's not some dream."

"You could take that kind of thing too far."

"Eva's gone. My comrades – all gone. Revolution's gone. Sooner or later, so will I…Ozymandias."

"Pardon?"

"Ozymandias. A poem. Shelley, I think."

"I didn't know you read English?"

"A bit. Not very well though…When I was young, I headed west. You see, I fancied myself an artist, so I put together the fare to head to Paris. I was taken into an atelier as an apprentice for an Englishman. Worked for him for six months before I learned that I was never going to be good at it.

"He couldn't speak German or Hungarian, and neither one of us was particularly good at French. He was my mentor, so I had to learn English.

"He taught me by having me memorize poetry – Keats, Byron – but that one poem, Ozymandias, that stuck in my head."

Merich grinned. "I met a traveler from an antique land…" he intoned.

"A-ha!" exclaimed Licht. "You know it! Bravo!"

"Yes. I have to confess I'm partial to it too."

Licht paused to take another draw of his cigarette. "It's strange, really," he said. "When we were fighting – the old king, the old republic, the Nazis – that poem was my inspiration. I had this overwhelming sense that all our enemies were going to end up that way – you know – buried in the sand."

Merich began to laugh.

"What's so funny?"

"I have to confess - I used to think the same thing too."

Licht nodded his bemusement. "Well," he said thoughtfully, "I suspect I'll be lucky to have even one broken down statue left before this is over."

"You'll have your life," volunteered Merich.

Licht's smile started to dissipate. "This defense," he began, "has been a fool's errand from the very beginning. No offense, but your talents – whatever they are - are not enough to stop the inevitable.

"At some point I got caught up with your optimism, but reality – this place – it's made me tired. I want an end more than anything else."

Even after all of their meetings, the endless flow of documents, and the diary, Merich still found himself put off guard by Licht's defeatism. "This isn't like you, Johann. You've fought every step – with me and against me. It's probably a case of nerves – it'll pass as we get into it," he said reassuringly. It was the first time that he had addressed Licht by his given name, up to now avoiding any sense of familiarity. Why he did this he could not understand.

"Think what you believe," he continued, "but it's my duty to get the best deal for you – and I think that we have that. That's why I'm here."

Licht smiled and nodded for him to proceed.

"Yesterday, I met with the Minister, and he presented me with new evidence."

"About?"

"About your time in Moscow, and please – don't deny it. They know everything."

Licht frowned and, removing his spectacles, rubbed his eyes. "I don't see what this has to do with anything," he said.

"Well, it seems that the charges relate to that period of time, so they would prefer to prosecute Stern for them."

"Stern's gone, so that's a meaningless gesture," Licht said derisively.

"They have Stern…at least, they will have him here within a day or two."

Licht paused for a moment, then began to laugh. "I didn't know that the powers of your Ministry extended beyond the grave! Bravo!" he intoned as he began to slowly, mockingly, clap his hands.

"Stern's not dead," replied Merich, keeping an even tone. "Apparently the devil's not ready for him just yet. I can show you the proof if you don't believe me."

Licht stopped laughing. He bent his head forward, staring at the cobblestone underfoot. "Where did he turn up?" he asked.

"Ecuador. Called himself Steinbrucker, a plantation owner from Paraguay who emigrated before the war."

"Are they sure it's him?"

Merich looked back past Licht to the guard. "You sure you want to have this conversation now?" he asked.

"Now - later - what's the difference?"

He shrugged, then continued. "South America's swarming with people hunting Nazis - government agents, private contractors. If you came within the last ten years and speak German, then you've got a tail.

"Herr Steinbrucker was a pretty busy man. Too busy to run a plantation, it seems. Steinbrucker's son was away at school in Buenos Aires, but then the money stopped. He heads back home and finds that his father's gone - money, passport, personal effects as well. Within a couple of weeks, the old man shows up - stuffed in a sealed oil drum out on the far end of the plantation. Neck, legs, arms - all broken.

"The son calls the authorities, and hires some detectives. Within a couple of months, they find a Helmut Steinbrucker making the rounds in Quito. Apparently, he got rough with a girl one night - put a gash in one cheek.

"They caught him running a printing press for an underground newspaper - socialist, of course. They arrested him, photographed and fingerprinted him, then started to run the records against him. Nothing showed up for known Nazi sympathizers, but the Gestapo records for occupied territories were still quite extensive. Stern's arrests and surveillance reports were confirmation enough."

"He's alive, then," said Licht.

"Somewhere between London and Vienna right now, as far as I know," replied Merich. "Ministry officials are taking custody of him from there. I suspect he'll be here within a couple of days."

A furrow appeared across Licht's forehead. He blinked rapidly for a moment or so, then turned to look up at the turret that stood past and over Merich's shoulder. "It still means nothing. Stern was my deputy. I was still in charge," he said softly.

Merich shook his head "Almost a thousand miles away? In a hospital bed, pumped full of morphine? The magistrates won't accept that claim."

"Accept, don't accept – it makes no difference to me."

"Well, it's irrelevant. The government has altered the charges."

"Meaning?"

"Meaning that the death penalty has been taken of the table."

"That means I have another twenty-five to thirty years here?" asked Licht rhetorically. "Thank you for the kind offer, but I'd just as soon be dead."

"There may be the possibility of going into exile."

"Where? Russia? East Germany? No, I don't think that is a possibility. Your masters would never agree to that. They would never be satisfied that I wasn't plotting a return…Yes, I've heard about the bombings, and I know what they are thinking – kill me and all hell breaks loose, but keep me under lock and key, and they'll always have the ability to threaten them. No, they'll leave me here."

Merich shook his head. "I don't think so - there's no percentage in it. Besides, they really want to put a noose around Stern's neck – so much so that they're willing to forgo putting one on you."

Licht grimaced, as he lifted a hand to rub his eyes. "You know," he said thoughtfully, "I hear a great deal about this new government of yours. The guards talk about it all the time."

Merich had not grown used to Licht's frequent segues, but resigned himself to them nevertheless. He sighed, and gestured for Licht to make his point.

"They all talk about it," Licht continued, "but they say very different things. Some talk about freedom, some talk about getting rich, and others talk about getting revenge. The funny thing is that they all agree on one thing."

"And what is that?"

"They agree that so far you've let them all down."

"Well, democracy shouldn't be confused with some polite parlor talk," countered Merich. "They have a right to their opinions – at least now they do."

"Perhaps," said Licht. "Then again, they're only opinions, aren't they?"

"Yes," replied Merich hastily. "They are opinions – everyone has opinions. Can we please get on with this? I have to leave and we've agreed on nothing."

"That's because there is no agreement."

"We can agree that Stern is an animal and should be put down."

"We agree that Stern is an animal, yes, but I do not agree that he should be, as you say 'put down'."

"Not even if it will save your own neck?"

"Especially so."

"What about your wife, then?" asked Merich.

"What about her?"

"She hated Stern, didn't she?"

"She didn't particularly like his company, if that's what you mean. A lot of people felt that way."

"Did you ever ask her why?"

"I know why," he said. "I know exactly why – I take it you know too."

"I have the arrest report, if that's what you mean," said Merich.

Licht grinned. "You know; Hugo ran agents into Austria looking for that file. He didn't think I knew…but I did. I have to say I'm impressed. You dug up something no one else has seen for over ten years."

"You just have to know where to look."

"Or who to look for?"

"Perhaps."

"I usually don't like priests, but I liked him," he declared. "I never mentioned him."

Merich stopped walking. He paused, then looked at Licht. "You didn't," he replied. "Look, I need to tell you."

"Tell me what?"

Merich said nothing. He stared at the ground.

"Tell me what?" repeated Licht, his expression becoming tense.

"We found some surveillance records – pre-war," he said calmly. "They were hidden away in the University Archives. Guess they were forgotten."

"Until now – how fortunate."

"I've spent months looking high and low for documents, papers. I wasn't the only one either. There's a small army out there scouring through boxes."

Licht said nothing. He stared intently at Merich for a moment. Then, he said "That's your problem... Your army's busy rifling through boxes, while bandits are sniping at trucks on the road. You need to set priorities…So, ask me."

"Ask you what?" Merich asked cautiously.

"Man rapes my wife," said Licht. "I do nothing. I'm head of state – most powerful man in the land. I know where the proof is. I say nothing."

"I'm your lawyer. That's beyond my remit."

"You're a man," countered Licht. "You're a man with a woman. You love her. Surely you know what you'd do."

Merich looked straight at Licht. "I'd kill the bastard," he said coolly. "I'd do it with my bare hands, and I'd make it hurt – a lot."

"Of course you would!" announced Licht. "Who wouldn't?"

"You...you wouldn't."

"That bothers you."

Merich paused, then shook his head. "Would it surprise you if I said no," he replied.

"Actually, yes – yes, it would."

"I understand why you chose to do nothing. I know it was complicated – I'm not naïve. That doesn't explain now. Stern has no power. You're in control."

"Control?" laughed Licht. "Alex, do you see those men, those guards watching us?" he asked. He pointed up to the dozen or so men who stood watch from the guard towers and the iron walkways connecting them.

"Uh, yes. What of them?"

"If you were to come here every night, you would not see the same guard twice. Do you know why that is so?"

"Probably the policy of the warden," said Merich. "I can't say for sure."

"Yes, it's the warden's policy – a policy of fear. You see, every guard is restricted so that they spend no more than a shift or two with me. On one hand, they're afraid that if I'm paired with one of them long enough, I'll get their pity and they'll help me escape."

"And on the other hand?"

"On the other hand, they're afraid that one of them will take the opportunity to kill me before your judges gets the chance!" Licht began to laugh, self-satisfied. "You know, they're very good shots. Even in this light, any one of them could put a bullet in my forehead and not even come close to touching you...Then again, you're my lawyer – they may want to shoot you instead!"

Merich felt a chill go up his spine. He stopped walking, turning to look straight into Licht's eyes. "What's your point?" he asked quietly, firmly. "Do you want to die? Is that it?"

"Want to? No…only a fool wants that.

"Tomorrow, I'll get more guards – different ones - and the next day, and the day after that. But you know, there aren't that many prison guards in this country. Sooner or later, some of them will be back, the security won't be so tight, and then…some fresh faced boy with a score to settle will take his chance."

"Sounds like false bravado to me," replied Merich.

"No…no, it's not. You see, I'm really not afraid to die. It'll happen eventually. The only question is when.

"Understand that what I fear – what everyone fears - is the unknown, the randomness of it all. Hundreds of gypsy women make a living reading palms. I'm no different. Everything I've done up to now, good or bad, has been of my own volition. The day I came here was the day I stopped being in control."

"I'm sorry, but that's a piss poor excuse for failure if I've ever heard one," replied Merich.

"And you don't mean to fail, do you?" said Licht. "I know your story. If you were honest with yourself, you'd know the truth."

"Being?"

"Being that you've never did anything for an ideal. You do it to prove some stubborn point. You do nothing on principle – it's all based on a dare."

"You're daft - my job is to save your life," said Merich.

"That's not your job," countered Licht. "That's your feeble attempt at grabbing control. I've done it for so long, you don't think I can see it?"

Merich was unable to hide his irritation. "I don't have time for this foolishness," he muttered. "It's self-indulgent, pure and simple. Like it or not, I have a case to prepare for. You can choose to help yourself or not."

"You haven't heard a word I've said, have you?" said Licht. "This case isn't about me. It's about what people think I am. I'm a dead man however you choose to look at it.

"No, it's all about you – your ego, your demons. You're putting me through all of this to satisfy your own needs. You don't think you were man enough to stand up to Stern when you could, so you need to be punished. I understand that – hell, I think I'd be that way myself."

"You're turning it around," said Licht. "That's all you lawyers do. You turn things around."

"Seriously?!" exclaimed Merich. "This trial is about you! This mess of a country is about you! What Stern is, what he'll be – that's you! My job – yes, my job – is to find some shred, some redeeming sliver of humanity in your sorry body! For what it's worth, I know it's there. I see it even if you don't. You want to fight, but you don't mind dying to make up for the things you could've or should've done – and that starts and stops with Stern!

"Look, what you do after the trial is your own business. All I can tell you is that you'll live if you want to – only if you want to…For what it's worth, I can't see how you could if you didn't take the chance to put that mad dog down for good."

Licht's eyes grew deep and anguished. His jaw began to clench, as he turned to the guard. "I want to go back to my cell, please," he said calmly.

"Johann, we need to…"

"I'm tired, Alex," he said quietly. "Good night."

He walked a dozen feet away in the direction of his minder when Merich spoke.

"There was a baby," he said.

Licht stopped, but did not turn around. "You're lying," he intoned.

"Am I?" asked Merich. "When have I lied to you before?"

Licht remained still, his back still to Merich. "She wasn't pregnant," he asserted. "I would have known."

"Or should have known?" argued Merich, his voice growing louder. "When did you find out about what he did? A month later? A year? Five years?"

"You have no proof," said Licht, holding his position. "You've got nothing."

"You want a medical report? You think they keep those kind of things laying around? I have all the proof I need."

"Why are you doing this? What are you trying to gain?"

"Because…I want justice," stated Merich, clearing his throat. "You should want it to."

Licht began to walk again. "I said I was tired," he called out. "You need to leave."

CHAPTER 31

Merich had been so consumed by crafting the latest draft of his opening statement that he had not bothered to shut his office door. Few people ventured down the hallway in the course of a day, and he had learned over the years to tune out superfluous noises, like the errant echoes or the rhythmic tapping of shoes against the floor. The immediate knock on the glass pane in the door was another matter. Not bothering to move his head from its bowed position, he raised his gaze, peering over the frames of his reading glasses.

"Bruno," he said as he maneuvered to pull himself up. "This is a bit of a surprise."

Stolzer came fully into the room, casually pulling off his leather gloves, finger by finger. "Please," he insisted. "Sit."

"Look, I know why you're here," began Merich. "I'm only surprised that Emi told you anything."

"I would be too," came the reply. "Actually, Jaromir gave me all of the details."

"Yes...I learned that he can actually talk."

"He saved your life."

"Yes...yes, he did," sighed Merich. "He still doesn't sit right with me, but...I owe him. I can't deny that. I suppose that I have you to thank as well?"

Stolzer moved to sit in the chair opposite. "You could have thanked me by not getting yourself in this situation to begin with," he said matter-of-factly. "Alex, I think that we need to clear the air between us."

"About Emi?"

"She's a grown woman. I learned long ago not to involve

myself in her affairs. She would never forgive me, and besides, despite you behaving like a sonofabitch, I still have my hopes."

"So, I should thank you for this dispensation?" asked Merich with an airy tone.

"You should stop behaving like a sullen brat," countered Stolzer.

"I beg your pardon?"

"You heard me. For the longest time you've made it a point to offend my family - to offend me."

"Look, I'm quite busy preparing for my case, and..."

"If you put as much effort into that as you do insulting me, I should think you might perform a minor miracle."

"No thanks to you," argued Merich. "I believe that Mama Stolzer is the only one who hasn't tried to rip me apart for taking it."

"It's a foolish exercise and you know it...Tell me, Alex, do you know what a 'Forlorn Hope' is?"

"I'm sure that you will tell me," commented Merich dryly.

"They were British soldiers that volunteered for an important task, yes, but almost always impossible to do. They were asked to volunteer, because it was tantamount to suicide."

"Not the same."

"Isn't it?"

"I'm doing this to become a judge," explained Merich, "not a corpse."

"From where I stand, you're not doing this to get appointed to the bench, and you'll likely end up in a shallow grave anyway. You're cannon fodder. You just don't realize it."

"Everyone's entitled to their opinions - doesn't mean I have to take them."

Stolzer shook his head, and began to laugh derisively. "You sound just like Franz when he'd get worked up about something or other."

Merich could feel his face become flushed. "You have no right!" he snapped, as he reached out and pointed his fountain pen at him. "You have no right to talk about him!"

"The hell I don't!" barked back Stolzer. "I loved your father! He was a brother to me, but that doesn't mean I didn't see him for what he could be!"

"You can stop right now!" cautioned Merich.

"He was sanctimonious!" continued Stolzer. "Holier than thou!"

"He was a great man!" screamed back Merich. His voice travelled out into the cavernous hallway and echoed.

A moment passed before Stolzer said, in a lower tone, "I didn't say he wasn't, but ask yourself what it was worth."

Merich clenched his jaw. "Say what you mean, Bruno."

"No man becomes great without paying a price - their money, their standing. The people around them pay a price too."

The frustration grew on Merich's face. Still, he found he could say nothing.

"You know I'm right, Alex," continued Stolzer. "He paid dearly, but so did your mother...so did you."

"I'm alive, Bruno. That's all that matters."

"That's not all. You've changed. Not for the better."

"That's your opinion," argued Merich. "Things aren't wrong just because you don't like them."

"Look in the mirror. If I didn't know you, I'd think you were a street beggar. Half the time you look like you're going to collapse from something or another."

Merich removed his reading glasses and set them on top of the legal pad. "I'm fine," he insisted. "I've been a bit under the weather, but this time of year is bad for everybody."

"Worse for some...Tell me, do you still..."

"No. No, I don't," interrupted Merich, the intensity beginning to creep back into his voice. "Not for a couple of months. I find other ways to deal with the pain."

Stolzer shrugged. "I've known men who have been hooked on the stuff," he observed. "Just like you. It starts out with taking the edge off, then..."

"It's morphine, Bruno! For God's sake, you act like I spent all my nights in some opium den with whores..."

"You don't need to be defensive."

"And you don't need to come into my office and talk about that!" snapped Merich. "All I need is for Hartz to find out."

"You're a fool if you think he doesn't know," said Stolzer. "I suspect that's why he picked you for the case. He thinks the pressure will get to you, and you'll go looking for a needle."

Merich swallowed nervously, clearing his throat as if to set himself back on the offensive. "I know where all of this is coming from," he said coolly.

"Really? Well do enlighten me."

"Jealousy."

Stolzer shook his head. "Of you?" he laughed. "I hardly think so..."

"Of my father," interrupted Merich, the confidence beginning to return to his voice. "He didn't need to bribe or threaten anyone - he didn't lie to them. They still followed him, no matter what. He had respect, and you hated him for that."

Stolzer paused for a brief moment, his eyes beginning to narrow as a smile began to cross his mouth. He resembled a wild beast that had every confidence that his prey was his and his alone. "Maybe I am jealous," he intoned. "After all, I never did have his knack with people...You know, he could get so passionate about things. A few well-placed words and they were ready to sign up for whatever he was selling. I never had that."

"That's what made him different."

"Different - not better."

"That's your opinion," argued Merich.

"It's the truth. I'm a capitalist - that means that I don't get something without giving something. People follow me, but they get money, homes, jobs in return. The people that followed Franz got nothing - except for some broken bones for their trouble."

"They have their integrity."

"Do they? Do they though? Do you?"

"Yes. I think I do," declared Merich.

Stolzer sighed heavily, then leaned back in the chair. "How's Olga then?" he asked casually.

Merich began to feel the anger swell back up in him. His face felt hot and flushed. "You have no right - no right whatsoever!" he snapped.

Stolzer found his moment, and took it. He quickly lurched forward and pounded his fist against the desk. Merich's glasses rattled off the note pad. "The hell I don't, boy!" he barked back. "Smart as you are, and you never figured out how Havasy gives your mother such care on what you pay them?!"

"I don't know what you're talking about!" defended Merich.

"I'm talking about the thousands of crowns I pay Janousek every month! I'm talking about the special room so she doesn't try to fling herself out the window again!"

Merich felt ill. The room felt claustrophobic to him. The anger left him as quickly as it came. "You're full of it!" he spat.

Stolzer leaned in even closer, his gaze only softening enough to allow him to retain the momentum. "Alex...I made a promise to your father - to look out for your mother, and you. Even if you and Emi...you're a son to me. Hate me if you want, but I made a promise, and I'm damn well keeping it - in spite of you."

Merich sat quietly, like a whelped puppy. He lowered his gaze to the floor as he attempted to absorb everything.

Stolzer slowly rose from the chair, and turned to leave. "You're angry and you're arrogant - and that's not going to make life easy for you," he said as he pulled his gloves back on, methodically inserting each finger into their set place. "Make your own choices, but I refuse to have you look down your nose at me. Some of us choose to keep our integrity in our own way - you remember that!"

He passed out of the office, leaving the door open. Merich staring out into the hallway, listening to the steady, confident cadence of heel clicks that echoed all the way to the lift at the end.

CHAPTER 32

The Kriegstat was a former royal palace that had, at one time, possessed one of the continent's foremost museums of fine art and antiquities. Its patrons, in a desire to elevate the stature of a capital, and a nation newly emerged from direct Habsburg control, endowed the Musee with the wherewithal to procure the finest works of sixteenth and seventeenth century European artists. Acquisitions also extended into Egypt, Palestine, Syria and Persia, where a number of well-financed expeditions were launched in competition with the Austrians, Germans, French and Britons.

Two major wars, a revolution, and finally a counter revolt, had taken a massive toll on the once proud institution. Most of the collection had been looted or damaged a dozen times over. Now, as capital life had developed some degree of stability, the task of rebuilding the Kriegstat had begun in earnest.

This was, in fact, Emi's greatest challenge - to return the Musee to something approximating its former splendor. Starting with only a dozen or so stylized pieces that celebrated the proud peasant worker in various poses of victorious defiance, it was not going to be an easy task.

Emi was a missionary, bringing the gospel of aesthetics to the people. Beauty, colour, grace and elegance were to be her legacy. Merich always wondered whether she was motivated by some higher sense of altruism, or simply a desire not to see the ugliness that often appears from without and within. Increasingly, she would spend more time here than elsewhere, which only served to reinforce his opinion even further.

During the time in Switzerland, Emi had enrolled in the Universität Zürich to study Art History and Conservation. By the time the Stolzers had prepared for their return, she had completed her Baccalaureate and was well into a term of her graduate work, researching the expressionist painters of *Der Blaue Reiter.*

Merich often listened politely as she spoke of her well-established interest in Kandinsky. He admired the painter's one piece, which had become the group's namesake, but disliked much of the rest. Once, in an unguarded moment, he had told Emi that his paintings looked like pictures of scrap iron that a junk dealer had assembled, that they never looked like anything real. This revelation devolved into a debate of such surprising intensity that Merich avoided further contributions to this topic in the future. If time or circumstance made such a policy of neutrality untenable, he stuck with his well-rehearsed joinder - that *Der Blaue Reiter* itself was actually very good.

Emi's reasons for returning from Switzerland were neither articulated to nor fully understood by him. Bruno Stolzer was a man used to getting his way in every regard, but in the case of his daughter, he was often outmatched, or at least forced into an accommodation. The men in Emiliane Stolzer's life rarely agreed on things. On the subject of her return, though, they had presented a united front. Regrettably, they had been woefully mismatched in the effort.

The Kriegstat was decimated. To this point, no-one could dispute or accuse of being an overstatement. War had resulted in multiple rounds of looting – from the escaping emigres, from the Nazis, and from the Red Army. Years of fighting armies and insurgencies had also taken its toll on the building, which had been nearly as badly abused as Nyitny. Windows were easily reglazed, and walls replastered. The collection was another matter. It was virtually non-existent.

The previous regime had commissioned a number of 'artists' to produce new works, rather than attempt to repatriate what they considered to be 'bourgeois affectations'. They had gone so far as to create an artists' commune to the north of the capital, christening it *'Kis Epreskert'*, in homage to the colony outside Budapest it had been modelled after. All the commissions were intended 'to glorify the revolution and the class struggle'. The sharp edges and stultified figures were reminiscent of the Soviet style of approved art that had proliferated over the past two decades. Indeed, many of the pieces had arrived on loan from the Hermitage, that once proud centre of Russian art and culture.

Merich surmised that while Emi loved Switzerland, she loved a challenge even more. It was the only explanation for her return to a place she barely remembered and that could not have been more inhospitable to her ilk. The Gallery gave her the kind of professional opportunity that rarely presented itself in a lifetime. His theory was that it was enticement enough for her to return.

After convincing her father to serve as a patron for this project, she arrived back in the capital with money and a dozen pieces of work – two Picassos, a Goya, one Rembrandt, a Van Gogh, an El Greco, and a Vermeer among them. There were also firm commitments for another dozen individual pieces, paintings and sculptures alike. The current collection was removed to storage, with the pieces that had been on loan having been politely returned to Moscow with the sincerest of best wishes.

In recognition of the generosity of the Stolzers, Emi had been made the Chief Curator of the Gallery. Political considerations had led to retaining the presiding director, but it was well understood that his jurisdiction would be confined to the simple logistics and mechanics of running the facility, keeping the lights on and the staff paid. Emi was not disappointed. She did not crave the authority or the title, let alone the tedium that an administrator needed to deal with. She loved her work and was well satisfied to stick to it, provided that she was left alone - and she was.

The main lobby of the museum was a rotunda, crowned by a dome in the classic neo-gothic style. Its inside was adorned by a massive fresco depicting a representation of the Nine Muses – a swirl of vivid colours and pale fleshy tones. Around its perimeter was a band of gold, inlaid with a pattern familiar in middle eastern art – meant not only to honour the eastern traditions of learning, but as a reminder of the nation's struggle to thwart the ever frequent encroachments of Ottoman armies.

Supporting the structure were a network of stone spines that ran down to merge into massive columns, strategically placed around its outer edges. Halfway between the cupola and the floor were a series of balconies and parapets that threaded around the circumference.

Along the balconies, long metal staffs protruded horizontally, from which banners of vibrant color and various design hung down to about thirty feet from the floor. They were the heraldic colours of each of the old provincial regions, all of whom now existed in name and history only.

The museum was a quiet place, save for the voices that scarcely rose above a dull din, and the intermittent clicking of shoe heels as patrons made their way across the polished marble floor.

An usher had directed Merich to Emi's office on the third floor. In fact, it was not an office, but a studio that doubled for that purpose. Much of her job had centered on the restoration of pieces that had seen damage from war and neglect. It was painstakingly slow and he wondered how she could have summoned the patience and concentration to deal with it.

Emi stood with her back to Merich, speaking with a colleague. Their attention was drawn to a large canvas braced against the far wall. A couple of ladders and a small scaffold were positioned to the left, clearly intended for the work on the top leading edge.

"Beautiful place," he called out, his voice carried by a slight echo in the cavernous room.

Emi halted her conversation and turned around. She paused for a moment. "That's right," she finally answered back coolly. "You've never been here."

Merich bowed his head down slightly, as if to make careful note of every step. He moved to within a dozen feet of her. "I don't know what to say."

"You had plenty to say before."

"Well, I owe you an apology…"

"Damn right you do!" she snapped, her voice creating a small echo in the room. Merich looked out from the corner of his eye to watch Emi's colleague bid a timely exit from through a side door.

"Look," he began again, taking a deep breath, "you need to understand…"

"Understand?!" she said mockingly. "You behaved like a brute! If you want to apologize, then get on with it, but don't you dare ask me to understand!"

"Okay – I'm sorry. No lawyer tricks. Just I'm sorry."

Emi paused as she looked straight at him. A pained expression came across her face. "I can't do this, Alex. This is too hard," she said.

"What's too hard?"

"This…you," she said, shaking her head. "I've tried – really hard. I can't try harder."

"I'm not asking you to," insisted Merich.

"But you are," she argued. "You don't see it, but you are! Every time you go off on something, you drag me along!"

"That's not true."

"You came back here. I didn't hear from you for weeks on end. I didn't know if you were still alive. Did you know I asked Father to have someone find out if you were dead? I used to wait, and I always – always - thought the worst. Then, I come back here, and I see you with your leg…"

Emi stopped, feeling the emotion begin to well up inside. Merich felt empty and ashamed. He stepped forward to embrace her.

"Don't!" she protested. She stepped back and held out her hand. "Don't you dare touch me!"

"I'm sorry…"

"You're sorry? I'm sorry! Sorry for this, sorry for that - we're all so goddamn sorry, aren't we?! This miserable place has nothing but sorry people!"

Merich bowed his head, staring in the direction of Emi's feet. "What do you want from me?" he sighed.

Emi paused, her eyes darting all about the cavernous room. "Nothing…I don't know," she rambled. "Different time…different place."

"It's life, Emi – life's hard," he said calmly. "You can't fix people like these paintings. We don't hold still and pose for you."

"That's what you think? You think that I'm spoiled?"

"What I think is that you've lived different from everybody else," he explained. "We don't have a clean and tidy life. It's dirty and it's ugly - you have to know that."

Emi shook her head. "That's funny, coming from you," she said. "You hide behind this thing called the law. You don't accept life any more than anyone else. You're even worse – you make people do things. Conform or go to prison."

Merich began to laugh mockingly. "You're kidding me!" he remarked. "I haven't the power to control anything or anyone – not you, not even my own life!"

"But that's what you want, isn't it?" she countered. "Control. You want to control me. I mean, that's why you took that case without asking me. You knew I'd say no, so you thought you'd drag me along anyway!"

"What's the alternative? Work for your father? Taking cases

only if you think I should? You're the controlling one - not me!"

"Don't you dare turn this around on me!" screamed Emi, her voice reverberating with a fierce tempo that felt like it was coming from every direction at once. "Don't you dare! You made choices and they affect all of us! You just pretend they don't! You have no idea how much of my life has revolved around you. That's bad enough, but you don't even give a damn what it does to us - to me!"

Merich felt beaten from the barrage, as if his spirit had been siphoned from his veins. He had seen Emi angry before, even furious. This furious burst crossed into a territory he neither recognized nor desired to travel. He hung his head down and paused to think. "No. I never wanted that," he finally said. "Even if I could, I don't want that responsibility…I shouldn't have come here. I'm sorry…I know it's not much, but I mean it." With that, he turned to walk away. He managed a couple of paces before she spoke.

"Alex, wait... We can't just leave things like this," she said quietly "I really don't want it left like this."

Merich stopped and turned around. "You've said your piece. I've said mine," he shrugged. "I've got nothing to add."

"You just don't understand…"

"What I understand is either you love me or you don't," he said solemnly. "No conditions - not whether I do things the way you want, or whether you do it my way. Did I behave dreadfully to you? Yes – I admit it and I will always feel ashamed for it. Should I have talked to you before I agreed to the case? Yes – I should have. I admit that…but you know I was going to take it anyway – even if you said not to. I can't promise you that it won't happen again…I can't help the way I am."

"It'll be the death of you," said Emi.

"What did your father tell you?" he asked.

"Enough…I made him tell me," she volunteered. "He didn't want to, but I made him."

Merich grinned slightly. "You didn't make him," he declared. "He wanted you to know. He wanted me to know that you knew."

"This isn't about him, is it? This isn't about telling things that happened already?"

"No…I suppose not," he said. "For what it's worth, I still love you – very much."

Emi shook her head. "It's worth something," she replied, "but I'm not sure it's enough…You asked me why I pulled back – why I didn't want to rush into marriage. Don't you see? I couldn't say it, not without making you…I just couldn't…I'm sorry."

Merich paused, staring into Emi's eyes. "Be happy," he said quietly, then turned and made his way out of the room.

Emi remained in place, long after the echo of Merich's cane tapping against the marble floor disappeared into the ether.

CHAPTER 33

As the car pulled into the main courtyard, Merich was surprised by the appearance of Szatmáry, accompanied by two guards. He had not laid eyes on the Deputy Warden since his first visit, and based on that meeting, he did not expect to see him again. For a brief moment, he wondered if the diary had become an issue, and whether he would be in need of a ride back to the city. He could feel the hairs on the back of his neck stand up as the driver slowly wheeled the sedan up to where the men were standing. One of the guards stepped forward and opened the door.

"Hello, Szatmáry," said Merich cautiously, as he steadied himself out of the car and onto his feet. "To what do I owe this reception?"

"Herr Merich," came the perfunctory reply. "Could I have a word with you?"

Merich felt a pit form in his stomach. "Yes...of course," he hesitated. "We'll have to make it quick - I need to get back before dark, and I have a lot to cover..."

"Please - Herr Merich. I won't take much of your time. I promise."

Merich shrugged and, nodding his assent, followed Szatmáry and his retinue into the main entrance. Szatmáry's office was located, mercifully, up a short flight of steps, and the men were remarkably patient as Merich gingerly made his way up.

Once inside the office, Szatmáry instructed the guards to wait in the hall. He then gestured for Merich to have a seat at the desk opposite to him. The desk was empty, save for an envelope that sat in front of the warden. Merich noticed the writing on the outside that bore his name.

"Herr Merich, there's no pleasant way to put this...Your client, Herr Licht, was found dead in his cell this morning."

Merich's expression grew grim, his eyes narrowing. "I was here a couple of days ago," he said slowly. "He was in good health as far as I could see."

"And he was," concurred Szatmáry. "I assure you that he was in excellent condition."

"But you say he's dead."

"Yes. The morning shift came to deliver his meal. They found him hanging - a trouser belt."

"Inmates aren't allowed belts," commented Merich.

Szatmáry sighed. "Yes," he conceded. "Rest assured that we are investigating."

"He wasn't wearing one any other time," continued Merich.

"I know - believe me - this has my full attention...I have to say, though, that it appears to be a suicide. This was left in the cell." With that, Szatmáry slid the envelope across the desk to Merich. "It's addressed to you."

Merich made no move. He quickly glanced at the envelope, then looked back at Szatmáry. "No suicide's complete without a note, is it?" he observed wryly.

"I know that this is an awkward situation..."

"Awkward!" chided Merich. "Hanging from a belt he didn't have before, and a note. Please tell me that this is not your idea of an investigation because it's sure as hell not mine!"

"I assure you that we...I... will find the answers to this."

"I'm sure you'll find answers," mocked Merich. "I just want to know if they're to the right questions?"

Szatmáry was beginning to find surer footing. "Meaning?" he asked pointedly.

"Have you decided on suicide? Are you ruling out murder?"

"Herr Merich, regardless of what you might think of me - or this place - we will handle this matter professionally. We collect evidence with an open mind, and let it lead the conclusion."

"He was the head of the bloody country!" he snapped. "From the first day I set foot in this place, it's been a joke! Don't talk to me about professionalism! If you were handling this professionally, you wouldn't have slid that envelope over to me like that! Tell me - how many sets of greasy fingerprints am I going to find on it?"

Szatmáry scowled at him. He rose from his seat, and yanked open the centre drawer of the desk. Pulling out a set of latex surgical gloves, he tossed them at Merich, hitting him in the chest. "It's a sealed envelope, Merich. Provided you put those on, there should only be one set of prints on the letter inside." With that, he proceeded to make his way out of the office.

"You have five minutes, counsellor," he barked, as he opened the door to pass through. "I still have a prison to run." As Szatmáry left the room, Merich could hear him instruct one of the guards in the hall to escort him to the infirmary once he had finished up.

Merich once again turned his attentions back to the envelope that lay before him. After putting on the gloves, he took a letter opener that lay on the desk and proceeded to open it along the top seam.

The letter was written on some of the paper he had brought Licht:

Dear Merich,

I have no great wisdom to reveal - you seem to know enough already. As for the rest of the world, they all divide between those who don't know or don't care. I have nothing for them.

I still do not know if you are any good as a lawyer, but I can tell you that you are the closest thing that I've had to a friend in a very long time. I would like to think that you might have felt the same as well.

I only have advice - avoid politics, quit the law. Bury yourself in the arms of the woman you love. If you lose what will kill you, you've lost nothing.

Licht

Merich stared at the note, the all too familiar handwriting was shaky, but deliberate. Simple words, uncomplicated thoughts that masked a determined intent. Simple lines on a page revealing more than what Szatmáry's investigation would reveal.

He folded the letter up and replaced it in the envelope, which he put back on the desk. He removed the gloves slowly, then balled them up and threw them at Szatmáry's vacant chair. He got up from his chair and made his way out of the office.

The guard who had waited in the hallway patiently led Merich down the corridor, the steps, and back out into the cobblestoned yard. He pointed to a single storey annex on the other side. "Just over there, Herr Merich," he said. "The doctor is waiting for us."

Every tentative step on the grease covered cobblestone made the journey across the yard slow and labored. More than a couple of times Merich had insisted that his escort slow their pace. Every step grew the building in size and stature. Every step created a new variation of the image he expected to find. Every step carried nervous anticipation on its heel.

A man wearing a white smock greeted him at the door. The front of the gown had the dull reddish brown stains of old blood. A surgical mask hung around his neck like a pouched amulet. He was young – younger than Merich, or so he appeared. He introduced himself as Kornheiser, or at least that is what Merich thought he had heard.

Young. Young and innocent. Innocent and young, he thought to himself. As they were brought inside the cinderblock structure, Merich could not help but stare at him. *You're either brilliant or incompetent and connected. No one like you becomes a doctor unless you're one or the other.*

The doctor led the men to a door just inside the corridor. He opened it to pitch black darkness. His hand scraped against the left side of the door frame. Florescent lights slowly came to life with a stubborn crackle and hum of electricity.

The room was cold and antiseptic. The walls were clad with white tiles, which gave the look of old pearls when the light hit their glazed edges. It was empty, save for a chrome topped stool, a table on wheels that held a tray full of surgical tools, and a massive bench that supported what lay beneath a large white sheet. Merich noticed the floor was sloped ever so slightly inward, funneling toward a dull and dirty drain that sat in the middle. It all reminded him of a slaughtering room in an abattoir.

Its sinister purpose was masked by the pungent odour of ammonia and solvents. The smell was a frontal assault, a challenge to those who would question whether all had been rendered sterile. For a brief moment, Merich gagged from the overpowering stench. There was a difference between clean and pure, and he knew it.

"Please," said the doctor, as he gestured for Merich to come inside. He walked over to the bench and gently drew back the shroud.

Merich had no formal training in the field of forensics, but time and circumstance were a worthy teacher. He saw the purplish black bruising that extended across Licht's throat, the bloody abrasions that traced over his trachea. He looked at the bare shoulders, the arms and wrists. There was plenty of scarring, but nothing fresh. No struggle.

The doctor coughed to clear his throat. "The plan," he intoned, "is to perform an autopsy. As he didn't have any family, we'll need your agreement."

Merich remained staring at Licht for a few moments longer before turning back. "I have no objections," he answered quietly.

"You'll need to sign a release," said the doctor. "Before you leave, that is."

"Yes…of course…I'll want a copy of the report, and the list of evidence – photos – all of it."

"I'll see to it that everything is sent to your office," assured the doctor. "If you'll follow me, we can take care of the paperwork."

"Actually," replied Merich. "I'd like to stay for a while longer."

"If you wish…"

"Alone."

"I'm afraid that's not possible," frowned the doctor. "The rules are quite clear…"

"He's still my client," interrupted Merich. "I haven't signed off on anything yet. Those same rules say I'm entitled to consult with him in private."

"He's dead."

"Either leave me be, or bring Szatmáry down here!" snapped Merich.

The doctor's jaw clenched. "I'm going to have a guard posted," he said efficiently.

"Fine," answered Merich with equal resolve. "Just make sure he knows what side of the door to stand on."

CHAPTER 34

"Hello, Alex."

Merich slowly raised his head as if waking up from a long slumber. "Georg," he muttered in acknowledgment.

Hartz came fully into the office, gently closing the door behind him. "For what it's worth," he began, "I'm sorry to hear about your client."

Merich remained frozen in place. "Thanks - I think," he replied nonplussed. "The prison doctor asked me about an autopsy. I said they wouldn't get any argument from me."

"Yes, I know. I just had a word with the prison. It'll be sometime late tomorrow."

Merich's face began to register some concern. "Shouldn't he get on with it now?" he asked. "I can't think this is going to stay quiet long – not with the imbeciles running that place…"

"It's not exactly a secret how you feel about them," interrupted Hartz. "Nevertheless, I expect you to act like an adult…Anyway, the doctor will start once his assistants arrive."

"I don't follow. It's an autopsy. Surely he isn't going to kill him all over again."

Hartz cleared his throat, a reflex Merich knew meant that the old man was reaching the end of his tether. "Tonight we're expecting a couple of doctors to fly in from Berlin," he said in a controlled tone. "An American and a Russian. They'll observe the whole thing."

Merich rolled his eyes, cocking his head toward the ceiling.

"Covering your ass, Georg?" he sighed.

"Covering all our asses. Yours too, if you must know" grunted Hartz as he lowered himself into the chair opposite. "I want no misunderstandings."

"You may get them anyway. You've got a teenager there pretending to be a doctor..."

"He's no greener than you," defended Hartz. "Besides, no one leaves the room without all three signatures on the report. Then, we'll release it to the papers for good measure."

"Assuming it's a suicide," added Merich.

"Any reason why it shouldn't be?"

Merich paused, lowering his head ever so slightly. "None of us will ever know for sure, but I think he did it," he said quietly. Hartz nodded. "Under the circumstances, it's the best we can hope for," he said. "You know that, don't you?" It was not a question. Merich began to shift in his chair. His eyes darted around the room, searching for something that could pull him out of place and time. All he could find were the piercing eyes of the old man, staring at him, telling him not to bother looking for an exit. "I've still got a problem," he sighed in resignation. "Getting my head around it."

"Well, I suppose you were close enough to him," conceded Hartz. "I would think that you would have figured him out."

"I thought I did...I mean, he genuinely wanted to fight – at least part of him did. He fought with me enough over how we were going to go into trial, what the strategy was."

"When did you see him last?"

"Couple of days ago. Got there late, so I stayed the night at the prison."

"No clue what happened. Nothing said?"

Merich sat silently at the desk. He thought about the conversation, about all that he had said. He thought about the very last words he spoke to Licht – words that he had tried to push back to the corner of his mind almost from the moment they had passed his lips. "Nothing," he finally said. "I didn't say anything."

Hartz studied Merich carefully. "I meant him," he said. "What did he say?"

Merich's face felt flushed. He clenched his jaw. "He said he was tired," he stated. "Then he walked away – Really, Georg – do we have to do this right now?"

Hartz paused for a moment, then leaned forward and clasped his hands on the edge of the desk. "This was your first case, Alex. A real case - not one of those dress up moot affairs. A real client, life and death.

"Through it all, you have these peaks and valleys. One minute, they want to take on the world. Next time you see them; they want to step in front of a train. A defense counsel has to do more than fight a case. Sometimes they have to fight their client's moods. The bigger the client, the bigger the crime - and the swings. You had the luck to start with the biggest."

"Luck, or your plan?" asked Merich.

"Your luck, my plan," replied Hartz. "Regardless, you should be proud of how you've handled it. You have a promising road ahead."

"In front of the bench, or on it?" asked Merich. "I presume this changes our...understanding?"

"Perhaps," said Hartz. "You lived up to your end of the bargain. Too bad Licht didn't."

"Let off on a technicality - you're a real credit to your profession," Merich replied.

"It's yours as well."

"Not bloody likely. Not politics at least."

Hartz relaxed his gaze as he took in a deep breath. "Despite what you think, I still have people to answer to," he said. "Half of them are already wondering why your client's dead. Not a good time to be asking for a reward for services rendered."

"I have a piece of paper with your name on it, Georg." Hartz smiled slyly. "Through all of this," he laughed, "the times we've met – I saw my old friend. It was like having Franz back. I forgot how much I missed him...Now all I'm seeing is Bruno."

"The appeal to emotion," replied Merich. "After all of these years, you've discovered your sentimental side. I'm surprised you don't retire and take up poetry or something."

Hartz cocked his head to the side ever so slightly. "As I would like to think that we are still friends, I don't mind telling you that you've got more nerve than you should." The casual tone was a thin disguise for the intent.

Merich leaned in on the desk and, extending his hand, he tapped the desk with his index finger. "No," he replied intently. "What I have is a promise on a piece of paper. What I have are the scars that earned it. You told me not to use my father as a prop for favors. That works both ways."

Hartz was about to speak, but held back. He paused for a

moment, softening his expression. He reached into the pocket of his overcoat and extracted a small, thick vellum envelope. "Before I forget. I have this for you," he said as he laid it on the desk.

"What is it?" asked Merich.

"Your inheritance."

"Excuse me?"

Hartz leaned back in the chair and nodded his head in the direction of the envelope. "Johann Licht had no surviving relatives," he explained. "He left two notes - the one you saw at the prison, and one naming you as his beneficiary."

"Beneficiary? To what?"

"What's in the envelope. Everything else is gone - destroyed, seized."

Merich stared at the package on his desk.

"Are you going to open it?" asked Hartz.

"Why? I suspect you already know what's in it," he replied matter-of-factly.

Hartz smiled as he let forth a small sigh. "Well, I guess I'll leave you to it then," he said as he rose from the chair. "Oh, by the way," he added, "I'm placing you on a month's leave - paid, of course. Some things have come to my attention. Maybe you'll have your head screwed on straight by then."

Merich sat quietly as Hartz left the office, closing the door behind him. He waited until the dark silhouette in the glass pane grew larger and greyer, and then faded completely. He stared at the package for a moment, then took it in hand and opened it.

The familiar patent leather cover came into view, the faint scratches and blemishes. He felt a reflex in his chest as if he were to choke. He pushed it back and down, as he placed the diary on the desk. Old habits, he thought.

Leaning back in his chair, he propped an elbow on one of the armrests, his hand cradling his chin. The room was silent, save for the gurgling and spitting of the steam pipe overhead. The journey from his study to the desk consumed every synapse. He wondered whether it would have revealed itself in some other way had things been different.

He slowly moved his hand out and toward the book, sliding it toward him. Opening the cover, he leafed through the book to find the place where the writing ended.

"November 6, 1948

"The biggest protests to date started today - at least that is what I'm being told. They call them 'protests', but I'm not stupid. I don't have to see the activity to know that they go well beyond that. The city is under martial law, and I'm holed up in my apartments like a rat.

I'm too weak to fight Hugo anymore. The truth is that he stopped listening to me long ago, but at least he was always diplomatic about it. There's no more pretense now. Both he and the Cossack do what they damn well please. They've succeeded in culling the ranks of the Central Committee. The only people left are those supporting Hugo, and those too frightened to oppose him. The Plenary has become even more of a captive. The first thing he did after Eva was killed was put a security detail on every Minister. They were all too scared of being killed not to realize what was going on. Now, none of them can take a shit without him or that Russian bastard knowing.

A few days ago I tried to confront him. I told him that it had to end, that he was destroying the Revolution. He just stood there in front of me, banging his fist on my desk, yelling about how I was just a prop. He told me that dead or alive I was equal use to him.

Deep down, I've always understood that Hugo was a man lacking in many respects. I chose to ignore it because he served a greater purpose. I still must admit that we would never have accomplished what we did without him. I thought I could influence him - at the very least, exert some control. I was wrong.

I can see a half-dozen columns of smoke throughout the city from my windows. Every muscle in my body aches to go there, but there's no point. Stern has his guards posted at my door, and I've no doubt that I would be dead before I reached the grand staircase. Right now, I could care less what happens to me. The only thing stopping me is to deprive him of the chance to kill me and blame it on the partisans.

At this point, I honestly don't believe that I'll last the week. The fighting is too intense to be an isolated event. This time it's organized, and it's substantial. If the rumours about the defections in the army are true, then the fighting will turn this city into another Warsaw or Stalingrad. I suspect they are, as I managed to learn that some of the EBI that were attached to infantry units as political officers were found in Podrovice, in the west, hanging from light poles along the main street. When I think of how hard I fought to keep this country from being razed to the ground, it saddens me to no end.

So much of my life is now contingent on the whims of others - where I go, what I say. I have become a slave in a country where my picture hangs in every government office. It's nothing less than perverse.

No matter what happens, I've resolved to myself one thing - I want to die on my own terms."

Merich closed the book, then sat at his desk in silence. He remained until the sun surrendered to the night.

CHAPTER 35

Janousek stood waiting as the taxi pulled up to the front step. It was not often that his presence was specifically requested, although he always tried to make himself available. He watched Merich as he exited the vehicle.

"Herr Doktor," said Merich, turning for a moment to pay the driver his fare.

"Herr Merich. Good to see you again."

As the taxi pulled away, Merich hobbled up the couple of steps leading to the landing. "How is she?" he asked.

"Calm," said Janousek. "Calm today. Calm for the past week for that matter."

"Does she..."

"No. She doesn't remember any of it. It might as well have been a lifetime ago."

Merich nodded his head in a thoughtful pose. He leaned into his cane slightly to adjust the weight on his feet. "Well, in any event, I appreciate you letting me come," he said.

Janousek smiled kindly. "As I said on the telephone, if I thought that last episode was to be repeated, I'd never allow it," he replied.

"I understand...I hope you know - I didn't..."

"There's no need to explain," interrupted the doctor. "You know, every day we run into rational people who react to what we say or do in pretty dramatic ways. Just imagine if their minds were impaired in some way. Like I said before, I suspected you'd tell her. I could have asked you not to say anything beforehand. The fault's mine as much as anyone's."

"Be that as it may, I could have used some discretion,"

admitted Merich. "It's not like I don't know how she gets."

"She's your mother. You're not exactly objective about her," replied Janousek, placing a hand on Merich's shoulder.

"But I'm not blind to the reality, either, Herr Doktor. She's in this place for a reason."

Janousek nodded, and gestured for Merich to join him inside.

The two men proceeded through the doors and into the lobby. They headed a few paces in the direction of the staircase when Merich stopped walking. "Doktor," he began. "I need to ask...Well, it might seem strange."

"Strange is pretty relative, Herr Merich," said Janousek. "There isn't a day where I don't have to suspend disbelief at least once."

Merich raised his gaze toward the staircase for a moment. "I've thought about this place - and others," he said in a distracted tone. "People here get called crazy - my apologies for using the word."

"I understand. Please."

"My question is how do you know?

"If a patient is ill?" asked Janousek.

"Well, yes...I mean, a broken bone or a cough is obvious, but this...I don't know."

Janousek thought for a moment. He glanced over at the nurse standing at the front desk, then back to Merich. "I'm a psychiatrist, so I have to answer a question with another question - you're a lawyer, correct?"

"So I'm told," smiled Merich.

"Well, how do you know innocence from guilt?"

"Evidence, of course," came the reply.

"But what passes for evidence?" pressed the doctor.

"Well...it depends."

"On what?"

"I don't know," shrugged Merich "...different things...factors."

Janousek extended his hands out, palms up, as if he were carrying a large object. "Herr Merich, there are two handkerchiefs covered with grease and blood. One is proof of a murder, and one is proof of a mishap. Which is which?"

Merich shook his head. "Could be murder in both cases, or not at all," he answered. "I would need to know more."

"Yes, of course. Now consider my situation. You see a

woman crying - did she lose something? Yes, of that I'm sure, but what? A pet? A necklace? A lover? Her hold on reality?"

"I've never found it that easy to pigeonhole people," replied Merich, "and I suspect it's not that simple for you either."

"Not simple at all," replied the doctor. "I mean, I can make a diagnosis, but I can't always cure...You could win a case, but did you get justice?"

"Honestly - I don't know. I only hope to God that would be the outcome."

"Then we aren't so different. Sometimes the best thing to do is recognize that life makes all of us sad at some point. You know, people never question laughter - only tears."

"That sounds like the kind of thing that only a psychiatrist would bother pondering," observed Merich.

Janousek gave a weak smile as he shook his head. "You'd be surprised how many don't," he replied. "We're trained to see sadness as some sort of defect. I never questioned that view through school – only when I left to come here.

"One day, I went out into the grounds after checking on some patients. I overheard the families, the visitors, as they were coming and going. It occurred to me that they were the ones crying, arguing...obsessing. Nobody living here had a care in the world. They'd just talk about the sun, the rain, whatever they were going to eat that day.

"My training told me that it was my duty to protect the world from illnesses of the mind, and they told me what to look for. I assumed it meant keeping patients away from the world. That day, I wondered whether it might just be the other way around."

"That's strange way of looking at things," observed Merich.

"Perhaps," answered Janousek. "I came to this hospital in 1928. Some of the patients have been here longer than that. During the Depression, we kept going. When the Nazis came, we found ways of getting by. Same with the Russians and the last government. There were countless times where I thought this place - my life - would be a waste. One errant artillery shell that could have hit us, one military commander who decided that we weren't worth saving or tolerating - that's all it would have taken.

"I've laughed, I've cried, and I've seen a side of myself that I've only ever seen in some of the patients here. What kept me going is the sense that I'm needed, that if I were gone tomorrow, someone would be affected."

Merich grimaced. "I envy you - you heal people," he replied.

"It's easy to find a purpose in that."

"I don't heal people," countered Janousek. "They heal themselves. I only show them the power they have to do it...But that's only a vocation. We are sons and daughters, mothers and fathers, lovers. We're more than what we're paid to do."

"Do you have a family?" asked Merich.

Janousek paused for a moment. "I used to," he shrugged. "Like a lot of other people...but I have my patients, and my colleagues. I feel their pain, celebrate their happiness. They're close to my heart, so I don't mind."

Merich gave a weak grimace. "I envy you that," he said.

"You have your mother - you have others. That's more than enough."

"If you say so."

"Most people would say so," said Janousek, "but it's not for me to judge...Let me take you up to Olga." The doctor began to walk toward the staircase. It took but a moment for him to realize that he was walking alone. He turned around to see Merich standing in place.

"I'm not going up," said Merich.

"I don't understand?"

"I came to talk to you."

"That's fine," said the doctor, gesturing toward the staircase. "You can visit your mother, and then we can discuss whatever you want..."

"Sorry - I'm not making myself clear," interrupted Merich. "I'm not coming back."

Janousek walked back toward Merich. "If this is about the last time..."

"No - not entirely...Look, I fully intend to make sure she's taken care of. Her expenses will be covered."

"She needs more than that, Herr Merich," insisted Janousek.

"Yes...she does. Not from me. I don't have it to give." Janousek looked straight at Merich, who, in turn, tried averting his eyes away from the doctor. "I get the idea there's more to this than you're saying," he said solemnly.

Merich shook his head. "I don't want to get into it," he said. "I know it seems odd. Believe me, I've thought about it for a while now."

"It isn't odd at all," sighed the doctor. "There's more than a few of our residents whose families made that choice. But they've never set foot in this place after they bring them here – not even to pay the bill. You've been coming for almost two years?"

"And from what I've seen, I'm certain she'll be in good hands," offered Merich. "After all, they're part of your life - you said so yourself."

"So, this is your decision?" he asked.

Merich said nothing. He looked straight into Janousek's eyes for a brief moment, then nodded.

"Well," sighed the doctor, "you'll want to at least go up to say goodbye."

Merich looked past Janousek, up at the staircase. He took a long draw of breath, then turned back. "Herr doktor...I said my goodbyes a long time ago," he said. "Let's just leave it at that."

The doctor nodded his head. "I don't agree, but I understand," he said thoughtfully, as he extended his hand. "I can't push you. I hope...I hope that I see you again."

"Thank you. You're a good man," said Merich, as he turned and hobbled toward the door. The tap of his cane seemed to be the only noise in the cavernous lobby.

"Can I at least call you a taxi?" Janousek called out.

Merich paused for a moment, then turned. "Actually," he replied, "I think I'm going to take a walk."

CHAPTER 36

Merich did not know what compelled him to head to the river edge. It was crowded and congested, a mass of anarchy where only stevedores and pickpockets were in their element. The cobblestones were slick with the greasy filament that came from years of barrel slop and dull moist vapor.

He looked up and to his right, to the Stanislaus Bridge. He had purposefully avoided it. Nothing waited for him at the end, nothing accessible, nothing welcome. Merich stared dolefully at the crude, massive stone arches that straddled the fast flow of water. If he had nowhere to go, then any destination was as good as the next. He turned and made his way to the span's end a block over.

The vendors had already packed up their wares and moved on, leaving the crossing uncharacteristically naked and quiet. Merich was grateful for the respite from crowds. He hobbled carefully down the centre, veering over to the left as he made his way to the midpoint of the first of the arches. He opened his carrying bag, and after extracting its contents, he sat it down to his right, against the column that supported the statue of St. Vitus.

He had meant to take the diary, but had also taken out a copy of Ehrlich's *"Grundlegung der Soziologie des Rechts"*. It had been one of the texts his father had given him when he left with the Stolzers, and the one that Franz had quizzed him on the most when he had returned.

Merich placed the two books side by side on the capstone of the bridge wall. For what felt like an eternity, he stared at them – eyes to one, and then the other. It made him feel tired, so tired, on the inside. His brain tried to formulate a reason for what his body was doing, but none came. Coincidence? Premonition? Maybe nothing.

He took a deep breath and with a sweep of his right hand, one of the books slipped off its perch. It tumbled, end over end, until it hit the water. Its heft produced a moderate splash and wave which was carried out quickly past the bridge by the speed of the current. Merich took a moment to watch the wake get absorbed back into the dark blue. Gone.

Without ceremony, he picked up the remaining book, slipped it back into his bag and began the long walk home.

It took almost two hours for him to walk the distance to his building. Not a minute of the journey passed without him wanting to hail a cab. A couple of times, he had done just that, managing to get one to pull over. Each time, however, he would lean in through the opened passenger side window, apologize for the mistake, and continue on his way. He began to take some form of pleasure from the sharp needles of pain that stabbed into his savaged thigh, like a fighter tasting the salty tang of a blooded mouth.

Exhausted, Merich moved slowly and carefully up the staircase like a climber who checked his ropes before moving a yard in any direction.

Once he had mastered the challenge, once he had gotten past his front door, he pulled out one of the chairs at the kitchen table to sit. He sighed and slumped on the table, burying his head in his arms like a schoolboy serving a detention. He remained there, immobile and fatigued, until he could feel the throbbing pulse in his leg deaden into the familiar dullness.

Raising himself from the table, he pressed his palms downward on the edge of its top and thrust himself to a standing position. Then, steadying himself against the walls that led down the hall to his toilet, he made his way to prepare a bath.

The scalding water gave a momentary bite to Merich's flesh as he slipped himself carefully into the tub. The water was like a harsh, yet repentant lover, with the angry heat giving way to a warm envelopment. He watched as the steam hung over him like the early morning fog.

Merich shifted his leg, bending it ever so slightly as to accommodate his move deeper in. The water rose to about an inch or two from the lip of the tub. A couple of errant waves rippled and crested with his momentum, allowing a thin skimming to move over and trickle on the tile floor. The heat made the muscle flex almost pleasurable for him.

Everything below his chin and jawline was immersed in the warm caress of water. It was raw, primal, and safe.

Merich lie still for a moment, the drip of the faucet his only true companion. The sound of his breath overtook all else. His brain began to race, his body craving warmth above all.

Suddenly, he closed his eyes and plunged beneath the surface. The water buffeted his face like a blast of hot air from a radiator. He fought the urge to swallow hard, and tried to relax himself in the lightness and solitude of immersion. Within moments, his body began to lobby for air. *Not yet*, said the brain - *not yet*. Each passing second made the debate more pointed, more heated. *Not yet, not just yet.*

Merich's lungs began to ache, enlisting the spasming throat for some compassion. Still, the brain stood resolute. Not yet - don't take this from us.

Mere seconds turned the tide. The brain became heavy and dull. It lowered its vigilance as the body pleaded in concert - give us air, give us light. He pushed himself up through the warmth, taking a greedy gasp of air and steam. Merich began to cough and choke, as he attempted to right himself in the tub.

Quickly, he looked about the room. Nothing. The plain light bulb, free of frivolous adornment, was his only companion and witness. He tilted his head back and stared at the ceiling.

Once the water began to cool, Merich began the labored task of pulling himself up and out of the tub. Without bothering to dry himself, he donned his dressing gown and slippers. He reached down to pull the stopper from the drain, then after shutting off the light switch, made his way to the bedroom.

Merich glanced at the clock on his dressing stand. It was wrong - it was much later than what it said.

CHAPTER 37

Merich woke from his uneasy slumber at a quarter past three in the morning. Desperately, he wanted to sleep. His mind craved it. So did his body. The nervous energy robbed him of the respite.

For the next two hours, he stared at the ceiling. Flickers of light from the street below pried their way up and over the closed curtain. They drew their narrow beams in like slender fingers, beckoning him forth. He wanted to resist their charm, but the darkness no longer held his fascination. No longer able to justify his position, he pulled himself up from his bed. The familiar throb in his leg and hip could do no more than slow his ascent. It was the one fight that he was unwilling to relent to. Hobbling to his wardrobe, he took a simple cotton shirt and trousers from their hangars. After socks, shoes and overcoat, he made his way out of the flat, the building, and into the dark blue of the dying dusk.

He had not seen another living soul for at least two blocks, just the damp chill and the dew that had deposited from the midnight mist. He made his way over to a stretch of the street where small shops and cafés stood cheek to jowl. A group of revelers, weighed down by fatigue and alcohol, made their way along the sidewalk, with the odd detour into the storm gutter. The sudden drop in elevation and wet feet brought them back to their true path, often with a lusty spate of profanity. They stumbled past some early risers, the sober and serious who were busy preparing their wares for prospective customers. Merich was neither, and he felt the dispassionate curiosity in it all that came with his station. *A shopkeeper, or a drunk. Pick your place and make your peace,* he thought to himself. *At least you know what you are, where you belong.*

He looked upward. The light had finally reached enough of an intensity as to make the clouds visible once again, faint chalk lines of soft blue against bruised black. Neither light nor dark, neither black nor white. Nothing on the street felt as authentic and inviting as the canopy above.

He made his way to a small park across the street. Stumps marked the spots where large trees once stood, branches that used to cradle the modest plot from the assault from around and above. They endured much, but could not withstand the naked need of those who feared succumbing to the bitter cold. Their fate was sealed in the countless funeral pyres that had kept alive rich and poor alike. Trees and shrubs, the fountain and the walkways – all revealed the abuse of desperation.

Merich sat down on a rusted bench set off to one side against a wrought iron fence. It groaned its discontent as he shifted his weight. He placed his hands deep into the pockets of his coat and pulled his shoulders in. He tried to inoculate himself from the late spring frost that refused to relent while hope remained. *Expediency was the great leveler*, he thought to himself. *Nothing could avoid that.*

For a full hour, he sat on the bench, staring, glancing, then closing his eyes. He tried to conjure a vision more comforting. He wondered if his deal still stood. It was not his fault. He also knew that no piece of paper could stand up against the old man once he had set his mind. The thought of it all began to make him feel queer and uncomfortable inside. This was not him.

As the day began in earnest, Merich watched the street slowly fill with people. Carefully, he lifted himself from the bench, steadying between the cane and the back of the seat. The early morning dampness had sunk into his leg. It made him wince as he poked his cane forward. Nothing more was to be gained. It was time to go.

Slowly, he hobbled home. People passed him, some nearly knocking him over. Others stared at him - at his cane - as he continued on his path. He felt exposed – naked and weak. Naked and pitied. He arrived at his building, passing through the front entrance as quickly as his leg permitted. Judgmental eyes could not pierce stone and plaster.

Merich pulled himself up the staircase. For once, though, the corridor was quiet. The only sound was that of the semi-rhythmic tap of his cane against each step. The world had paused.

He reached into the oversized pockets of his overcoat, fumbling for his keys. His coat – his father's coat – felt larger on him than normal. It felt like an oversized blanket tossed over a boy's bare shoulders.

His hands were still cold from his travels, aching from the tips. They felt clumsy, almost alien. The keys fell away the moment they emerged from the pocket. They dropped to the floor with a soft metallic jingle as they caught the edge of the narrow carpet that ran along the hall.

Merich groaned as he used his cane to lower himself to the floor. Legs stiffened by the cold damp refused to relent. He dropped to the floor hard. His right knee drove into the floor like an angry fist. The sudden shot of pain pulled the breath from his chest. The cane glanced back and hit the back of his head, then rolled off to the floor. He was reduced to his hands and knees. *This is how it began.*

After a moment, he recovered his senses and took hold of the keys that sat a couple of inches from his hand. He pulled himself around, sitting upright with his back braced against the wall just to the right of his door. Mind and body refused anything more.

Merich could feel the rush deep in his chest coming up again. He swallowed hard to keep it down, push it back to where it came. He had fought this battle before, and he always won. He looked about, down the hall way to the stairs, then at himself, his splayed legs, the scuffs and dirt that stained his pants and shoes. He was alone. Completely alone.

He stared at the carpet on the floor. What looked to be a bed of plush crimson from above now showed flecks of dirt and discoloured matter that conformed to the numerous boot prints that compressed its pelt.

Nothing else had worked to this point. It was time for something different - a change. Merich chose not to fight.

Time slowed to a crawl. The release compensated for the pain. He wondered why he had not come to this revelation before.

Minutes had passed when the door to his flat suddenly opened. A part of him still registered surprise, but it did not matter. He closed his eyes and bowed his head. *Just finish it...Please...*

"My God – what's wrong?"

Merich craned his neck and looked up, his bloodshot eyes stinging and wet. "Please...I'm begging you. Don't...," he sobbed.

Emi knelt down, and said nothing. She placed her hand gently against Merich's tear- stained cheek. Instinctively, desperately, he nuzzled it like a kitten searching out his mother. She held it there for a minute, before slowly pulling back.

"Come inside, love," she murmured as she rose to her feet.

Holding out her arm, she sought to steady Merich as he pulled himself up.

He stopped, returning to his place against the wall. "You should leave," he choked. "This is no good for you."

"No... This is where I need to be."

"I didn't think I'd see you again..." he cried.

"You need to stop," she counseled.

"You heard?"

"Yes," she nodded. "I know what happened. I'm sorry - I can't feel sad for him. I can't feel anything. I never could. It's you...I won't let him take you with him. I won't."

Merich grimaced. "It's a mess - all of it. I can't make it right," he gasped, shaking his head.

Emi crouched in front of Merich. She gently grasped both his hands in hers. "Then don't," she counseled. "If you can't, then don't even try. You're allowed that."

He looked deeply, sorrowfully, into her eyes. "I wasn't...I wasn't wrong...Was I?"

She smiled, gently clasping his hands in hers. "No... No, you weren't," she assured. "Let's go inside."

ABOUT THE AUTHOR

B. H. Cameron is a husband and father of two living on land settled by his great-great grandfather.

A graduate of Queen's University and St. Lawrence College in Kingston, Ontario, he has held positions with the Government of Canada, noted political pollster Nik Nanos, and on the staff of a member of the Ontario Legislature. He has also worked on national campaign tours for two Canadian Prime Ministers, Joe Clark and Brian Mulroney.

In 1997, Cameron served as a member, and contributing writer, to the Community Editorial Board of the Kingston Whig-Standard newspaper. In 2013, he joined the Advisory Board of Commonwealth Exchange, a London, UK based policy and research group.

In October, 2014 he was elected to municipal office, serving as a Councillor for the Township of Central Frontenac, in eastern Ontario.

His first book, "The Case for Commonwealth Free Trade", was released in 2005.

www.ingramcontent.com/pod-product-compliance
Lightning Source LLC
Chambersburg PA
CBHW072209170626
46813CB00003B/857